THE SUPERNATURAL
STORIES OF MONSIGNOR
ROBERT H. BENSON

THE SUPERNATURAL STORIES OF MONSIGNOR ROBERT H. BENSON

THE LIGHT INVISIBLE
A MIRROR OF SHALOTT

COACHWHIP PUBLICATIONS
Landisville, Pennsylvania

The Supernatural Stories of Monsignor Robert H. Benson
Copyright © 2010 Coachwhip Publications

The Light Invisible, published 1903
A Mirror of Shalott, published 1907

ISBN 1-61646-004-0
ISBN-13 978-1-61646-004-4

Cover: Cemetery © Jean Schweitzer

Coachwhipbooks.com

THE LIGHT INVISIBLE

A MIRROR OF SHALOTT

THE LIGHT INVISIBLE

PREFACE

My friend, whose talk I have reported in this book so far as I am able, would be the first to disclaim {as indeed he was always anxious to do) the role of an accredited teacher, other than that which his sacred office conferred on him.

All that he claimed {and this surely was within his rights) was to be at least sincere in his perceptions and expressions of spiritual truth. His power, as he was at pains to tell me, was no more than a particular development of a faculty common to all who possess a coherent spiritual life. To one Divine Truth finds entrance through laws of nature, to another through the medium of other sciences or arts; to my friend it presented itself in directly sensible forms. Had his experiences, however, even seemed to contravene Divine Revelation, he would have rejected them with horror: entire submission to the Divine Teacher upon earth, as he more than once told me, should normally precede the exercise of all other spiritual faculties. The deliberate reversal of this is nothing else than Protestantism in its extreme form, and must ultimately result in the extinction of faith.

For the rest, I can add nothing to his own words. It is of course more than possible that here and there

I have failed to present his exact meaning; but at least I have taken pains to submit the book before publication to the judgment of those whose theological learning is sufficient to reassure me that at least I have not so far misunderstood my friend's words and tales, as to represent him as transgressing the explicit laws of ascetical, moral, mystical, or dogmatic theology.

To these counsellors I must express my gratitude, as well as to others who have kindly given me the encouragement of their sympathy.

R. B.

The Green Robe

"To see a world in a grain of sand,
And a heaven in a wild flower;
Hold infinity in the palm of your hand,
And eternity in an hour."

Blake

The old priest was silent for a moment. The song of a great bee boomed up out of the distance and ceased as the white bell of a flower beside me drooped suddenly under his weight.

"I have not made myself clear," said the priest again. "Let me think a minute." And he leaned back.

We were sitting on a little red-tiled platform in his garden, in a sheltered angle of the wall. On one side of us rose the old irregular house, with its latticed windows, and its lichened roofs culminating in a bell-turret; on the other I looked across the pleasant garden where great scarlet poppies hung like motionless flames in the hot June sunshine, to the tall living wall of yew, beyond which rose the heavy green masses of an elm in which a pigeon lamented, and above all a tender blue sky. The priest was looking out steadily before him with great childlike eyes that shone strangely in his thin face under his white hair. He was dressed in an old cassock that showed worn and green in the high lights.

"No," he said presently, "it is not faith that I mean; it is only an intense form of the gift of spiritual perception that God has given me; which gift indeed is common to us all in our measure. It is the

11

faculty by which we verify for ourselves what we have received on authority and hold by faith. Spiritual life consists partly in exercising this faculty. Well, then, this form of that faculty God has been pleased to bestow upon me, just as He has been pleased to bestow on you a keen power of seeing and enjoying beauty where others perhaps see none; this is called artistic perception. It is no sort of credit to you or to me, any more than is the colour of our eyes, or a faculty for mathematics, or an athletic body.

"Now in my case, in which you are pleased to be interested, the perception occasionally is so keen that the spiritual world appears to me as visible as what we call the natural world. In such moments, although I generally know the difference between the spiritual and the natural, yet they appear to me simultaneously, as if on the same plane. It depends on my choice as to which of the two I see the more clearly.

"Let me explain a little. It is a question of focus. A few minutes ago you were staring at the sky, but you did not see the sky. Your own thought lay before you instead. Then I spoke to you, and you started a little and looked at me; and you saw me, and your thought vanished. Now can you understand me if I say that these sudden glimpses that God has granted me, were as though when you looked at the sky, you saw both the sky and your thought at once, on the same plane, as I have said? Or think of it in another way. You know the sheet of plate-glass that is across the upper part of the fire-place in my study. Well, it depends on the focus of your eyes, and your intention, whether you see the glass and the fire-plate behind, or the room reflected in the glass. Now can you imagine what it would be to see them all at once? It is like that." And he made an outward gesture with his hands.

"Well," I said, "I scarcely understand. But please tell me, if you will, your first vision of that kind."

"I believe," he began, "that when I was a child the first clear vision came to me, but I only suppose it from my mother's diary. I have not the diary with me now, but there is an entry in it describing how I said I had seen a face look out of a wall and had run indoors from the garden; half frightened, but not terrified. But I remember nothing of it myself, and my mother seems to have thought it must have been a waking dream; and if it were not for what has happened to me since perhaps I should have thought it a dream too. But now the other explanation seems to me more likely. But the first clear vision that I remember for myself was as follows:

"When I was about fourteen years old I came home at the end of one July for my summer holidays. The pony-cart was at the station to meet me when I arrived about four o'clock in the afternoon; but as there was a short cut through the woods, I put my luggage into the cart, and started to walk the mile and a half by myself. The field path presently plunged into a pine wood, and I came over the slippery needles under the high arches of the pines with that intense ecstatic happiness of home-coming that some natures know so well. I hope sometimes that the first steps on the other side of death may be like that. The air was full of mellow sounds that seemed to emphasise the deep stillness of the woods, and of mellow lights that stirred among the shadowed greenness. I know this now, though I did not know it then. Until that day although the beauty and the colour and sound of the world certainly affected me, yet I was not conscious of them, any more than of the air I breathed, because I did not then know what they meant. Well, I went on in this glowing dimness, noticing only the trees that might be climbed, the squirrels and moths that might be caught, and the sticks that might be shaped into arrows or bows.

"I must tell you, too, something of my religion at that time. It was the religion of most well-taught boys. In the foreground, if I may put it so, was morality. I must not do certain things; I must do certain other things. In the middle distance was a perception of God. Let me say that I realised that I was present to Him, but not that He was present to me. Our Saviour dwelt in this middle distance, one whom I fancied ordinarily tender, sometimes stern. In the background there lay certain mysteries, sacramental and otherwise. These were chiefly the affairs of grown-up people. And infinitely far away, like clouds piled upon the horizon of a sea, was the invisible world of heaven whence God looked at me, golden gates and streets, now towering in their exclusiveness, now on Sunday evenings bright with a light of hope, now on wet mornings unutterably dreary. But all this was uninteresting to me. Here about me lay the tangible enjoyable world—this was reality: there in a misty picture lay religion, claiming, as I knew, my homage, but not my heart. Well; so I walked through these woods, a tiny human creature, yet greater, if I had only known it, than these giants of ruddy bodies and arms, and garlanded heads that stirred above me.

"My path presently came over a rise in the ground; and on my left lay a long glade, bordered by pines, fringed with bracken, but itself a folded carpet of smooth rabbit-cropped grass, with a quiet oblong pool in the centre, some fifty yards below me.

"Now I cannot tell you how the vision began; but I found myself, without experiencing any conscious shock, standing perfectly still, my lips dry, my eyes smarting with the intensity with which I had been staring down the glade, and one foot aching with the pressure with which I had rested upon it. It must have come upon me and enthralled me so swiftly that my brain had no time to reflect. It was no work, therefore, of the imagination, but a clear and sudden vision. This is what I remember to have seen.

"I stood on the border of a vast robe; its material was green. A great fold of it lay full in view, but I was conscious that it stretched for almost unlimited miles. This great green robe blazed with embroidery. There were straight lines of tawny work on either side which melted again into a darker green in high relief. Right in the centre lay a pale agate stitched delicately into the robe with fine dark stitches; overhead the blue lining of this silken robe arched out. I was conscious that this robe was vast beyond conception, and that I stood as it were in a fold of it, as it lay stretched out on some unseen floor. But, clearer than any other thought, stood out in my mind the certainty that this robe had not been flung down and left, but that it clothed a Person. And even as this thought showed itself a ripple ran along the high relief in dark green, as if the wearer of the robe had just stirred. And I felt on my face the breeze of His motion. And it was this I suppose that brought me to myself.

"And then I looked again, and all was as it had been the last time I had passed this way. There was the glade and the pool and the pines and the sky overhead, and the Presence was gone. I was a boy walking home from the station, with dear delights of the pony and the air-gun, and the wakings morning by morning in my own carpeted bedroom, before me.

"I tried, however, to see it again as I had seen it. No, it was not in the least like a robe; and above all where was the Person that wore it? There was no life about me, except my own, and the insect life that sang in the air, and the quiet meditative life of the growing things. But who was this Person I had suddenly perceived? And then it came upon me with a shock, and yet I was incredulous. It could not be the God of sermons and long prayers who demanded my presence Sunday by Sunday in His little church, that God Who watched me like a stern father. Why religion, I thought, told me that all was vanity and unreality, and that rabbits and pools and glades were nothing compared to Him who sits on the great white throne.

"I need not tell you that I never spoke of this at home. It seemed to me that I had stumbled upon a scene that was almost dreadful, that might be thought over in bed, or during an idle lonely morning in the garden, but must never be spoken of, and I can scarcely tell you when the time came that I understood that there was but one God after all."

The old man stopped talking. And I looked out again at the garden without answering him, and tried myself to see how the poppies were embroidered into a robe, and to hear how the chatter of the starlings was but the rustle of its movement, the clink of jewel against jewel, and the moan of the pigeon the creaking of the heavy silk, but I could not. The poppies flamed and the birds talked and sobbed, but that was all.

The Watcher

"Il faut d'abord rendre l'organe de
la vision analogue et semblable à
l'objet qu'il doit contempler."
Maeterlinck

On the following day we went out soon after breakfast and walked up and down a grass path between two yew hedges; the dew was not yet off the grass that lay in shadow; and thin patches of gossamer still hung like torn cambric on the yew shoots on either side. As we passed for the second time up the path, the old man suddenly stooped and pushing aside a dock-leaf at the foot of the hedge lifted a dead mouse, and looked at it as it lay stiffly on the palm of his hand, and I saw that his eyes filled slowly with the ready tears of old age.

"He has chosen his own resting-place," he said. "Let him lie there. Why did I disturb him?"—and he laid him gently down again; and then gathering a fragment of wet earth he sprinkled it over the mouse. "Earth to earth, ashes to ashes," he said, "in sure and certain hope"—and then he stopped; and straightening himself with difficulty walked on, and I followed him.

"You seemed interested," he said, "in my story yesterday. Shall I tell you how I saw a very different sight when I was a little older." And when I had told him how strange and attractive his story had been, he began.

16

"I told you how I found it impossible to see again what I had seen in the glade. For a few weeks, perhaps months, I tried now and then to force myself to feel that Presence, or at least to see that robe, but I could not, because it is the gift of God, and can no more be gained by effort than ordinary sight can be won by a sightless man; but I soon ceased to try.

"I reached eighteen years at last, that terrible age when the soul seems to have dwindled to a spark overlaid by a mountain of ashes—when blood and fire and death and loud noises seem the only things of interest, and all tender things shrink back and hide from the dreadful noonday of manhood. Some one gave me one of those shot-pistols that you may have seen, and I loved the sense of power that it gave me, for I had never had a gun. For a week or two in the summer holidays I was content with shooting at a mark, or at the level surface of water, and delighted to see the cardboard shattered, or the quiet pool torn to shreds along its mirror where the sky and green lay sleeping. Then that ceased to interest me, and I longed to see a living thing suddenly stop living at my will. Now," and he held up a deprecating hand, "I think sport is necessary for some natures. After all the killing of creatures is necessary for man's food, and sport as you will tell me is a survival of man's delight in obtaining food, and it requires certain noble qualities of endurance and skill. I know all that, and I know further that for some natures it is a relief—an escape for humours that will otherwise find an evil vent. But I do know this—that for me it was not necessary.

"However, there was every excuse, and I went out in good faith one summer evening intending to shoot some rabbit as he ran to cover from the open field. I walked along the inside of a fence with a wood above me and on my left, and the green meadow on my right. Well, owing probably to my own lack of skill, though I could hear the patter and rush of the rabbits all round me, and could see them in the distance sitting up listening with cocked ears, as I stole along the fence, I could not get close enough to fire at them with any hope of what I fancied was success; and by the time that I had arrived at the end of the wood I was in an impatient mood.

"I stood for a moment or two leaning on the fence looking out of that pleasant coolness into the open meadow beyond; the sun had at that moment dipped behind the hill before me and all was in shadow except where there hung a glory about the topmost leaves of a beech that still caught the sun. The birds were beginning to come in from the fields, and were settling one by one in the wood behind me, staying here and there to sing one last line of melody. I could hear the quiet rush and then the sudden clap of a pigeon's wings as he came home, and as I listened I heard pealing out above all other sounds the long liquid song of a thrush somewhere above me. I looked up idly and tried to see the bird, and after a moment or two caught sight of him as the leaves of the beech parted in the breeze, his head lifted and his whole body vibrating with the joy of life and music. As some one has said, his body was one beating heart. The last radiance of the sun over the hill reached him and bathed him in golden warmth. Then the leaves closed again as the breeze dropped but still his song rang out.

"Then there came on me a blinding desire to kill him. All the other creatures had mocked me and run home. Here at least was a victim, and I would pour out the sullen anger that had been gathering during my walk, and at least demand this one life as a substitute. Side by side with this I remembered clearly that I had come out to kill for food: that was my one justification. Side by side I saw both these things, and I had no excuse—no excuse.

"I turned my head every way and moved a step or two back to catch sight of him again, and, although this may sound fantastic and overwrought, in my whole being was a struggle between light and darkness. Every fibre of my life told me that the thrush had a right to live. Ah! he had earned it, if labour were wanting, by this very song that was guiding death towards him, but black sullen anger had thrown my conscience, and was now struggling to hold it down till the shot had been fired. Still I waited for the breeze, and then it came, cool and sweet-smelling like the breath of a garden, and the leaves parted. There he sang in the sunshine, and in a moment I lifted the pistol and drew the trigger.

"With the crack of the cap came silence overhead, and after what seemed an interminable moment came the soft rush of something falling and the faint thud among last year's leaves. Then I stood half terrified, and stared among the dead leaves. All seemed dim and misty. My eyes were still a little dazzled by the bright background of sunlit air and rosy clouds on which I had looked with such intensity, and the space beneath the branches was a world of shadows. Still I looked a few yards away, trying to make out the body of the thrush, and fearing to hear a struggle of beating wings among the dry leaves.

"And then I lifted my eyes a little, vaguely. A yard or two beyond where the thrush lay was a rhododendron bush. The blossoms had fallen and the outline of dark, heavy leaves was unrelieved by the slightest touch of colour. As I looked at it, I saw a face looking down from the higher branches.

"It was a perfectly hairless head and face, the thin lips were parted in a wide smile of laughter, there were innumerable lines about the corners of the mouth, and the eyes were surrounded by creases of merriment. What was perhaps most terrible about it all was that the eyes were not looking at me, but down among the leaves; the heavy eyelids lay drooping, and the long, narrow, shining slits showed how the eyes laughed beneath them. The forehead sloped quickly back, like a cat's head. The face was the colour of earth, and the outlines of the head faded below the ears and chin into the gloom of the dark bush. There was no throat, or body or limbs so far as I could see. The face just hung there like a down-turned Eastern mask in an old curiosity shop. And it smiled with sheer delight, not at me, but at the thrush's body. There was no change of expression so long as I watched it, just a silent smile of pleasure petrified on the face. I could not move my eyes from it.

"After what I suppose was a minute or so, the face had gone. I did not see it go, but I became aware that I was looking only at leaves.

"No; there was no outline of leaf, or play of shadows that could possibly have taken the form of a face. You can guess hew I tried to force myself to believe that that was all; how I turned my head this way and that to catch it again; but there was no hint of a face.

"Now, I cannot tell you how I did it; but although I was half beside myself with fright, I went forward towards the bush and searched furiously among the leaves for the body of the thrush; and at last I found it, and lifted it. It was still limp and warm to the touch. Its breast was a little ruffled, and one tiny drop of blood lay at the root of the beak below the eyes, like a tear of dismay and sorrow at such an unmerited, unexpected death.

"I carried it to the fence and climbed over, and then began to run in great steps, looking now and then awfully at the gathering gloom of the wood behind, where the laughing face had mocked the dead. I think, looking back as I do now, that my chief instinct was that I could not leave the thrush there to be laughed at, and that I must get it out into the clean, airy meadow. When I reached the middle of the meadow I came to a pond which never ran quite dry even in the hottest summer. On the bank I laid the thrush down, and then deliberately but with all my force dashed the pistol into the water; then emptied my pockets of the cartridges and threw them in too.

"Then I turned again to the piteous little body, feeling that at least I had tried to make amends. There was an old rabbit hole near, the grass growing down in its mouth, and a tangle of web and dead leaves behind. I scooped a little space out among the leaves, and then laid the thrush there; gathered a little of the sandy soil and poured it over the body, saying, I remember, half unconsciously, 'Earth to earth, ashes to ashes, in sure and certain hope'— and then I stopped, feeling I had been a little profane, though I do not think so now. And then I went home.

"As I dressed for dinner, looking out over the darkening meadow where the thrush lay, I remember feeling happy that no evil thing could mock the defenceless dead out there in the clean meadow where the wind blew and the stars shone down."

We reached in our going to and fro up the yew path a little seat at the end standing back from the path. Opposite us hung a crucifix, with a pent-house over it, that the old man had put up years before. As he did not speak I turned to him, and saw that he was looking steadily at the Figure on the Cross; and I thought how He who bore our griefs and carried our sorrows was one with the heavenly Father, without whom not even a sparrow falls to the ground.

The Blood-Eagle

"And this I know: whether the one True Light
Kindle to Love or Wrath—consume me quite,
One glimpse of It within the Tavern caught
Better than in the Temple lost outright."
                                        Omar Khayyam

One night when I went to my room I found in a little shelf near the window a book, whose title I now forget, describing the far-off days when the religion of Christ and of the gods of the north strove together in England. I read this for an hour or two before I went to sleep, and again as I was dressing on the following morning, and spoke of it at breakfast.

"Yes," said the old man, "that was one of my father's books. I remember reading it when I was a boy. I believe it is said to be very ill-informed and unscientific in these days. My parents used to think that all religions except Christianity were of the devil. But I think St. Paul teaches us a larger hope than that."

He said nothing more at the time; but in the course of the morning, as I was walking up and down the raised terrace that runs under the pines beside the drive, I saw the priest coming towards me with a book in his hand. He was a little dusty and flushed.

"I went to look for something that I thought might interest you, after what you said at breakfast," he began, "and I have found it at last in the loft."

We began to walk together up and down.

21

"A very curious thing happened tome," he said, "when I was a boy. I remember telling my father of it when I came home, and it remained in my mind. A few years afterwards an old professor was staying with us; and after dinner one night, when we had been talking about what you were speaking of at breakfast, my father made me tell it again, and when I had finished the professor asked me to write it down for him. So I wrote it in this book first; and then made a copy and sent it to him. The book itself is a kind of irregular diary in which I used to write sometimes. Would you care to hear it?"

When I had told him I should like to hear the story, he began again.

"I must first tell you the circumstances. I was about sixteen years old. My parents had gone abroad for the holidays, and I went to stay with a school friend of mine at his home not far from Ascot. We used to take our lunch with us sometimes on bright days—for it was at Christmas time—and go off for the day over the heather. You must remember that I was only a schoolboy at the time, so I daresay I exaggerated or elaborated some of the details a little, but the main facts of the story you can rely upon. Shall we sit down while I read it?"

Then when we had seated ourselves on a bench that stood at the end of the terrace, with the old house basking before us in the hot sunshine, he began to read.

"About six o'clock in the evening of one of the days towards the end of January, Jack and I were still wandering on high, heathy ground near Ascot. We had walked all day and had lost ourselves; but we kept going in as straight a line as we could, knowing that in time we should strike across a road. We were rather tired and silent; but suddenly Jack uttered an exclamation, and then pointed out a light across the heath. We stood a moment to see if it moved, but it remained still.

"'What is it?' I asked. 'There can be no house near here.'

"'It's a broomsquire's cottage, I expect,' said Jack.

"I asked what that meant.

"'Oh! I don't know exactly,' said Jack; 'they're a kind of gipsies.'

"We stumbled on across the heather, while the light grew steadily nearer. The moon was beginning to rise, and it was a clear night, one of those windless, frosty nights that sometimes come after a wet autumn. Jack plunged at one place into a hidden ditch, and I heard the crackling of ice as he scrambled out.

"'Skating to-morrow, by Jove,' he said.

"As we got closer I began to see that we were approaching a copse of firs; the heather began to get shorter. Then, as I looked at the light, I saw there was a fixed outline of a kind of house out of which it shone. The window apparently was an irregular shape, and the house seemed to be leaning against a tall fir on the outskirts of the copse. As we got quite close, our feet noiseless on the soft heather, I saw that the house was built altogether round the fir, which served as a kind of central prop. The house was made of wattled boughs, and thatched heavily with heather.

"I felt more and more anxious about it, for I had never heard of 'broomsquires,' and also, I confess, a little timid; for the place was lonely, and we were only two boys. I was leading now, and presently reached the window and looked in.

"The walls inside were hung with blankets and clothes to keep the wind out; there was a long old settle in one corner, the floor was carpeted with branches and blankets apparently, and there was an opening opposite, partly closed by a wattled hurdle that leaned against it. Half sitting and half lying on the settle, was an old woman with her face hidden. An oil-lamp hung from one of the branches of the fir that helped to form the roof. There was no sign of any other living thing in the place. As I looked Jack came up behind and spoke over my shoulder.

"'Can you tell us the way to the nearest high-road?' he asked.

"The old woman sat up suddenly, with a look of fright on her face. She was extraordinarily dirty and ill-kempt. I could see in the dim light of the lamp that she had a wrinkled old face, with sunken dark eyes, white eyebrows, and white hair; and her mouth began to mumble as she looked at us. Presently she made a violent gesture to wave us from the window.

"Jack repeated the question, and the old woman got up and hobbled quietly and crookedly to the door, and in a moment she had come round close to us. I then saw how very small she was. She could not have been five feet tall, and was very much bent. I must say again that I felt very uneasy and startled with this terrifying old creature close to me and peering up into my face. She took me by the coat and with her other hand beckoned quickly away in every direction. She seemed to be warning us away from the copse, but still she said nothing.

"Jack grew impatient.

"'Deaf old fool!' he said in an undertone, and then loudly and slowly, 'Can you tell us the way to the nearest highroad?'

"Then she seemed to understand, and pointed vigorously in the direction from which we had come.

"'Oh! nonsense,' said Jack, 'we've come from there. Come on this way,' he said, 'we can't spend all night here.' And then he turned the side of the little house and disappeared into the copse.

"The old woman dropped my coat in a moment, and began to run after Jack, and I went round the other side of the house and saw Jack moving in front, for the firs were sparse at the edge of the wood, and the moonlight filtered through them. The old woman, I saw as I turned into the wood, had stopped, knowing she could not catch us, and was standing with her hands stretched out, and a curious sound, half cry and half sob came from her. I was a little uneasy, because we had not treated her with courtesy, and stopped, but at that moment Jack called.

"'Come on,' he said, 'we're sure to find a road at the end of this.'

"So I went on.

"Once I turned and saw the little old woman standing as before; and as I looked between the trees she lifted one hand to her mouth and sent a curious whistling cry after us, that somehow frightened me. It seemed too loud for one so small.

"As we went on the wood grew darker. Here and there in an open patch there lay a white splash of moonlight on the fir needles, and great dim spaces lay round us. Although the wood stood on high ground, the trees grew so thickly about us that we could see nothing of the country round. Now and then we tripped on a root, or else caught in a bramble, but it seemed to me that we were following a narrow path that led deeper and deeper into the heart of the wood. Suddenly Jack stopped and lifted his hand.

"'Hush!' he said.

"I stopped too, and we listened breathlessly. Then in a moment more,

"'Hush!' he said, 'something's coming,' and he jumped out of the path behind a tree, and I followed him.

"Then we heard a scuffling in front of us and a grunting, and some big creature came hurrying down the path. As it passed us I looked, almost terrified out of my mind, and saw that it was a huge pig; but the thing that held me breathless and sick was that there ran nearly the whole length of its back a deep wound, from which the blood dripped. The creature, grunting heavily, tore down the path towards the cottage, and presently the sound of it died away. As I leaned against Jack, I could feel his arm trembling as it held the tree.

"'Oh!' he said in a moment, 'we must get out of this. Which way, which way?'

"But I had been still listening, and held him quiet.

"'Wait,' I said, 'there is something else.'

"Out of the wood in front of us there came a panting, and the soft sounds of hobbling steps along the path. We crouched lower and watched. Presently the figure of a bent old man came in sight, making his way quickly along the path. He seemed startled and out of breath. His mouth was moving, and he was talking to himself in a low voice in a complaining tone, but his eyes searched the wood from side to side.

"As he came quite close to us, as we lay hardly daring to breathe, I saw one of his hands that hung in front of him, opening and shutting; and that it was stained with what looked black in the moonlight. He did not see us, as by now we were hidden by a great bramble bush, and he passed on down the path; and then all was silent again.

"When a few minutes had passed in perfect stillness, we got up and went on, but neither of us cared to walk in the path down which those two terrible dripping things had come; and we went stumbling over the broken ground, keeping a parallel course to the path for about another two hundred yards. Jack had begun to recover himself, and even began to talk and laugh at being frightened at a pig and an old man. He told me afterwards that he had not seen the old man's hand.

"Then the path began to lead uphill. At this point I suddenly stopped Jack.

"'Do you see nothing?' I asked.

"Now I scarcely remember what I said or did. But this is what my friend told me afterwards. Jack said there was nothing but a little rising ground in front, from which the trees stood back.

"'Do you see nothing on the top of the mound? Out in the open, where the moonlight falls on her?'

"Jack told me afterwards that he thought I had gone suddenly mad, and grew frightened himself.

"'Do you not see a woman standing there? She has long yellow hair in two braids; she has thick gold bracelets on her bare arms. She has a tunic, bound by a girdle, and it comes below her knees: and she has red jewels in her hair, on her belt, on her bracelets; and her eyes shine in the moonlight: and she is waiting,—waiting for that which has escaped.'

"Now Jack tells me that when I said this I fell flat on my face, with my hands stretched out, and began to talk: but he said he could not understand a word I said. He himself looked steadily at the rising ground, but there was nothing to be seen there: there were the fir-trees standing in a circle round it, and a bare space in the middle, from which the heather was gone, and that was all. This mound would be about fifteen yards from us.

"I lay there, said Jack, a few minutes, and then sat up and looked about me. Then I remembered for myself that I had seen the pig and the old man, but nothing more: but I was terrified at the remembrance, and insisted upon our striking out a new course through the wood, and leaving the mound to our left. I did not know myself why the mound frightened me, but I dared not go near it. Jack wisely did not say anything more about it until afterwards. We presently found our way out of the copse, struck across the heath for another half-mile or so, and then came across a road which Jack knew, and so we came home.

"When we told our story, and Jack, to my astonishment, had added the part of which I myself had no remembrance, Jack's father did not say very much; but he took us next day to identify the place. To our intense surprise the house of the broomsquire was gone; there were the trampled branches round the tree, and the smoked branch from which the oil lamp had hung, and the ashes of a wood-fire outside the house, but no sign of the old man or his wife. As we went along the path, now in the cheerful frosty sunshine, we found dark splashes here and there on the brambles, but they were dry and colourless. Then we came to the mound.

"I grew uneasy again as we came to it, but was ashamed to show my fear in the broad daylight.

"On the top we found a curious thing, which Jack's father told us was one of the old customs of the broomsquires, that no one was altogether able to explain. The ground was shovelled away, so as to form a kind of sloping passage downwards into the earth. The passage was not more than five yards long; and at the end of it, just where it was covered by the ground overhead, was a sort of altar, made of earth and stones beaten flat; and plastered into its surface were bits of old china and glass. But what startled us was to find a dark patch of something which had soaked deep into the ground before the altar. It was still damp."

When the old man had read so far, he laid down the book.

"When I told all this to the Professor," he said, "he seemed very deeply interested. He told us, I remember, that the wound on the pig identified the nature of the sacrifice that the old man had begun to offer. He called it a 'blood-eagle,' and added some details which I will not disgust you with. He said too that the broomsquire had confused two rites—that only human sacrifices should be offered as 'blood-eagles.' In fact it all seemed perfectly familiar to him: and he said more than I can either remember or verify."

"And the woman on the rising ground?" I asked.

"Well," said the old man, smiling, "the Professor would not listen to my evidence about that. He accepted the early part of the story, and simply declined to pay any attention to the woman. He said I had been reading Norse tales, or was dreaming. He even hinted that I was romancing. Under other circumstances this method of treating evidence would be called 'Higher Criticism,' I believe."

"But it's all a brutal and disgusting worship," I said.

"Yes, yes," said the old man, "very brutal and disgusting; but is it not very much higher and better than the Professor's faith? He was only a skilled Ritualist after all, you see."

"—For faith, that when my need is sore,
Gleams from a partly-open door,
And shows the firelight on the floor—"
             A Canticle of Common Things

We were sitting together one morning in the common sitting-room in the centre of the house. There had been a fall of rain during the night, and it was thought better that the old man should not sit in the garden until the sun had dried the earth—so we sat indoors instead, but with the great door wide open, that looked on to a rectangle of lawn that lay before the house. Once a drive had led to this door through a gate with pedestals and stone balls, that stood exactly opposite, about fifteen yards away, but the drive had long been grassed over; although even now it showed faintly under two slight ridges in the grass that ran from the gate to the door. Otherwise the lawn was enclosed by a low old brick wall, almost hidden by a wealth of ivy, against which showed in rich masses of colour the heads of purple and yellow irises and tawny wallflowers.

The old man had been silent at breakfast. He had offered the Holy Sacrifice as usual that morning in the little chapel upstairs, and I had noticed at the time even that he seemed pre-occupied: and at breakfast he had talked very little, letting every subject drop as I suggested it; and I had understood at last that his thoughts were far away in the past; and I did not wish to trouble him.

29

We were sitting in two tall carved chairs at the doorway, his
feet were wrapped in a rug, and his eyes were looking steadily and
mournfully out across towards the ironwork gate in the wall. Tall
grasses of the patch of uncut meadow outside leaned against it or
pushed their feathery heads through it; and I saw presently that
the priest was looking at the gate, letting his eyes rove over every
detail of climbing plant, iron-work and the old brickwork—and not,
as I had at first thought, merely gazing into the dim distances of
the years behind him.

Suddenly he broke the long silence.

"Did I ever tell you," he asked, "about what I saw out there in
the garden? It looks ordinary enough now: yet I saw there what I
suppose I shall never see again on this side of death, or at least not
until I am in the very gate of death itself."

I too looked out at the gate. The atmosphere was full of that
"clear shining after rain" of which King David sang—it was air made
visible and radiant by the union of light and water, those two most
joyous creatures of God. A great chestnut tree blotted out all beyond the gate.

"Tell me if you can," I said. "You know how I love to hear those
stories."

"Years ago, as perhaps you know, not long after my ordination
I was working in London. My father lived here then, as his father
before him. That coat of arms in the centre of that iron gate was
put up by him soon after he succeeded to the property. I used to
come down here now and then for a breath of country air. I hardly
remember any pleasure so keen as the pleasure of coming into this
glorious country air out of the smoke and noise of London—or of
lying awake at night with the rustle of the pines outside my window instead of the ceaseless human tumult of the town.

"Well, I came down here once, suddenly, on a summer evening,
bearing heavy news. I need not go into details; it would be useless
to do that—but it will be enough to say that the news did not personally affect me or my family. It was a curious series of circumstances that led me to be the bearer of such news at all—but it was
to a lady who happened by the merest chance to be staying with

my family. I scarcely knew her at all—in fact I had only seen her once before. The news had come to my ears in London, and I had heard that the one whom it most concerned did not know it—and that they dared not write or telegraph. I volunteered of course to take the news myself.

"It was with a very heavy heart that I walked up from the station—the road seemed intolerably short. I may say that I knew that the news would be heartbreaking to her who had to hear it. I came in by the gate at the end of the avenue" (he waved his hand round to the right) "and passed right down to the back of the house, behind us. This door at which we are sitting had been the front door, but the drive had just been turfed over, and we used the door at the back instead, and this lawn here was very muck as you see it now, only the drive still showed plainly like a long narrow grave across the grass.

"As I came in through the door at the back, she was coming out, with a book and a basket-chair to sit in the garden. My heart gave a terrible throb of pain—for I knew that by the time my business was done there would be no thought of a quiet evening in the garden, and that look of serene happiness would be wiped out of her face—and all through what I had to say. For a moment she did not recognise me in the dark entry and stood back as I came in, and then—

"'Why it is you,' she said; 'you have come home. I did not know you were expected.'

"I breathed a moment steadily to recover myself.

"'I was not expected,' I said; and then, after a moment: 'May I speak to you?'

"'Speak to me? Why, certainly. In the garden or here?'

"'In here,' I answered, and went past her and pushed open the door into this room.

"She came past me, and stood here by the door still holding the book, with her finger between the leaves.

"Now you are wondering, I expect, why I did not get some other woman to break the news to her. Well, I had debated that ever since I had volunteered to be the bearer of these tidings: and partly because

I was afraid of being cowardly—call it pride if you will—and partly for other reasons which I need not mention, I felt I was bound to fulfil my promise literally. It might be, I thought too, that she would prefer the news to be known by as few people as possible. At least, whether I judged rightly or wrongly, here was my task before me.

"She stood there," the old man went on, pointing to the door-post on the right, "and I here," and he pointed a yard further back, "and the door was wide open as it is now, and the fragrant evening air poured past us into the room. Her face would be partly in shadow; but in her eyes there was just a dawning wonder at my abruptness, with perhaps the faintest tinge of anxiety, but no more.

"'I have come,' I said slowly, looking out into the garden, 'on a very hard errand.' I could not go on. I turned and looked at her. Ah! the anxiety had deepened a little. 'And—and it concerns you and your happiness.' I looked again, and I remember how her face had changed. Her lips were a little open, and her eyes shone wide open, half in shadow and half in light, and there were new and terrible little lines on her forehead. And then I told her.

"It was done in a sentence or two, and when I looked again her lips had closed and her hand had clenched itself into the moulding of the doorpost. I can see her rings now blazing in the light that poured over the chestnut tree (it was lower then) into the room. Then her lips moved once or twice—her hand unclenched itself hesitatingly—and she went steadily across the room. There was a great sofa there then, and when she reached it she threw herself face downwards across the arm and back.

"And I waited at the doorway, looking out at the iron gate. Sorrow was new to me then. I had not learnt to understand it then, or to be quiet under it. And as I looked I knew only that there was a terrible struggle going on in the room behind. There in front of me was a garden full of peace and sweetness and the soft glow of sunset light; and there behind me was something very like hell—and I stood between the living and the dead.

"Then I remembered that I was a priest, and ought to be able to say something—just a word of the Divine message that the Saviour brought—but I could not. I felt I was in deep waters. Even God seemed far away, intolerably serene and aloof; and I longed with all my power for a human person to pray and to bear a little of that strife behind me, from which I felt separated by so wide a gulf. And then God gave me the clear vision again.

"You see the iron gate," the old man went on, pointing. "Well, right between those posts, but a little above them, outlined clearly against the chestnut tree, beyond, was the figure of a man.

"Now I do not know how to explain myself, but I was conscious that across this material world of light and colour there cut a plane of the spiritual world, and that where the planes crossed I could look through and see what was beyond. It was like smoke cutting across a sunbeam. Each made the other visible.

"Well, this figure of a man, then, was kneeling in the air, that is the only way I can describe it—his face was turned towards me, but upwards. Now the most curious thing that struck me at the time was that he was, as it were, leaning at a sharp angle to one side; but it did not appear to be grotesque. Instead the world seemed tilted; the chestnut tree was out of the perpendicular; the wall out of the horizontal. The true level was that of the man.

"I know this sounds foolish, but it showed me how the world of spirits was the real world, and the world of sense comparatively unreal, just as the sorrow of the woman behind me was more real than the beams overhead.

"And again, compared with the kneeling figure, the chestnut tree and the gate seemed unsubstantial and shadowy. I know that men who see visions tell us that it is usually the other way. All I can say is that it was not so with me. This figure was kneeling, as I have said; his robe streamed away behind him—a great cloak— drawn tightly back from the shoulders, as if he were battling with a strong wind—the Wind of Grace, I suppose, that always blows from the Throne. His arms were stretched out in front of him, but opened sufficiently to let me see his face; and his face will be with me till I die, and please God afterwards. It was beardless, and bore the unmistakable character of a priest's face.

"Now you know how close the intensest pain and the intensest joy lie together. Their lines so nearly meet. In this man's face they did meet. Anguish and ecstasy were one. His eyes were open, his lips parted. I could not tell whether he was old or young. His face was ageless, as the faces of all are who look upon Him who inhabits eternity. He was praying. I can say no more than that. He had opened his heart to this woman's sorrow. He had made it his own: and it met there, in petition if you wish to call it so, or in resignation if you prefer that name for it, or in adoration—you may call it what you will—all that is true, but each is inadequate—but that sorrow met there with his own purified will, which itself had become one with the eternal will of God. I tell you I know it.

"I looked at him, and in my ears was a sobbing from the room behind; but as I looked the glory of anguish deepened on his face, and the sobbing behind me slackened and ceased, and I heard a whispering and the name of God and of His Son, and then the sight before me had passed; and there stood the chestnut tree again as real and as beautiful as before; and when I turned the woman was standing up, and the light of conquest was in her eyes.

"She held out her hand to me, and I stooped and kissed it, but I dared not take it in my own, for she had been in heavenly places. I had seen her sorrow carried and laid before the throne of God by one greater than either of us, and something of his glory rested upon her."

The old man's voice ceased. When I turned to look at him he was looking steadily again at the iron gate in the wall, and his eyes were shining like the radiant air outside. "I do not know," he said in a moment, "whether she is alive or dead, but I offered the Holy Sacrifice this morning for her peace in either state."

Pœna Damni

"All their sins stand before them,
and produce in their essences
remorse, eternal despair and a
hostile will against God. For
such a soul there is no remedy.
It cannot come into the light of
God. . . . Even if St. Peter had
left many thousand keys upon
earth, not a single one of them
could open Heaven for it."
            A German Mystic

We were sitting at dinner one evening when the priest, who
had been talkative, seemed to fall into a painful train of thought
that silenced him. He grew more and more ill at ease, and was obviously relieved when I threw my cigarette away and he was able
to propose a move to the next room. Presently his distress seemed
to pass; and then, as we sat near the fireplace, he explained himself.

"I must ask your pardon," he said, "but somehow I fell into a
very dreadful train of thought. It was suggested to me, I think, by
the red lamp on the table and the evening light through the windows, and the silver and glass. (You know the power of association!) I went through one of the most fearful moments of my life
under just those circumstances."

I was silent, as the priest seemed to have more to say.

"It has affected my nerves," he said, "and it would be rather a relief to tell you. Would you mind if I did so?"

On my assurance that it would greatly interest me, he began.

"It is a fashion among those who do not really accept Revelation as revelation to believe in a kind of Universalism. Quite apart from authority, this doctrine contravenes, as you of course know, the reality of man's free will. The incident of which I wish to tell you concerns the way in which I first caught a glimpse of that for myself.

"A good many years ago I made the acquaintance of a man in the West of England, under circumstances that I need not describe further than saying that he seemed to have confidence in me. He asked me to stay with him in his country house, and I went down from London for the inside of a week. I found him living the usual country life, fishing and so forth; for it was summer when I visited him. It was a fine old house that he lived in, surrounded by coverts. He had a charming wife and two or three children, and at first I thought him extremely happy and contented.

"Then I thought that I noticed that things were not so well with him. The cottages on his estate were ill-cared for, and that is always a bad sign. From one or two small signs, such as you can guess, I found that the tone among his servants was not what it should be; and one or two horrid pieces of cruelty came under my notice. I know this sounds as if I were a sort of spy, greedy for information; but all that I can say is, that these signs were unmistakable and obvious, and came to me, of course, unsought and unexpected. Then I saw that his domestic relations were not right. I do not know how else to describe all this than by saying that there seemed a kind of blight upon his surroundings. Nothing was absolutely wrong, and yet all was just wrong.

"At first I thought that I myself was depressed or jaundiced in some way; but at last I could not continue to believe that; and on the Friday of my stay, the last day, I became finally certain that something was horribly wrong with the man himself. Then that evening he opened his heart to me, so far as it was possible for him to do so.

"His wife, with the two daughters, had left us after dessert and gone into the garden, and we remained in the dining-room. The windows looked to the west, across a smooth sloping lawn, with the lake at the end; beyond that rose up a delicate birch wood, and beyond that again a soft green sky, where the sun had set, deepening into a liquid evening blue overhead, in which a star or two glimmered. I could see, as I looked out, the white figures of his wife and daughters against the shining surface of the lake at the end of the lawn.

"After he had lit his cigarette, and had a glass or two of wine, suddenly he opened his heart to me, and told me an appalling story that I could not tell you. I sat and watched his strong sinewy hand rise and fall with the cigarette, under the red lamplight; I glanced at his quiet well-bred face with the downcast eyes and the long moustache, and I wondered whether it was possible really for such a tale to be true; but he spoke with a restrained conviction that left no room for doubt. What I gathered from the story was this;— that he had identified himself, his whole will, his whole life practically, with the cause of Satan. I could not detect as he talked that he had ever seriously attempted to detach himself from that cause. It has been said that a saint is one who always chooses the better of the two courses open to him at every step; so far as I could see this man had always chosen the worse of the two courses. When he had done things that you and I would think right, he had always done them for some bad reason. He had been continuously aware, too, of what was happening. I do not think that I have ever heard such a skilful self-analysis. Now and then, as I saw the gulf of despair towards which his talk was leading, I interrupted him, suggesting alleviations of the horror—suggesting that he was pessimistic—that he had acted often under misconceptions—and the like; but he always met me with a quiet answer that silenced me. In fact," said the priest, who was beginning to tremble a little, "I have never thought it possible that a heart could be so corrupt and yet retain so much knowledge and feeling.

"When he had finished his story he looked at me for a moment, and then said:

"'Lately I have seen what I have lost, and what I shall lose; and I have told you this to ask if the Christian Gospel has any hope for such as I am.'

"Of course I answered as a Christian priest must answer, for I honestly thought that here was the greatest miracle of God's grace that I had ever seen. When I had finished I lifted my eyes from the cloth and looked up. His fingers, while I was speaking, had been playing with an apostle spoon, but as I looked up he looked up too, and our eyes met."

As the priest said this, he got up, and leaned his head against the high oak mantelpiece, and was silent a moment. Then he went on:

"God forgive me if I was wrong—if I am wrong now—but this is what I think I saw.

"Out of his eyes looked a lost soul. As a symbol, or a sign, too, his eyes shone suddenly with that dull red light that you may see sometimes in a dog's eyes. It was the *pœna damni* of which I had read, which shone there. It was true, as he had said, that he was seeing clearly what he had lost and would lose; it was the gate of heaven opening to one who could not enter in. It was the chink of light under the door to one who cried, 'Lord, Lord, open to me,' but through the door there came that answer, 'I know you not.' Ah! it was not that he had never known before what God was, and His service and love; it was just his condemnation that he had known: that he had seen, not once or twice but again and again, the two ways, and had, not once nor twice but again and again, chosen the worse of those two; and now he was powerless.

"I tell you I saw this for a moment. There was this human face, so well-bred, with its delicate lines, looking almost ethereal in the soft red light of the lamp: behind him, between the windows hung a portrait of an ancestor, some old Caroline divine in ruff and bands. Through the windows was that sweet glory of evening—with the three figures by the lake. Here, between us, was the delicate soothing luxury of cleanliness and coolness and refreshment, such as glass and silver and fruit suggest: and there for one second in this frame of beauty and peace looked the eyes of one who desired even a drop of living water to cool his tongue, for he was tormented in a flame.

"And I saw all this; and then the room began to swim and whirl, and the table to tilt and sway, and I fell, I suppose, forward, and sank down on to the floor. When I recovered there were the men in the room, and the anxious face of my host looking down on me.

"I had to return to town the next morning. I wrote to him a long letter the following week, saying that I had been ill on the evening on which he had given me his confidence: and that I had not said all that I could say: and I went on, giving the lie to what I had thought I had seen, speaking to him as I should speak to any soul who was weary of sin and desired God.

"Indeed I thought it most possible, as I wrote the letter, that I had had a horrible delusion; and that all could be well with him. I got an answer of a few lines, saying that he must apologise for having troubled me with such a story; adding that he had greatly exaggerated his own sin; that he too had been over-excited and unwell: and that he too trusted in a God of Love—and begging me not to refer to the conversation again."

The priest sat down again.

"Now you may of course accept this version of it, if you will. I only would to God that I could too."

"Should it be burdensome for
thee ... she will for thy sake
herself raise me up when I chance
to fall, and console me when
sorrowing."
                St. Leander of Seville

The following letter will explain itself. The original was read to me by my friend on one of those days during my stay with him; and he allowed me, at my request, to make a copy. The sermon referred to in the first sentence of the letter was preached in a foreign watering-place on Christmas Day.

"Villa —

"December 29, 18—

"Reverend and Dear Sir,

"I listened with great attention to your sermon on Christmas Day; I am getting on in years, and I am an invalid; so you will understand that I have few friends—and I think none who would not think me mad if I told them the story that I am proposing to tell you. For many years I have been silent on this subject; since it always used to be received with incredulity. But I fancy that you will not be incredulous. As I watched you and listened to you on Christmas Day, I thought I saw in you one to whom the supernatural was more than a beautiful and symbolical fairy-story, and one who held it

40

not impossible that this unseen should sometimes manifest itself. As you reminded us, the Religion of the Incarnation rests on the fact that the Infinite and the Eternal expresses Himself in terms of space and time; and that it is in this that the greatness of the Love of God consists. Since then, as you said, the Creation, the Incarnation, and the Sacramental System alike, in various degree, are the manifestation of God under these conditions, surely it cannot be 'materialistic' (whatever that exactly means), to believe that the 'spiritual' world and the personages that inhabit it sometimes express themselves in the same manner as their Maker. However, will you have patience with me while I tell you this story? I cannot believe that such a grace should be kept in darkness.

"I was about seven years old when my mother died, and my father left me chiefly to the care of servants. Either I must have been a difficult child, or my nurse must have been a hard woman: but I never gave her my confidence. I had clung to my mother as a saint clings to God: and when I lost her, it nearly broke my heart. Night after night I used to lie awake, with the firelight in the room, remembering how she would look in on her way to bed; when at last I slept it seems to me now as if I never did anything but dream of her; and it was only to wake again to that desolate emptiness. I would torture myself by closing my eyes, and fancying she was there; and then opening them and seeing the room empty. I would turn and toss and sob without a sound. I suppose that I was as near the limit that divides sanity from madness as it is possible to be. During the day I would sit on the stairs when I could get away from my nurse, and pretend that my mother's footsteps were moving overhead, that her door opened, that I heard her dress on the carpet: again I would open my eyes, and in self-cruelty compel myself to understand that she was gone. Then again I would tell myself that it was all right: that she was away for the day, but would come back at night. In the evenings I would be happier, as the time for her return drew nearer; even when I said my prayers I would look forward to the moment, into which I had cheated myself in believing, when the door would open, after I was in bed, and my mother look in. Then as the time passed, my false faith would break down, and I would sob myself to sleep, dream of her, and sob myself awake again. As I look back it appears to me as if this went on for months: I suppose, however, in reality, it could not have been more than a very few weeks, or my reason would have given way. And at last I was caught on the edge of the precipice, and drawn lovingly back to safety and peace.

"I used to sleep alone in the night-nursery at this time, and my nurse occupied a room opening out of it. The night-nursery had two doors, one at the foot of my bed, and one at the further end of the room, in the corner diagonally opposite to that in which the head of my bed stood. The first opened upon the landing, and the second into my nurse's room, and this latter was generally kept a few inches open. There was no light in my room, but a night-light was kept burning in the nurse's room, so that even without the firelight my room was not in total darkness.

"I was lying awake one night (I suppose it would be about eleven o'clock), having gone through a dreadful hour or two of misery, half-waking and half-sleeping. I had been crying quietly, for fear my nurse should hear through the partly opened door, burying my hot face in the pillow. I was feeling really exhausted, listening to my own heart, and cheating myself into the half-faith that its throbs were the footsteps of my mother coming towards my room; I had raised my face and was staring at the door at the foot of my bed, when it opened suddenly without a sound; and there, as I thought, my mother stood, with the light from the oil-lamp outside shining upon her. She was dressed, it seemed, as once before I had seen her in London when she came into my room to bid me good-night before she went out to an evening party. Her head shone with jewels that flashed as the firelight rose and sank in the room, a dark cloak shrouded her neck and shoulders, one hand held the edge of the door, and a great jewel gleamed on one of her fingers. She seemed to be looking at me.

"I sat up in bed in a moment, amazed but not frightened, for was it not what I had so often fancied? and I called out to her:

"'Mother, mother!'

"At the word she turned and looked on to the landing, and gave a slight movement with her head, as if to some one waiting there, either of assent or dismissal, and then turned to me again. The door closed silently, and I could see in the firelight, and in the faint glimmer that came through the other door, that she held out her arms to me. I threw off the bed-clothes in a moment, and scrambled down to the end of the bed, and she lifted me gently in her arms, but said no word. I too said nothing, but she raised the cloak a little and wrapped it round me, and I lay there in bliss, my head on her shoulder, and my arm round her neck. She walked smoothly and noiselessly to a rocking-chair that stood beside the fire and sat down, and then began to rock gently to and fro. Now it may be difficult to believe, but I tell you that I neither said anything, nor desired to say anything. It was enough that she was there. After a little while I suppose I fell asleep, for I found myself in an agony of tears and trembling again, but those arms held me firmly, and I was soon at peace; still she spoke no word, and I did not see her face.

"When I woke again she was gone, and it was morning, and I was in bed, and the nurse was drawing up the blind, and the winter sunshine lay on the wall. That day was the happiest I had known since my mother's death; for I knew she would come again.

"After I was in bed that evening I lay awake waiting, so full of happy content and certainty that I fell asleep. When I awoke the fire was out, and there was no light but a narrow streak that came through the door from my nurse's room. I lay there a minute or two waiting, expecting every moment to see the door open at the foot of my bed; but the minutes passed, and then the clock in the hall below beat three. Then I fell into a passion of tears; the night was nearly gone, and she had not come to me. Then, as I tossed to and fro, trying to stifle my crying, through my tears there came the misty flash of light as the door opened, and there she stood again. Once again I was in her arms, and my face on her shoulder. And again I fell asleep there.

"Now this went on night after night, but not every night, and never unless I awoke and cried. It seemed that if I needed her desperately she came, but only then.

"But there were two curious incidents that occurred in the order in which I will write them down. The second I understand now, at any rate; the first I have never altogether understood, or rather there are several possible explanations.

"One night as I lay in her arms by the fire, a large coal suddenly slipped from the grate and fell with a crash, awaking the nurse in the other room. I suppose she thought something was wrong, for she appeared at the door with a shawl over her shoulders, holding the night-light in one hand and shading it with the other. I was going to speak, when my mother laid her hand across my mouth. The nurse advanced into the room, passed close beside us, apparently without seeing us, went straight to the empty bed, looked down on the tumbled clothes, and then turned away as if satisfied, and went back to her room. The next day I managed to elicit from her, by questioning, the fact that she had been disturbed in the night, and had come into my room, but had seen me sleeping quietly in bed.

"The other incident was as follows. One night I was lying half dozing against my mother's breast, my head against her heart, and not, as I usually lay, with my head on her shoulder. As I lay there it seemed to me as if I heard a strange sound like the noise of the sea in a shell, but more melodious. It is difficult to describe it, but it was like the murmuring of a far-off crowd, overlaid with musical pulsations. I nestled closer to her and listened; and then I could distinguish, I thought, innumerable ripples of church bells pealing, as if from another world. Then I listened more intently to the other sound; there were words, but I could not distinguish them. Again and again a voice seemed to rise above the others, but I could hear no intelligible words. The voices cried in every sort of tone—passion, content, despair, monotony. And then as I listened I fell asleep. As I look back now, I have no doubt what voices those were that I heard.

"And now comes the end of the story. My health began to improve so remarkably that those about me noticed it. I never gave way, during the day at any rate, to those old piteous imaginings; and at night, when, I suppose, the will partly relaxes its control, whenever my distress reached a certain point, she was there to comfort me. But her visits grew more and more rare, as I needed her less, and at last ceased. But it is of her last visit, which took place in the spring of the following year, that I wish to speak.

"I had slept well all night, but had awakened in the dark just before the dawn from some dream which I forget, but which left my nerves shaken. When in my terror I cried out, again the door opened, and she was there. She stood with the jewels in her hair, and the cloak across her shoulders, and the light from the landing lay partly on her face. I scrambled at once down the bed, and was lifted and carried to the chair, and presently fell asleep. When I awoke the dawn had come, and the birds were stirring and chirping, and a pleasant green light was in the room; and I was still in her arms. It was the first time, except in the instance I have mentioned, that I had awakened except in bed, and it was a great joy to find her there. As I turned a little I saw the cloak which sheltered us both—of a deep blue, with an intricate pattern of flowers and leaves and birds among branches. Then I turned still more to see her face, which was so near me, but it was turned away; and even as I moved she rose and carried me towards the bed. Still holding me on her left arm she lifted and smoothed the bedclothes, and then laid me gently in bed, with my head on the pillow. And then for the first time I saw her face plainly. She bent over me, with one hand on my breast as if to prevent me from rising, and looked straight into my eyes; and it was not my mother.

"There was one moment of blinding shock and sorrow, and I gave a great sob, and would have risen in bed, but her hand held me down, and I seized it with both my own, and still looked in her eyes. It was not my mother, and yet was there ever such a mother's face as that? I seemed to be looking into depths of indescribable tenderness and strength, and I leaned on that strength in those moments of misery. I gave another sob or two as I looked, but I was quieter, and at last peace came to me, and I had learnt my lesson.

"I did not at the time know who she was, but my little soul dimly saw that my own mother for some reason could not at that time come to me who needed her so sorely, and that another great Mother had taken her place; yet, after the first moment or so, I felt no anger or jealousy, for one who had looked into that kindly face could have no such unworthy thought.

"Then I lifted my head a little, I remember, and kissed the hand that I held in my own, reverently and slowly. I do not know why I did it, except that it was the natural thing to do. The hand was strong and white, and delicately fragrant. Then it was withdrawn, and she was standing by the door, and the door was open; and then she was gone, and the door was closed.

"I have never seen her since, but I have never needed to see her, for I know who she is; and, please God, I shall see her again; and next time I hope my mother and I will be together; and perhaps it will not be very long; and perhaps she will allow me to kiss her hand again.

"Now, my dear sir, I do not know how all this will appear to you; it may seem to you, though I do not think it will, merely childish. Yet, in a sense, I desire nothing more than that, for our Saviour Himself told us to be like children, and our Saviour too once lay on His Mother's breast. I know that I am getting an old man, and that old men are sometimes very foolish but it more and more seems to me that experience, as well as His words, tells me that the great Kingdom of Heaven has a low and narrow door that only little children can enter, and that we must become little again, and drop all our bundles, if we would go through.

"That, dear and Reverend Sir, is my story. And may I ask you to remember me sometimes at the altar and in your prayers? for surely God will ask much from one to whom He has given so much, and as yet I have nothing to show for it; and my time must be nearly at an end, even if His infinite patience is not.

"Believe me,

"Yours faithfully,

"— —."

"Lo, I am free! I choose the pain thou bearest:
Thou art the messenger of one who waits;
Thou wilt reveal the hidden face thou wearest
When my feet falter at the Eternal Gates."
Old Foes

We were at tea one afternoon on the little low, tiled platform that marked the site of an old summer-house. Tall hurdles covered with briar-roses on the further side of the path fenced off the rest of the garden from us, and the sun had just sunk below the level of the house, throwing both ourselves and the garden into cool shadow. The servant had brought out the tea-things, but he presently returned with something of horror on his face. The old man looked up and saw him. "What is it, Parker?" he asked.

"There's been an accident, sir. Tom Awcock at the home farm has been drawn into some machine, and they say he must lose both arms, and maybe his life."

The old man turned quite white, and his eyes grew larger and brighter.

"Is the doctor with him?" he asked, in a perfectly steady voice.

"Yes, sir, and they've sent a message, Would you be good enough to step down? The rector's away, and Tom's mother's crying terrible. But not yet, sir. About seven o'clock, they say. It won't be over till then, and there's no immediate danger."

"Tell them I will be there at seven," said the clergyman.

47

Parker went back to the house, and presently we heard the foot-steps of a child running down the drive towards the farm.

"How shocking it is!" I said in a moment or two.

"Ah!" said the old man, smiling, "I have learnt my lesson. It is not really so shocking as you think. Does that sound very hard?"

I said nothing, for it seemed to me that all the consolations of religion could not soften the horror of such things. If such agonies are necessary as remedies or atonements, at least they are terrible.

"I learnt my lesson," the old man went on, "down the road there outside the hedge—down by the bridge. Would you like to hear it? Or are you tired of an old dreamer's stories?" and he smiled at me.

"Now I know you think that I am hard—that I am a little apart maybe from human life—that I cannot understand the blind mis-ery of those who suffer in ignorance; yet you would be the first, I believe, to think that Mrs. Awcock's consolations are unreal, and that when she tells me that she knows there is a wise purpose be-hind, she is only repeating what is proper to say to a clergyman. But that is not so; that old threadbare sentence is intensely real to these people, and, I hope, to myself too. For there is nothing that I desire more than to be a child like them. It is the apparent pur-poselessness that distresses you: it is the certainty of a deliberate purpose that comforts me. Well, shall I tell you what I saw?"

I was a little distressed at what looked like callousness, but I told him I would like to hear the story.

"I was standing one evening—it would be about five years ago—in the field down there near the stream. You remember the bridge there, over which the road goes, just outside the hedge. I love run-ning water, and I went slowly up and down by the side of the beck. There were children on the road, coming back from school, and they stopped on the bridge to look at the water, as children and old men will. They did not see me, as the field is a little below the road, and besides their backs were turned to me. I could see a pink frock or two, and a pair of stout bare legs. Two girls were taking their brother home—he was between them, a hand clasped by each of the sisters. I suppose the eldest girl would be about nine, and the boy five. They were talking solemnly, and I could hear every word.

"Why are children always supposed to be gay? There is no solemnity in the world to be compared to the solemnity of a little boy, or of his sister who has charge of him.

"One of the girls said, 'Look, Johnny, there are little fishes down there.'

"'When I am a man'—Johnny began, very slowly.

"'Look, Johnny,' said the other girl, 'there's a blue flower.'

"Up to this I remember every word. But then I began to watch Johnny.

"The girls went on talking, but they leaned over more, and I could not hear them plainly. Johnny stealthily withdrew a hand from each of his sisters, and began to look for a stone to throw at the fishes or the blue flower, I suppose; for man is lord of Creation. I could see him presently through the hedge digging patiently with his fingers and loosening a stone that was firm in the road. And at that moment I heard a far-away shout and the distant bark of a dog.

"The evening was wonderfully still every leaf hung quiet: and there were far-off clouds heaping themselves up in the west, tower over tower. We had a thunderstorm that night, I remember. The brook was quiet, just slipping noiselessly from pool to pool.

"Still Johnny was digging and the girls were talking. Then out of the village above us came again far-off noises. I could hear a rumble and the clatter of hoofs, then a cry or two more, and the nearer terrified yelp of a dog. But the girls were intent on the brook—and Johnny on the stone.

"Even now I did not understand what was happening: but I grew uneasy—and with great difficulty, for I was an old man even then, tried to scramble up the high bank by the bridge. As I reached the top I saw that one of the girls had gone. She had run, I suppose, off the bridge down by the side of the road. The other girl was still standing—but looking in a frightened way up the hill. Down the hill came the loud rumble of a cart and the clatter of hoofs, terribly near.

"The girl by the side of the road began to scream to her sister, who darted off, and then remembered Johnny and turned. Johnny got up too and ran to the parapet and stood against it.

"I was shouting too by now, through the hedge: but I could do nothing more, nothing more, because the hedge was high and thick, and I was an old man. Then in a moment I remembered that shouting would only distract them, and I stopped. It was useless. I could do absolutely nothing. But it was very hard.

"Then I saw the galloping body of a horse through the branches, with a butcher's cart that rocked behind him. There was no one on the cart.

"Now there was room for the cart to pass the boy safely. By the wheelmarks, which I looked at afterwards, there were three clear feet—if only the boy had stood still.

"The girls seemed petrified as they stood, one in act to run, the other crouching and hiding her face against the hedge. The cart was now within ten yards, as I could see, though I was still staring at Johnny. Then this is what I saw.

"Somewhere behind him over the parapet of the bridge there was a figure. I remember nothing about it except the face and the hands. The face was, I think, the tenderest I have ever seen. The eyes were downcast, looking upon the boy's head with indescribable love, the lips were smiling. One hand was over the boy's eyes, the other against his shoulder behind. In a moment the memory of other stories I had heard came to mind—and I gave a sob of relief that the boy was safe in such care.

"But as the iron hoofs and rocking wheels came up, the hand on the boy's shoulder suddenly pushed him to meet them; and yet those tender eyes and mouth never flinched, and the child took a step forward in front of the horse, and was beaten down without a cry: and the cart lurched heavily, righted itself, and dashed on out of sight.

"When the cloud of dust had passed, the little body lay quiet on the road, and the two girls were clinging to one another, screaming and sobbing, but there was nothing else.

"I was as angry at first as an old man could be. I nearly (may He forgive me for it now!) cursed God and died. But the memory of that tender face did its work. It was as the face of a mother who nurses her first-born child, as the face of a child who kisses a

wounded creature, it was as I think the Father's Face itself must
have been, which those angels always behold, as He looked down
upon the Sacrifice of His only Son.

"Will you forgive me now if I seemed hard a few minutes ago?
Perhaps you still think it was hardness that made me speak as I
did. But, for myself, I hope I may call it by a better name than
that."

"In her all longings mix and meet;
　Dumb souls through her are eloquent,
She feels the earth beneath her feet
　Vibrate in passionate intent;
Through her our tides of feeling roll
And find their God within her soul."
　　　　　　The Contemplative Soul

One evening about this time, on coming indoors for tea, I found the old man seated at the open door that looked on to the lawn, with a book on his knees, and his finger between the pages. He held the book towards me as I came near him, and showed me the title, "The Interior Castle."

"I have just been reading," he said, "Saint Teresa's description of the difference between the intellectual and the imaginative vision. It is curious how she fails really to express it, except to any one who happens to have had a glimpse already for himself of what she means. I suppose it is one of the signs of reality in the spiritual world that no one can ever describe so much as he knows."

I sat down.

"I am afraid I don't understand a word you are saying," I answered smiling.

For answer he opened the book and read Saint Teresa's curious gasping incoherent sentences—at least so I thought them.

"Still," I said, "I am afraid—"

"Oh," he said almost impatiently, "surely you know now; indeed you know it, but do not recognise it."

"Can you give me any sort of instance?" I asked.

He thought for a moment or two in silence; and then—

"I think I can," he said, "if you are sure it will not bore you."

He poured out tea for us both, and then began:

"Most of the tales I have told you are of the imaginative vision, by which I do not mean that the vision is in any way unreal or untrue, which is what most people mean by 'imaginative,' but only that it presents itself in the form of a visible picture. It seems chiefly the function of the imagination to visualise facts, and it is an abuse of that faculty to employ it chiefly in visualising fancies. But it is possible for spiritual facts to represent themselves vividly and clearly to the intellect instead, so that the person to whom the intellectual vision is given does not, so to speak, 'see' anything, but only 'apprehends' something to be true. However, this will become more clear presently.

"Some years ago I took my annual holiday in the form of a solitary walking tour. I will not tell you where I went, as there are others concerned in this story who would dislike intensely to be publicly spoken of in the way that I shall have to speak of them; but it is enough to say that I came at last to a little town towards sunset. My object in coming to this place was to visit a convent of enclosed nuns whose reputation for holiness was very great. I carried with me a letter of introduction to the Reverend Mother, which I knew would admit me to the chapel. I left my bag at the inn, and then walked down to the convent, which stood a little way out of the town.

"The lay sister who opened the door to me asked me to come into the parlour while she told the Reverend Mother; and after waiting a few minutes in the prim room with its bees-waxed floor and its religious engravings and objects, a wonderfully dignified little old lady, with a quiet wrinkled face, came in with my letter open in her hand. We talked a few minutes about various things, and I had a glass of cowslip wine in a thick-lipped wineglass.

"She told me that the convent was a very ancient foundation, that it had been a country house ever since the Dissolution of the Religious Houses, until about twenty years ago, when it had been acquired for the community. There still remained of the old buildings part of the cloisters, with the south transept of the old church, which was now the chapel; the whole, with a wall or two, forming the courtyard through which I had come. Behind the house lay the garden, on to which the window of the parlour looked; and as I sat I could see a black cross or two marking the nuns' graveyard. I made inquiries as to the way the time of the community was spent.

"'Our object,' said the old lady, 'is perpetual intercession for sinners. We have the great joy of the Blessed Sacrament amongst us in the chapel, and, except during the choir offices and Mass there is always a nun kneeling before It. We look after one or two ladies incurably ill, who have come to end their days with us, and we make our living by embroidery.'

"I asked how it was that she could receive strangers if the order was an enclosed one.

"'The lay sisters and myself alone can receive strangers. We find that necessary.'

"After a little more talk I asked whether I might see the chapel, and she took me out into the courtyard immediately.

"As we walked across the grass she pointed out to me the cloisters, now built up into a corridor, and the long ruined wall of the old nave which formed one side of the quadrangle. A grave-faced and stout collie dog had joined us at the door, and we three went together slowly towards the door in the centre of the west wall of the restored transept. The evening sun lay golden on the wall before us and on the ruined base of the central tower of the old church, round which jackdaws wheeled and croaked."

The old priest broke off and turned to me, with his eyes burning:

"What a marvellous thing the Religious Life is," he said, "and above all the Contemplative Life! Here were these nuns as no doubt they and their younger sisters are still, without one single thing that in the world's opinion makes life worth living. There is practically perpetual silence, there are hours to be spent in the chapel, no luxuries, no amusements, no power of choice, they are always rather hungry and rather tired, at the very least. And yet they are not sacrificing present happiness to future happiness, as the world always supposes, but they are intensely and radiantly happy 'now in this present time.' I don't know what further proof any one wants of Who our Lord is than that men and women find the keenest, and in fact their only joy, in serving Him and belonging to Him.

"Well, I remember that something of this sort was in my mind as I went across the courtyard beside this motherly old lady with her happy quiet face. She had been over fifty years in Religion, my friend had told me.

"At the door she stopped.

"'I will not come in,' she said, 'but you will find me in the parlour when you come out.'

"And she turned and went back, with the collie walking slowly beside her, his golden plumed tail raised high against her black habit.

"The door was partly open, but a thick curtain hung beyond. I pushed it quietly aside and stepped in. It seemed very dark at first, in contrast to the brilliant sunshine outside; but I presently saw that I was kneeling before a high iron-barred screen, in which was no door. On the left, in the further corner of the chapel, glimmered a blue light in a silver lamp before a statue of our Lady.

"Opposite me rose up the steps before the high altar; but not far away, because, as you remember, the chapel had once been the transept of a church, and the east wall, in the centre of which the high altar stood, was longer than both the south wall where a second altar stood, and the modern brick wall that closed it on the north. A slender crucifix in black and white and six thin tapers rose above the altar, and high above stood the Tabernacle closed by a white silk curtain, before which flickered a tiny red spark.

"I said a prayer or two, and then I noticed for the first time a dark outline rising in the centre of the space before the altar. For a moment I was perplexed, and then I saw that it was the nun whose hour it was for intercession. Her back was turned to me as she knelt at the faldstool, and her black veil fell in rigid lines on to her shoulders,

and mingled with her black serge habit below. There she knelt perfectly motionless, praying. I had not, and have not, a notion as to
her age. She might have been twenty-five or seventy.

"As I knelt there I thought deeply, wondering as to the nun's
age, how long she had been professed, when she would die, whether
she was happy; and, I am afraid, I thought more of her than of
Him Who was so near. Then a kind of anger seized me, as I compared in my mind the life of a happy good woman in the world
with that of this poor creature. I pictured the life, as one so often
sees it in homes, of a mother with her children growing up about
her, her hands busy with healthy home work, her life glorified by a
good man's love; as she grows older, passing from happy stage to
happy stage, comforting, helping, sweetening every soul she meets.
Was it not for this that women—and men too, I thought, rebuking
myself—were made? Then think of the sour life of the cloister—as
loveless and desolate as the cold walls themselves! And even, I
thought, even if there is a strange peculiar joy in the Religious
Life—even if there is an absence of sorrows and anxieties such as
spoil the happiness of many lives in the world—yet, after all, surely
the Contemplative Life is useless and barren. The Active Life may
be well enough, if the prayers and the discipline issue in greater
efficiency, if the priest is more fervent when he ministers outside,
and the sister of charity more charitable. Yes, I thought, the active
Religious Life is reasonable enough; but the Contemplative! After
all it is essentially selfish, it is a sin against society. Possibly it was
necessary when the wickedness of the world was more fierce, to
protest against it by this retirement; but not now, not now! How can
the lump be leavened if the leaven be withdrawn? How can a soul
serve God by forsaking the world which He made and loves?" . . .

"And so," said the priest, turning to me again, "I went on—poor
ignorant fool!—thinking that the woman who knelt in front of me
was less useful than myself, and that my words and actions and
sermons and life did more to advance God's kingdom than her
prayers! And then—then—at the moment when I reached that climax of folly and pride, God was good to me and gave me a little
light.

"Now, I do not know how to put it—I have never put it into words before, except to myself—but I became aware, in my intellect alone, of one or two clear facts. In order to tell you what those facts were I must use picture language; but remember they are only translations or paraphrases of what I perceived.

"First I became aware suddenly that there ran a vital connection from the Tabernacle to the woman. You may think of it as one of those bands you see in machinery connecting two wheels, so that when either wheel moves the other moves too. Or you may think of it as an electric wire, joining the instrument the telegraph operator uses with the pointer at the other end. At any rate there was this vital band or wire of life.

Now in the Tabernacle I became aware that there was a mighty stirring and movement. Something within it beat like a vast Heart, and the vibrations of each pulse seemed to quiver through all the ground. Or you may picture it as the movement of a clear deep pool when the basin that contains it is jarred—it seemed like the movement of circular ripples crossing and recrossing in swift thrills. Or you may think of it as that faint movement of light and shade that may be seen in the heart of a white-hot furnace. Or again you may picture it as sound—as the sound of a high ship-mast with the rigging, in a steady wind; or the sound of deep woods in a July noon."

The priest's face was working, and his hands moved nervously.

"How hopeless it is," he said, "to express all this! Remember that all these pictures are not in the least what I perceived. They are only grotesque paraphrases of a spiritual fact that was shown me.

"Now I was aware that there was something of the same activity in the heart of the woman, but I did not know which was the controlling power. I did not know whether the initiative sprang from the Tabernacle and communicated itself to the nun's will; or whether she, by bending herself upon the Tabernacle, set in motion a huge dormant power. It appeared to me possible that the solution lay in the fact that two wills co-operated, each reacting upon the other. This, in a kind of way, appears to me now true as regards the whole mystery of free-will and prayer and grace.

"At any rate the union of these two represented itself to me, as I have said, as forming a kind of engine that radiated an immense light or sound or movement. And then I perceived something else too.

"I once fell asleep in one of those fast trains from the north, and did not awake until we had reached the terminus. The last thing I had seen before falling asleep had been the quiet darkening woods and fields through which we were sliding, and it was a shock to awake in the bright humming terminus and to drive through the crowded streets, under the electric glare from the lamps and windows. Now I felt something of that sort now. A moment ago I had fancied myself apart from movement and activity in this quiet convent; but I seemed somehow to have stepped into a centre of busy, rushing life. I can scarcely put the sensation more clearly than that. I was aware that the atmosphere was charged with energy; great powers seemed to be astir, and I to be close to the whirling centre of it all.

"Or think of it like this. Have you ever had to wait in a City office? If you have done that you will know how intense quiet can coexist with intense activity. There are quiet figures here and there round the room. Or it may be there is only one such figure—a great financier—and he sitting there almost motionless. Yet you know that every movement tingles, as it were, out from that still room all over the world. You can picture to yourself how people leap to obey or to resist—how lives rise and fall, and fortunes are made and lost, at the gentle movements of this lonely quiet man in his office. Well, so it was here. I perceived that this black figure knelt at the centre of reality and force, and with the movements of her will and lips controlled spiritual destinies for eternity. There ran out from this peaceful chapel lines of spiritual power that lost themselves in the distance, bewildering in their profusion and terrible in the intensity of their hidden fire. Souls leaped up and renewed the conflict as this tense will strove for them. Souls even at that moment leaving the body struggled from death into spiritual life, and fell panting and saved at the feet of the Redeemer on the other side of death. Others, acquiescent and swooning in sin, woke and snarled at the merciful stab of this poor nun's prayers."

The priest was trembling now with excitement.

"Yes," he said; "yes, and I in my stupid arrogance had thought that my life was more active in God's world than hers. So a small provincial shopkeeper, bustling to and fro behind the counter, might think, if only he were mad enough, that his life was more active and alive than the life of a director who sits at his table in the City. Yes, that is a vulgar simile; but the only one that I can think of which in the least expresses what I knew to be true. There lay my little foolish narrow life behind me, made up of spiritless prayers and efforts and feeble dealings with souls; and how complacent I had been with it all, how self-centred, how out of the real tide of spiritual movement! And meanwhile, for years probably, this nun had toiled behind these walls in the silence of grace, with the hum of the world coming faintly to her ears, and the cries of peoples and nations, and of persons whom the world accounts important, sounding like the voices of children at play in the muddy street outside; and indeed that is all that they are, compared to her—children making mud-pies or playing at shop outside the financier's office."

The priest was silent, and his face became quieter again. Then in a moment he spoke again.

"Well," he said, "that is what I believe to have been an intellectual vision. There was no form or appearance or sound; but I can only express what was shown to me to be true, under those images. It almost seems to me as I look back now as if the air in the chapel were full of a murmurous sound and a luminous mist as the currents of need and grace went to and fro. But I know really that the silence was deep and the air dim."

Then I made a foolish remark.

"If you feel like that about the Contemplative Life, I wonder you did not try to enter it yourself."

The priest looked at me for a moment.

"It would be rash, surely, for a little shopkeeper of no particular ability to compete with Rothschild."

UNDER WHICH KING?

"All such knowledge as this,
whether it comes from God or
not, can be but of little profit
to the soul in the way of perfection,
if it trusts to it: yea, rather,
if it is not careful to reject it,
... it will bring upon it great
evil; ... for all the dangers
and inconveniences of the supernatural
apprehensions, and many
more, are to be found here."
The Ascent of Mount Carmel

Within a day or two of our conversation on St. Teresa, I asked the old priest about what is called "Quietism." A friend had given me an old copy of Molinos' *Spiritual Guide*, and I knew that the writer had been condemned and imprisoned for life, and yet I could not understand in what lay his crime.

"It is difficult to put into words," said the priest, "or even to understand, why certain sentences are condemned, since it is probably possible to parallel them from other Catholic mystics whose names are honoured. Yet the fact remains that the result of Molinos' teaching was neglect of the Sacraments and of external means of grace, which was not so in the case of the schools of other mystics."

"But I will tell you a story," he went on, "to illustrate the effect of certain kinds of mysticism; and I must leave you to judge whether my friend was right or wrong in what he decided, for I must tell you first that the incident did not happen to me. On the whole I may say that I have my own opinion on the subject, but I will not tell you what it is, as sometimes I am strongly inclined to change it. However, you shall hear the story. Shall we take a stroll on the terrace?"

And when we had reached it, he began:

"My friend was a priest of about thirty years of age (this happened some forty years ago). He was working in the country at the time, and had a great deal of leisure for reading, and this he chiefly occupied in the study of various mystics, and most of them of the Quietistic school. You know, too, that one of their characteristic lines of thought lies in the abandonment of all effort save that of adhering to God, and even that is to be a passive rather than an active effort. The soul must lie still, says one of them, and be drawn as if by a rope up the Mount of Perfection. The slightest movement will check or divert that swift and steady approach towards God.

"But my friend not only studied writers of this school intellectually, but he put himself more or less under their spiritual direction. He told me afterwards that it seemed to him that if he used the Sacraments faithfully, and if he found that his devotion towards them did not cool, he would be sufficiently protected against possible extravagances or heresies in his spiritual reading. His daily meditation, too, he told me, began to mean more to him than ever in his lifetime: the presence of God seemed more real and accessible, and, above all, the guidance of God in his daily life more apparent. The time that really matters, as he said to me once, is the time between our religious exercises; and in this time, too, God manifested Himself. In fact, from all that he said to me, I have very little doubt that his character and spiritual life were both deepened and purified, at any rate at first, by his devotional study of these mystics.

"One word more before I begin the actual story.

"I said just now that the guidance of God began to be more apparent in his daily life. There are two main ways of settling questions that come up for decision, and both ways are possible to a religious man. One way is to lay stress on the intellectual side, to weigh the arguments carefully, and decide, as it were, by reasoning alone: the other is to lay comparatively little stress on the arguments and the intellectual side generally, and to make the main effort lie in the aspiration of the will towards God for guidance. We may call them, roughly, the intellectual and the intuitive. Now of course my friend's mystical studies inclined him more and more towards the latter. He told me, in fact, that in the most ordinary questions—in his visiting his people—in his preaching—in his dealings with souls—he began more and more to refuse intellectual light, and to trust instead to the immediate interior guidance of the Holy Ghost. More than once, for example, he laid aside the sermon he had prepared, as he entered the pulpit, and preached from a text that had seemed to be suggested to him. Of course it was not so good from the literary point of view; but that, as he very justly said, is not the most important question in judging of a sermon. He seemed to find, he told me, that his spiritual power in every way developed, both in his interior life and in his dealings with others.

"In his conversations, too, he would allow long silences to come, if it did not seem to him that God moved him to speak; at other times he would drop conventional modes of speech and say things that, humanly judged, were calculated to do the very opposite of what he personally desired. Sometimes in such a case his wish was attained, and sometimes not; but in both cases he forced himself to regard it as if he had succeeded. In short, he acted and spoke in obedience to this interior drawing, and disregarded consequences entirely. And this, I need hardly say, is one road to interior peace.

"And then at last a startling thing happened.

"There had been some crime committed: I have not an idea what it was. Two men were involved in the consequences. One, whom we will call A., had committed the crime: but he could only be prosecuted if B., whom he had seriously injured, consented to take action. Now my friend was deeply interested in A., and he thought he knew that the one chance of A.'s salvation lay in his being allowed to go unpunished. But Lord B., who, by the way, was an Irish peer, of no importance himself, though his father had been well known, was a hard, vindictive man, and had publicly announced his intention of ruining A. In this state of affairs my friend was asked to intercede by A. and his friends.

"Lord B. lived in a large country-house some four or five miles from my friend's house. He was an unmarried man, but generally had his house fairly full of his friends, who did not bear the best possible reputation.

"My friend arrived at the house by appointment with B., whom he did not personally know, towards the close of a rainy autumn afternoon. In spite of his anxiety he had resolved to be guided as usual by the interior monitor whom he had learnt to trust, and he had hardly thought of a single argument which he could use. Yet he felt confident that he was right in coming, and equally confident that he would know what to say when the time came. As he got near the house this confident sense of guidance increased to an extent that almost terrified him. It seemed to him, as he walked under the dripping yellow branches, that a strong, almost physical, oppression carried him forward. As if in a dream he saw the manservant appear in answer to his ring, and heard, as from a great distance, the man tell him that Lord B. had come in a little while before, and was now expecting him in the smoking-room.

"On entering the house these curious sensations, which he hardly attempted to describe to me, seemed to diminish a little, and he felt cool and confident. He told me that the sense of oppression resting on him was dispelled, as if by a breeze, as he passed along the corridor on the ground floor on his way to the smoking-room in the west wing of the house.

"The servant threw open the door and announced him, and my friend went through, and the door closed behind him: but the moment he had crossed the threshold he felt that something was wrong.

"There was a circle of men, some in shooting costume, and some as if they had not been out all day, sitting in easy chairs round the fire, which was to the right of the door. My friend could see most of their faces, and Lord B.'s face among them, as he paused at the door; but not one offered to move, though all looked curiously at him.

"There was silence for a moment, and then Lord B. said suddenly and loudly:

"'Well, here's the parson at last, sermon and all.'

"And then two or three of the men laughed.

"My friend saw of course that Lord B. had arranged the interview in this way simply in order to insult him, and that he would not be able to speak to him in private at all, as he had hoped. There was, he told me, just one great heave of anger in his heart at this offensive behaviour; but he did his best to crush it down, and still stood without speaking. He had not, he said, an idea what to say or do, so he stood and waited.

"Lord B. got up in a moment and lit a cigarette with his back to my friend; and then turned and faced him, leaning against the mantelpiece.

"'Well,' he said, 'we're all waiting.'

"Still there was silence. One of the men beyond the fire suddenly laughed.

"'Now then,' said Lord B. impatiently, 'for God's sake say what you came to say, and go.'

"As this sentence ended my friend felt a curious sensation run over him, like those he had experienced in the park, but far stronger. He could never give me any description of it, except by saying that it seemed as if a force were laying hold of him in every remote fibre of his bodily and spiritual being. His own will seemed to give up the control into some stronger hand, and he felt a sense of being steadied and quieted.

"Then he was aware that his own voice said a single sentence of some half-dozen words; but though he heard each word, it was instantly obliterated from his mind. In his description of it all to me afterwards, he said it was like words that we hear immediately before we fall asleep in a lecture-room or a railway carriage: each word is English and intelligible, but the sentence conveys no impression.

"While his voice spoke for perhaps two or three seconds, his eyes were fixed on Lord B.'s face, and in that momentary interval he saw a terrible fear and astonishment suddenly stamped upon it. The mouth opened in loose lines and the cigarette fell out, and B.'s hands rose instinctively as if to keep my friend off. One of the men, too, at the further end of the circle suddenly sprang erect, with the same kind of imploring horror on his face.

"That was all that my friend had time to see; for the same power that had laid hold of him turned him immediately to the door, and he opened it and went out and down the corridor. As he went the strange sensation passed, but he felt the sweat prick to his skin and then pour down his face. He heard, too, as he reached the end of the corridor, a bell peal violently somewhere. He passed out into the hall, and even as he opened the front door a servant dashed past him through the hall and down the corridor, up which he had just come.

"He went straight home, feeling terribly tired and overwrought, and had to go to bed on reaching his house, tortured by neuralgia.

"Two hours later a note was brought by a groom from Lord B., written in a shaking hand, with an abject apology for his reception in the afternoon; an entreaty to him not to mention the subject again which he had spoken of in the sitting-room, with a scarcely veiled offer of a bribe, and an emphatic promise to withdraw all proceedings against A.

"On the following day he was told that Lord B. was supposed to be unwell, and that the house-party had been hurriedly broken up the night before.

"From that day to this he has never had an idea of what the sentence was that his voice spoke that worked such a miracle."

"That is a most curious story," I said. "What do you make of it?"

The priest smiled.

"I will tell you what my friend made of it. He gave up his study of mysticism, yet without in any sense condemning that line of thought of which I have spoken. His reasons, which he explained to me after coming to a decision, were that such a visitation might or might not be from God. If it were not from God, then that proved that he had been meddling with high things, and had somehow slipped under some other control. If it were from God, it might be that it was just for that very purpose that he had been brought so far, but that he dared not pursue that path without some distinct further sign. 'In any case,' he said, 'no soul can be lost by following the simple and well-beaten path of ordinary devotion and prayer.' And so he returned to intellectual forms of meditation, such as most Christians use. He died a few years ago, full of holiness and good works.

"But for you there are several opinions open. Either that it was an intensely strong case of hypnotic thought-transference from Lord B. to my friend, and that the latter only spoke mechanically of something that lay in the former's mind; or you may decide that the whole affair was of the Evil One, and that A. would have been all the better for prosecution, and that an evil being somehow found entrance into the strained nature of my friend, and used it for his own purposes; or that the prophetic gift was bestowed on him, but that the ordeal was too fierce and he too cowardly to claim it. And there are other solutions as well, no doubt possible.

"For myself I think I have formed my opinion; but I would prefer, as Herodotus says, to keep it to myself."

"Jesu, well ought I love Thee,
 For Thou me shewest Thy rood-tree,
 Thy crown of thorns, and nails three,
 The sharp spear that piercéd Thee."
                Swete Jhesu now wil I Synge

When the second post came in one morning I saw a letter addressed to the priest, in the trembling large characters of an old man's hand, lying upon the slab in the hall. When I came in to lunch I found the old clergyman with an open letter in his hand, and his face full of almost childish happiness.

"I have heard from my oldest friend," he said, making a little movement with the letter. "It is months since he has written. I have known him ever since we were boys."

We sat down to lunch, but he kept on referring to his friend, and to the pleasure the letter gave him.

"We are always planning to meet," he said to me presently. "But we never can manage it. We are both so old. He is much more active than I am, however. He is full of good works, while I, as you know, lead an idle life. I could not take charge of a church. It is all I can do now to serve my own little chapel upstairs."

"Where is he working?" I asked.

"I think perhaps you fancy he is in Holy Orders, but he is not. He has been on the Stock Exchange till a few years ago, and now he is living in the country, getting ready to die, as he tells me. But he is full of good works; his letter here has news about the village, and of a man whose acquaintance he has made in the reading-room there, which he himself built a year ago; but he is full of plans too, and asks my advice."

"It is not often you come across a business man like that," I said.

"No, he is wonderful, but he has been like that for years. He has done a great deal all his life among poor people in London. For years he never missed his two or three nights a week in some club, or on some committee, or visiting sick people."

I began to think that it might have been through the friendship of the priest that this man had been such a worker. But presently he began again.

"Perhaps the most wonderful thing was the way he first began to do such work. Let me see, have I mentioned his name? No? Then I can tell you, otherwise it would not be discreet; that is—" he added, "if you would care to hear."

I told him I should be very much interested.

"Then after lunch we will have coffee in the garden, and I will tell you."

When we had sat down under the shade of a wall, with the tall avenue of pines opposite us making a dark tangled frieze against the delicate sky, he began.

"What I am going to tell you now has been gathered partly from conversations with my friend: and partly from letters he has written to me. Years ago I jotted down the order of events, with names and dates, but that, of course, I fear I cannot show even to you. However, I know the story well, and you may rely on the main facts.

"I must tell you first that many years ago now, my friend, who was about forty years old, had lately become a partner in his father's firm: and of course was greatly occupied with all the details of business. It was a broker's firm, well established and did a good steady business. My friend at that time had no idea of doing any work outside his occupation. I heard him say in fact, about this time, that his work seemed to absorb all his energies and capacity. Then the first event of the series took place.

"He was coming home one frosty afternoon in December, between three and four o'clock, on the top of an omnibus. He was sitting in front and looking about him. He noticed a poorly-dressed man standing on the pavement on the right-hand side, as if he wished to cross. Then he began to cross, and came at last right up to the omnibus on which my friend was sitting, and paused a moment to let it pass. As he stood there, my friend watching him with that listless interest with which a tired man will observe details, a hansom cab moving quickly came in the opposite direction. It seemed as if the horse would run the man down. It was too sudden to warn him, but the man saw it, and to avoid the horse sprang quickly forward, his head half turned away, and his feet came between the front and back wheels of the omnibus. There was a jolt and a terrible scream, and my friend horrified leant far over the side to see. When the omnibus had passed the man stood for a moment on his crushed feet, and then swayed forward and fell on his face. My friend started up and made a movement to go to him, but several others had seen the accident and ran to the man, and a policeman was crossing quickly from the other side, so he sat down again and the omnibus carried him on.

"Now this horrible thing remained in my friend's mind, haunted him, shocked him profoundly. He could not forget the terrible face of pain that he had seen upturned for an instant, and his imagination carried him on in spite of himself to dwell on the details of those crushed feet. He wrote me a long letter a week or two afterwards, minutely describing all that I have told you.

"The following summer he was going down to the Kennington Oval one Saturday afternoon to see the close of some famous cricket match. He travelled by the Underground Railway as far as Westminster, and from there determined to walk at least across the Bridge. He walked on the right-hand side, and had reached the steps of St. Thomas' Hospital. He waited here a moment undecided whether to walk on or drive.

"As he waited, he half turned and saw a beggar sitting in the angle between the steps and the wall. There was a white dog beside him. The beggar's face was partly bandaged; but what caught my friend's attention most were his two hands. They were lying palms downwards on the beggar's knees, bandaged like his face, but in the centre of each was a dark spot, showing through the wrapping, as if there were a festering wound that soaked through from underneath. My friend looked at him in disgust for a moment: but terribly fascinated by those quiet suffering hands; and then he passed on. But during all that afternoon he could not forget those hands. I daresay he was overwrought and nervous. But his memory too went back to the accident by the Marble Arch. That night too, as he told me in a conversation afterwards, as he tossed about, his windows wide open to catch the night air, half waking visions kept moving before him of a man with crushed feet and bandaged hands, who moaned and lifted a drawn face to the sky.

"Early that autumn he was alone, except for the servants, in his father's house in London. A maid was taken ill. I forget the nature of the illness, but perhaps you will be able to identify it when I have finished. At any rate the girl grew quickly worse. One morning just before he started to the City the doctor, who had called early that morning, asked to have a word with him, and told him he thought he ought to operate immediately, and asked for his sanction.

"'Well,' said my friend, 'of course I must speak to the girl about it. Have you told her yet?'

"'No,' said the doctor, 'I thought I should mention it to you first. I understand that the girl has no relations in the world.'

"'Can you tell me the nature of the operation?' asked my friend.

"'It is not really serious. It is an incision in the right side,' and he added a few details explaining the case.

"'Well,' said my friend, 'we had better go upstairs together.'

"They went up and found the girl perfectly conscious and reasonable. She consented to the operation, which was fixed for that evening.

"But all that day the picture floated before his eyes of the quiet room at the top of the house, and the girl lying there waiting. And then the scene would shift a little. And he would see the girl after it was over, with a bandage against her side, and the knowledge of the little wound beneath. When he reached home, late in the evening, the doctor was waiting for him.

"'It has been perfectly successful,' he said, 'and I think she will recover.'

"Now, that evening, as my friend sat at the dinner-table alone, smoking and thinking, his old experiences came to his mind again. In less than a year he had seen three things, none of which seemed to have any very close relation to him, but each of which had deeply affected him. He told me afterwards that he began to suspect a design underlying them; but he had not a glimmer of light, strange as it may seem to you and me, as to the nature of that design. Within a month, however, I received a letter from him, from some place in the country where he was staying, describing the following incident.

"He had gone down from a Saturday to Monday to a friend's house in Surrey. On the Sunday afternoon he and his friend went for a walk through some woods. Autumn was in full glory, and the trees were blazing in red and gold: and the bramble branches were weighed down with purple fruit. As they walked together along a grass ride they heard shouts and laughter of children in the woods on one side. They could hear footsteps pattering through dry leaves, and the tearing and trampling of brushwood; and in a moment more a boy burst out of the thin hedge, tripped in a bramble, and rolled into the grass walk. He was up again in a moment laughing and flushed, but my friend saw across his forehead a little thin red dotted line where a thorn had scratched him. As the boy laughed up into their faces, he lifted his hand to his forehead.

"'Why it's wet,' he said, and then, looking at his fingers: 'Why, it's blood! I've scratched myself.'

"Other footsteps came running through the undergrowth, and the boy himself ran off down the road, and the footsteps in the wood stopped, retraced themselves and died away in faint rustlings up the hill. But as my friend had looked he had seen in his memory those other experiences of the last year. And all seemed to concentrate themselves on one Figure—with wounded feet and hands and side—and a torn forehead.

"My friend stood quiet so long that his companion spoke to him and touched his arm.

"'Yes, I am ready,' he said; 'let us go home.'

"The end of the letter I cannot quote to you. It is too intimate and personal. But it ended with a request to myself to give him an introduction to some friend who would give him work to do in some poor district. And work of that kind he has carried on ever since."

The old priest's voice ceased.

"There is one thing my friend did not know," he said after a moment. "When that particular operation on the side is performed, of which I have spoken, there comes out blood and water. A doctor will tell you so."

And then:

"That is my friend's story," he said. "Do you not think it re-markable?"

UNTO BABES

"Saint Bernard speaks of the words
of Job that he says: '*Abscondit
lucem in manibus*' (that is to say,
'God has light hid in His hands');
— 'Thou wot well, he that has a
candle a-light between his hands,
he may hide it and shew it at his
own will. So does our Lord to
His chosen.'"

The Abbey of the Holy Ghost

A few days after the conversation I have described my visit to the old man came to an end, and my work drew me back to London; but I left behind me a promise to return and spend Christmas at his house. He in the meantime would, he promised me, try to put together some other stories for me against the time that I should return. There were many others, he said, that he had come across in his life which he hoped would interest me, besides a few more personal experiences of his own.

And so I left him smiling and waving to me from his bedroom window that overlooked the drive (for I had to go by an early train), with the clean-shaven face of his old servant looking at me discreetly and gravely from the clear-glass chapel window next to the priest's room, where he had been setting things ready before his master was dressed.

It was a dark winter afternoon when I returned, a week or so before Christmas.

The coachman told me on my inquiry that his master seemed very much aged during the autumn and winter, that he had scarcely left the house since the leaves had fallen, except to sit for an hour or two in sunshiny weather in the sheltered angle of the wall where was the tiled platform that I have spoken of; and that he was afraid he had been suffering from depression. There had been days of almost complete silence, at least so Parker had told him, when the master had sat all day turning over letters and books and old drawers.

I reproached myself with having troubled the old man with demands for more stories; and feared that it had been in the attempt to please me that he had fallen brooding over the past, perhaps dwelling too much on sorrows of which I knew nothing.

As we passed under the pines that tossed their sombre plumes in the wind, the sun, breaking through clouds in an angry glory on my right, blazed on the little square-paned windows of the house on my left. The chapel-window on the top story seemed especially full of red light streaming from within, but the flame swept across the upper story as we drove past, and left the windows blank and colourless just before we turned the corner at the back of the house.

The old man met me in the hall, and I was startled to see the change that had come to him. His eyes seemed larger than ever, and there was a sorrow in them that I had not seen before. They had been the eyes of a stainless child, wide and smiling; now they were the eyes of one who was under some burden almost too heavy to be borne. In the stronger light of the sitting-room as the candles shone on his face, I saw that my impression had only been caused by a drooping of the eyelids, that now hung down a little further. But it looked a tired face.

He welcomed me, and said several charming things to me that I should be ashamed to quote, but he made me feel that he was glad that I had come; and so I was glad too. But he said among other things this:

"I am glad you have come now, because I think I shall have something further to tell you. I have had indications during this autumn that the end is coming, and I think that if I have to pass through a dark valley,—and I feel that I am at its entrance even now,—I think that He will give me His staff as well as His rod. But I am an old man and full of fancies, so please do not question me. But I am very glad," and he took my hand and stroked it for a moment, "very glad that you are here, because I do not think that you will be afraid."

During the following days he told me many stories, bringing out the old books and letters of which the coachman had spoken, and spelling out notes through his tortoiseshell glass, as he sat by the open fireplace in the central sitting-room, with the logs crackling and overrun with swift sparks as they rested on their bed of ashes. The door into the garden where the old drive had once been was now kept closed, and a heavy curtain hung over it.

We did not go out very much together—only in the early afternoons we would walk for an hour or so, he leaning on my arm and on a stick, up and down the terraced walk that lay next the drive under the pines, as the sunset burned across the hills like a far-away judgment. Some day perhaps I will write out some of the stories that he told me, although not all. I have the notes by me.

Here is one of them.

We were walking on one of these dark winter afternoons very slowly uphill towards the village that the priest might get a change from the garden. The morning had been gusty and wet, with sleet showers and even a sprinkle of pure snow as the sky cleared after lunch-time; and now the weather was settling down for a frost, and the snow lay thinly here and there on the rapidly hardening ground.

"It is remarkable," the old man was saying to me, "how in spite of our Lord's words people still think that faith is a matter more or less of intellect. Such a phrase as 'intelligent faith' is, of course, strictly most incorrect."

He stopped and looked at me as he said this, as if prepared for dispute. I did not disappoint him.

"You are very puzzling;" I said. "I cannot believe that you do not value intellect. Surely it is a gift of God, and therefore may adorn faith, as any other gift may do."

"Yes," he said, walking on, "it may adorn it; but it has nothing more to do with it really than jewels have to do with a beautiful woman. In fact, sometimes faith is far more beautiful unadorned, and it is quite possible to crush a delicate and growing faith with a weight of learned arguments intended to adorn and perfect it. Christian apologetics, it seems to me, are only really useful in the mouth of one who realises their entire inadequacy. You can demonstrate nothing of God. You can, by arguments, draw a number of lines that converge towards God, and render His existence and His attributes probable; but you cannot reach Him along those lines. Faith depends not on intellectual but on moral conditions. 'Blessed are the pure in heart,' said our Saviour, not 'Blessed are the profound or acute of intellect'— 'for they shall see God.' It is certainly true of intellectual as of all other riches that they who possess them shall find difficulty in entering into the kingdom of God."

"And so," I said, "you think that intellectual powers are not things to covet, and that education is not a very important question after all?"

"No more than wealth," he answered, "at least so far as you mean by education instruction in demonstrable facts or exact sciences. The point of our existence here is to know God. Well, you know for yourself how the race for wealth is ruining millions of souls to-day. No less surely is keen intellectual competition ruining souls. Mr. —, for instance," he said, naming a well-known critic and poet; "was there ever a man of keener and finer intellect, or of more unerring instinct in matters of literary taste? Well, once I talked with that man most of a day on all his own subjects; in fact, he did nearly all the talking, and I was astonished, I must confess, at the perfection of the training of his already brilliant powers. So much I could perceive, though of course I could not follow him. And of course there were many delicate shades of beauty, if not much more, invisible to me in his talk and criticism. His scale of intellectual beauty ran up out of my sight altogether. But what astonished me more was the coarseness and dulness of his spiritual instinct. I will not call him a child in matters of faith, because that would be high praise; but he was just an ill-bred boor. I have known many a Sussex villager of far purer and finer spiritual fibre. No, no; faith can and does exist quite apart from intellect; and to increase or develop the one often means the decrease and incoherence of the other. *Seigneur, donnez-moi la foi du charbonnier!*"

I must confess that this was a new point of view for me; and I am not sure now whether I do not still think it exaggerated and dangerous; but I said nothing, because it did seem to open up difficult questions, and also to throw light on other difficult questions. The priest turned to me again as he walked.

"Why, it must be so," he said; "if it were not, clever people would have a better hope of salvation than stupid people; and that is absurd—as absurd as if rich people should be nearer God than poor people. No, no; talents are distributed unevenly, it is true: to one ten and to another five; but each has one pound, all alike."

We had reached the top of the slope, and the towering hedges had gradually fallen away, so that we could now see far and wide over the country. Away behind us, as we paused for breath, we could see the misty Brighton downs, while in the middle distance lay tumbled wooded hills, with smoke beginning to curl up here and there from the evening fires of hidden villages. The sky was clear overhead, but in the west, where the sunset was beginning to smoulder, a few heavy clouds still lingered.

"And God sees all:" said the priest. "Can you put up with another story as we walk home again? I think I ought to be turning now."

We turned and began to retrace our steps downhill.

"This is not an experience of my own," he said. "It was told me by a friend of mine in Cornwall. He was the squire of a little village a few miles out of Truro, and lived there most of the year except a few weeks in the spring, when he would go abroad. He was a man of great learning and taste, but had the faith of a little child. It was like a spring of clear water to hear him speak of God and heavenly things.

"There was a boy in the village who was an idiot. His parents were dead, and he lived alone with his old grandmother, who was a strict Calvinist, and who regarded her grandson as hopelessly damned because his faith and his expression of it were not as hers. There were evident signs, she said, that God's inscrutable decrees were against him. The local preachers there would have nothing to do with the boy; and the clergyman of the parish, after an attempt or two, had given the child up as hopeless. I think my friend told me that the clergyman had tried to teach him Old Testament history.

"Well, the boy was a terrible and disgusting case. I will not go into details beyond saying that the boy's head had the look of a mule about it; his mother, I think, had had a fright shortly before his birth, and the boy used to think sometimes that he was a horse or mule, and the village children used to encourage him in it, and ride and drive him on the green, for he was quite harmless. And so he grew up, neglected and untaught, spending much of his time out of doors, and creeping home on all fours in the evening, snorting and stamping and neighing when he was much excited; and he would stable himself in a corner of the wide dark kitchen, and munch grass; while his grandmother sat in her high chair by the fire reading in her Bible, or looking over her spectacles at the poor misshapen body in the corner that held a damned soul.

"Now my friend hated to see this child. It was the one thing that troubled his faith. Those who have the faith of children have also the troubles of children; and this living example before his eyes of what looked like the carelessness of God, or worse, was a greater offence to my friend's faith than all infidel arguments, or the mere knowledge that such things happened.

"On a certain Christmas Eve my friend had been a long tramp over the hills with a guest who was staying with him for the shooting. They were returning through his own property towards evening, and were just dropping down from the hill. Their path lay along the upper edge of an old disused stone-quarry, whose entrance lay perhaps a hundred yards away from the valley-road that led into the village—so it was a lonely and unfrequented place. The evening was closing in; and my friend, as he led the way along the path, was trying to make out the outlines of stones and bushes on the floor of the quarry, which lay perhaps seventy feet below them. All at once his eye was caught by the steady glimmer of light somewhere in the dimness beneath, and the sound of a voice. He guessed at once that there were tramps below, and was angry at the thought that they must have wilfully disregarded the notice he had put up about making a fire so close to the wood: and he determined to turn them out, and, if need be, to give them shelter for the night in one of his own outhouses. So he stopped and explained to his friend which path would take him home, while that he himself intended to make his way along the lip of the quarry to the entrance, and then to go on into its interior where the tramps had made their camp; and he promised to be at the house five minutes after his friend.

"So they separated, and he himself soon found his way down a narrow overgrown path that brought him to the opening of the quarry.

"It was a good deal darker here, as the hill shadowed it from the west, and high trees rose on one side; but he was able to stumble along the stony path which led to the interior, though it grew darker still as he went. Presently he turned the corner of a tall boulder, and emerged into the kind of semi-circus that formed the heart of the quarry: before him, about a third way up the slope, burned the glimmer of light he had noticed from above, but even as he saw it it went out: my friend stood in the path and called out, explaining who he was, not threatening at all, but offering, if it was any one who wanted shelter, to provide it for the night. There was no answer, only the sound of scuffling in the dimness in front, and then the confused sound of footsteps scrambling: my friend ran forward, calling, and made out presently an oddly shaped thing scrambling over the silt and stone towards a shoulder of rock that stood out against the sky on his left (I think he said). He tried to follow, but it was too dark, and after he had stumbled once or twice, he gave up the pursuit. In a moment more the climbing figure stood out clear against the sky for an instant, and then disappeared: and the squire saw with a shock of disgust the mule-like head and tangled hair rising from the high shoulders of the village idiot, and his hands dangling on each side of him; and he heard a high-screaming neighing. But at least, he thought to himself, he would go and see what the boy had been doing.

"He made his way up the slope of silted gravel and mud that lay against the face of the rock, and at last reached a little platform apparently stamped and cut out at the top of the skree just where it touched the quarry-side. It was too dark for him to distinguish anything clearly, so he struck a match and held it in the still sheltered air while he looked about him. This is what he saw.

"There was a short halter, with a kind of rude head-stall, fastened to a rusty iron staple driven into the rock. There was a little pile of cut grass below it. There was a kind of mud trough constructed against the stone, with a little straw sprinkled in it and holly berries and leaves in front of it; but this showed signs of having been hastily trampled down, though parts of it survived: there were marks of hob-nailed boots in it here and there. So much my friend had noticed when the match burned his fingers: but just before he dropped it he noticed something else which made him open his box and light another match: and then he saw the end of a farthing taper sticking out of the ground into which it had been pushed, and another crushed into a ball. He drew out the first and lighted it, and then noticed this last thing. Quite plainly marked on the soft edge of the mud-trough, in a place which the hob-nailed boots had not touched, was the mark of a tiny child's naked foot, as if a baby had stood in the trough or manger, with one foot on the floor and another on the edge.

"Now I do not know what you think of this, but I know what my friend thought of it, and what I myself think of it. But before he went home he went first to the cottage where the boy lived and found him as usual tethered in the corner, with his grandmother nodding before the fire. The boy would do nothing but snort and stamp: and the grandmother could only say that ten minutes ago the boy had run in and gone straight to his corner as usual. The squire asked whether the boy had been trusted with a child by any one; but the grandmother said it was impossible. Nor indeed did he ever after hear a word of a child having been missed on that afternoon.

"Then, before he went home, he went to the little church, already decorated for the festival, and there with the fragrance of the holly and yew in the air about him, and the glimmer of a candle near the altar where the church-cleaner was sweeping, he praised the Holy Child whose Birth-night it was, and who had not disdained to lie in a manger and be adored by the beasts of the stall.

"The following morning on his way back from church he went to the quarry again with his friend to show him what he had seen; but the manger and the holly-berries and crumpled taper were all gone, and there was nothing to see but the iron staple and the platform beaten hard and flat."

We had reached the avenue of pines by now that led to the house, and turned in by the little garden-gate.

"The story seems to show," the priest added, "that intellect has not much to do with the knowledge of God; and that the things which He hides from the wise and prudent He reveals to babes."

The Traveller

"I am amazed, not that the Traveller
returns from that Bourne,
but that he returns so seldom."
The Pilgrims' Way

On one of these evenings as we sat together after dinner in front of the wide open fireplace in the central room of the house, we began to talk on that old subject—the relation of Science to Faith.

"It is no wonder," said the priest, "if their conclusions appear to differ, to shallow minds who think that the last words are being said on both sides; because their standpoints are so different. The scientific view is that you are not justified in committing yourself one inch ahead of your intellectual evidence: the religious view is that in order to find out anything worth knowing your faith must always be a little in advance of your evidence; you must advance *en échelon*. There is the principle of our Lord's promises. 'Act as if it were true, and light will be given.' The scientist on the other hand says, 'Do not presume to commit yourself until light is given.' The difference between the methods lies, of course, in the fact that Religion admits the heart and the whole man to the witness-box, while Science only admits the head—scarcely even the senses. Yet surely the evidence of experience is on the side of Religion. Every really great achievement is inspired by motives of the heart, and not of the head; by feeling and passion, not by a calculation of probabilities. And so are the mysteries of God unveiled by those who

82

carry them first by assault; 'The Kingdom of Heaven suffereth violence; and the violent take it by force.'

"For example," he continued after a moment, "the scientific
view of haunted houses is that there is no evidence for them beyond that which may be accounted for by telepathy, a kind of
thought-reading. Yet if you can penetrate that veneer of scientific
thought that is so common now, you find that by far the larger part
of mankind still believes in them. Practically not one of us really
accepts the scientific view as an adequate one."

"Have you ever had an experience of that kind yourself?" I
asked.

"Well," said the priest, smiling, "you are sure you will not laugh
at it? There is nothing commoner than to think such things a subject for humour; and that I cannot bear. Each such story is sacred
to one person at the very least, and therefore should be to all rev-
erent people."

I assured him that I would not treat his story with disrespect.

"Well," he answered, "I do not think you will, and I will tell
you. It only happened a very few years ago. This was how it began:

"A friend of mine was, and is still, in charge of a church in Kent,
which I will not name; but it is within twenty miles of Canterbury.
The district fell into Catholic hands a good many years ago. I received a telegram, in this house, a day or two before Christmas,
from my friend, saying that he had been suddenly seized with a
very bad attack of influenza, which was devastating Kent at that
time; and asking me to come down, if possible at once, and take his
place over Christmas. I had only lately given up active work, owing
to growing infirmity, but it was impossible to resist this appeal; so
Parker packed my things and we went together by the next train.

"I found my friend really ill, and quite incapable of doing anything; so I assured him that I could manage perfectly, and that he
need not be anxious.

"On the next day, a Wednesday, and Christmas Eve, I went down
to the little church to hear confessions. It was a beautiful old
church, though tiny, and full of interesting things: the old altar had
been set up again; there was a rood-loft with a staircase leading

on to it; and an awmbry on the north of the sanctuary had been fitted up as a receptacle for the Most Holy Sacrament, instead of the old hanging pyx. One of the most interesting discoveries made in the church was that of the old confessional. In the lower half of the rood-screen, on the south side, a square hole had been found, filled up with an insertion of oak; but an antiquarian of the Alcuin Club, whom my friend had asked to examine the church, declared that this without doubt was the place where in the pre-Reformation times confessions were heard. So it had been restored, and put to its ancient use; and now on this Christmas Eve I sat within the chancel in the dim fragrant light, while penitents came and knelt outside the screen on the single step, and made their confessions through the old opening.

"I know this is a great platitude, but I never can look at a piece of old furniture without a curious thrill at a thing that has been so much saturated with human emotion; but, above all that I have ever seen, I think that this old confessional moved me. Through that little opening had come so many thousands of sins, great and little, weighted with sorrow; and back again, in Divine exchange for those burdens, had returned the balm of the Saviour's blood. 'Behold! a door opened in heaven,' through which that strange commerce of sin and grace may be carried on—grace pressed down and running over, given into the bosom in exchange for sin! *O bonum commercium!*"

The priest was silent for a moment, his eyes glowing. Then he went on,

"Well, Christmas Day and the three following festivals passed away very happily. On the Sunday night after service, as I came out of the vestry, I saw a child waiting. She told me, when I asked her if she wanted me, that her father and others of her family wished to make their confessions on the following evening about six o'clock. They had had influenza in the house, and had not been able to come out before; but the father was going to work next day, as he was so much better, and would come, if it pleased me, and some of his children to make their confessions in the evening and their communions the following morning.

"Monday dawned, and I offered the Holy Sacrifice as usual, and spent the morning chiefly with my friend, who was now able to sit up and talk a good deal, though he was not yet allowed to leave his bed.

"In the afternoon I went for a walk.

"All the morning there had rested a depression on my soul such as I have not often felt; it was of a peculiar quality. Every soul that tries, however poorly, to serve God, knows by experience those heavinesses by which our Lord tests and confirms His own: but it was not like that. An element of terror mingled with it, as of impending evil.

"As I started for my walk along the high road this depression deepened. There seemed no physical reason for it that I could perceive. I was well myself, and the weather was fair; yet air and exercise did not affect it. I turned at last, about half-past three o'clock, at a milestone that marked sixteen miles to Canterbury.

"I rested there for a moment, looking to the south-east, and saw that far on the horizon heavy clouds were gathering; and then I started homewards. As I went I heard a far-away boom, as of distant guns, and I thought at first that there was some sea-fort to the south where artillery practice was being held; but presently I noticed that it was too irregular and prolonged for the report of a gun; and then it was with a sense of relief that I came to the conclusion it was a far-away thunderstorm, for I felt that the state of the atmosphere might explain away this depression that so troubled me. The thunder seemed to come nearer, pealed more loudly three or four times and ceased.

"But I felt no relief. When I reached home a little after four Parker brought me in some tea, and I fell asleep afterwards in a chair before the fire. I was wakened after a troubled and unhappy dream by Parker bringing in my coat and telling me it was time to keep my appointment at the church. I could not remember what my dream was, but it was sinister and suggestive of evil, and, with the shreds of it still clinging to me, I looked at Parker with something of fear as he stood silently by my chair holding the coat.

"The church stood only a few steps away, for the garden and churchyard adjoined one another. As I went down carrying the lantern that Parker had lighted for me, I remember hearing far away to the south, beyond the village, the beat of a horse's hoofs. The horse seemed to be in a gallop, but presently the noise died away behind a ridge.

"When I entered the church I found that the sacristan had lighted a candle or two as I had asked him, and I could just make out the kneeling figures of three or four people in the north aisle.

"When I was ready I took my seat in the chair set beyond the screen, at the place I have described; and then, one by one, the labourer and his children came up and made their confessions. I remember feeling again, as on Christmas Eve, the strange charm of this old place of penitence, so redolent of God and man, each in his tenderest character of Saviour and penitent; with the red light burning like a luminous flower in the dark before me, to remind me how God was indeed tabernacling with men, and was their God.

"Now I do not know how long I had been there, when again I heard the beat of a horse's hoofs, but this time in the village just below the churchyard; then again there fell a sudden silence. Then presently a gust of wind flung the door wide, and the candles began to gutter and flare in the draught. One of the girls went and closed the door.

"Presently the boy who was kneeling by me at that time finished his confession, received absolution and went down the church, and I waited for the next, not knowing how many there were.

"After waiting a minute or two I turned in my seat, and was about to get up, thinking there was no one else, when a voice whispered sharply through the hole a single sentence. I could not catch the words, but I supposed they were the usual formula for asking a blessing, so I gave the blessing and waited, a little astonished at not having heard the penitent come up.

"Then the voice began again."

The priest stopped a moment and looked round, and I could see that he was trembling a little.

"Would you rather not go on?" I said. "I think it disturbs you to tell me."

"No, no," he said; "it is all right, but it was very dreadful—very dreadful.

"Well, the voice began again in a loud quick whisper, but the odd thing was that I could hardly understand a word; there were just phrases here and there, like the name of God and of our Lady, that I could catch. Then there were a few old French words that I knew; '*le roy*' came over and over again. Just at first I thought it must be some extreme form of dialect unknown to me; then I thought it must be a very old man who was deaf, because when I tried, after a few sentences, to explain that I could not understand, the penitent paid no attention, but whispered on quickly without a pause. Presently I could perceive that he was in a terrible state of mind; the voice broke and sobbed, and then almost cried out but still in this loud whisper; then on the other side of the screen I could hear fingers working and moving uneasily, as if entreating admittance at some barred door. Then at last there was silence for a moment, and then plainly some closing formula was repeated, which gradually grew lower and ceased. Then, as I rose, meaning to come round and explain that I had not been able to hear, a loud moan or two came from the penitent. I stood up quickly and looked through the upper part of the screen, and there was no one there.

"I can give you no idea of what a shock that was to me. I stood there glaring, I suppose, through the screen down at the empty step for a moment or two, and perhaps I said something aloud, for I heard a voice from the end of the church.

"'Did you call, sir?'" And there stood the sacristan, with his keys and lantern, ready to lock up.

"I still stood without answering for a moment, and then I spoke; my voice sounded oddly in my ears.

"'Is there any one else, Williams? Are they all gone?' or something like that.

"Williams lifted his lantern and looked round the dusky church.

"'No, sir; there is no one.'

"I crossed the chancel to go to the vestry, but as I was half-way, suddenly again in the quiet village there broke out the desperate gallop of a horse.

"'There! there!' I cried, 'do you hear that?'

"Williams came up the church towards me.

"'Are you ill, sir?' he said. 'Shall I fetch your servant?'

"I made an effort and told him it was nothing; but he insisted on seeing me home: I did not like to ask him whether he had heard the gallop of the horse; for, after all, I thought, perhaps there was no connection between that and the voice that whispered.

"I felt very much shaken and disturbed; and after dinner, which I took alone of course, I thought I would go to bed very soon. On my way up, however, I looked into my friend's room for a few minutes. He seemed very bright and eager to talk, and I stayed very much longer than I had intended. I said nothing of what had happened in the church; but listened to him while he talked about the village and the neighbourhood. Finally, as I was on the point of bidding him good-night, he said something like this:

"'Well, I mustn't keep you, but I've been thinking while you've been in church of an old story that is told by antiquarians about this place. They say that one of St. Thomas à Becket's murderers came here on the very evening of the murder. It is his day, to-day, you know, and that is what put me in mind of it, I suppose."

"While my friend said this, my old heart began to beat furiously; but, with a strong effort of self-control, I told him I should like to hear the story.

"'Oh! there's nothing much to tell,' said my friend; 'and they don't know who it's supposed to have been; but it is said to have been either one of the four knights, or one of the men-at-arms.'

"'But how did he come here?' I asked, 'and what for?'

"'Oh! he's supposed to have been in terror for his soul, and that he rushed here to get absolution, which, of course, was impossible.'

"'But tell me,' I said. 'Did he come here alone, or how?'

"'Well, you know, after the murder they ransacked the Archbishop's house and stables: and it is said that this man got one of the fastest horses and rode like a madman, not knowing where he was going: and that he dashed into the village, and into the church where the priest was: and then afterwards, mounted again and rode off. The priest, too, is buried in the chancel, somewhere, I believe. You see it's a very vague and improbable story. At the Gatehouse at Mailing, too, you know, they say that one of the knights slept there the night after the murder.'

"I said nothing more; but I suppose I looked strange, because my friend began to look at me with some anxiety, and then ordered me off to bed: so I took my candle and went.

"Now," said the priest, turning to me, "that is the story. I need not say that I have thought about it a great deal ever since: and there are only two theories which appear to me credible, and two others, which would no doubt be suggested, which appear to me incredible.

"First, you may say that I was obviously unwell: my previous depression and dreaming showed that, and therefore that I dreamt the whole thing. If you wish to think that—well, you must think it.

"Secondly, you may say, with the Psychical Research Society, that the whole thing was transmitted from my friend's brain to mine; that his was in an energetic, and mine in a passive state, or something of the kind.

"These two theories would be called 'scientific,' which term means that they are not a hair's-breadth in advance of the facts with which the intellect, a poor instrument at the best, is capable of dealing. And these two 'scientific' theories create in their turn a new brood of insoluble difficulties.

"Or you may take your stand upon the spiritual world, and use the faculties which God has given you for dealing with it, and then you will no longer be helplessly puzzled, and your intellect will no longer overstrain itself at a task for which it was never made. And you may say, I think, that you prefer one of two theories.

"First, that human emotion has a power of influencing or saturating inanimate nature. Of course this is only the old familiar sacramental principle of all creation. The expressions of your face, for instance, caused by the shifting of the chemical particles of which it is composed vary with your varying emotions. Thus we might say that the violent passions of hatred, anger, terror, re-morse, of this poor murderer, seven hundred years ago, combined to make a potent spiritual fluid that bit so deep into the very place where it was all poured out, that under certain circumstances it is reproduced. A phonograph for example, is a very coarse parallel, in which the vibrations of sound translate themselves first into terms of wax, and then re-emerge again as vibrations when certain conditions are fulfilled.

"Or, secondly, you may be old-fashioned and simple, and say that by some law, vast and inexorable, beyond our perception, the personal spirit of the very man is chained to the place, and forced to expiate his sin again and again, year by year, by attempting to express his grief and to seek forgiveness, without the possibility of receiving it. Of course we do not know who he was; whether one of the knights who afterwards did receive absolution, which possibly was not ratified by God; or one of the men-at-arms who assisted, and who, as an anonymous chronicle says, '*sine confession et viatico subito rapti sunt.*'

"There is nothing materialistic, I think, in believing that spiritual beings may be bound to express themselves within limits of time and space; and that inanimate nature, as well as animate, may be the vehicles of the unseen. Arguments against such possibilities have surely, once for all, been silenced, for Christians at any rate, by the Incarnation and the Sacramental system, of which the whole principle is that the Infinite and Eternal did once, and does still, express Itself under forms of inanimate nature, in terms of time and space.

"With regard to another point, perhaps I need not remind you that a thunderstorm broke over Canterbury on the day and hour of the actual murder of the Archbishop."

"... quell' ombre orando, andavan sotto il pondo
simile a quel che talvolta si sogna,
disparmente angosciate tutte a tondo
e lasse su per la prima cornice,
purgando le caligine del mondo."

Il Purgatorie

As the days went on I became more reassured about my friend. Parker told me there was an improvement since I had come: and the shadow in his eyes seemed a little lightened. On Christmas Eve the Rector called, and they were shut up together in the chapel for an hour after tea; and the old man, I suppose, made his confession. He seemed brighter than ever that evening, and told me story after story after dinner, old tales of when he was a child.

On Christmas morning he celebrated the Holy Mysteries as usual in the chapel, and I received the Communion at his hands. We went to church in the brougham, and that was the last time the old priest was seen in public. There was intense curiosity about him in the village, as well as the greatest reverence and love for him, and I noticed a ripple of interest along the benches as we passed up to the Hall pew.

On the evening of Christmas Day he had provided a Christmas tree in the servants' hall; but we only looked in for a moment when the shouting was at its loudest, and he nodded at a child or two who caught sight of him, and I saw his whole face kindle with joy and tenderness, and then we went back to the fire in the sitting-room.

The morning of St. John's Day broke dark and heavy. We had to have candles at breakfast, and the old man seemed curiously changed and depressed again. He hardly spoke at all, and looked at me almost resentfully, like an overwrought child, when I failed to blow out the spirit lamp at the first attempt.

All day long the gloom outside seemed to gather, the sun went down in a pale sky barred with indigo, and the wind began to rise.

The old man, after a word or two, went to his room soon after dinner, and I understood from Parker, who presently came in, that the master was exceedingly sorry for his discourtesy, but that he did not feel equal to conversation, and intended to go to bed early, and that he would be obliged if I could manage to amuse myself alone that evening. But I too went upstairs early, feeling a little uneasy.

On the top landing of the north end of the house there are three doors: the central one is the chapel door; that on the right, approached by two little steep steps of its own, was the priest's room; that on the left opposite was my own room. As I went in, I noticed that a light shone from under the chapel door, and that his own door was wide open, showing the flickering light of the fire within. As I paused I saw Parker pass across the doorway, and called to him in a low voice.

"Yes, sir; he's fairly well, I think," he answered to my inquiry. "He is in the chapel just now, and is coming to bed directly. He told me just now, sir, too, to ask whether you would serve him to-morrow morning."

"Certainly," I said; " but are you sure he ought to get up? He has not been well all day."

"Well, sir," said Parker; "I will do my best to persuade him to stay in bed, and will let you know if I succeed, but I doubt whether the master will be persuaded."

As I crossed outside the chapel door to go to my own room I heard a murmur from within, with a word or two which I cannot write down.

Before I was in bed I heard the chapel door open, and foot-steps go up the little steps opposite, and the door close. Presently it opened again; and then a tap at my door.

"It's only me, sir," said Parker's voice. "May I speak to you a moment?" and then he came in with a candle in his hand.

"I'm not easy about him, sir," he said. "But he won't let me sleep in his room, as I asked. I've come to ask you whether you will let me lie down on your sofa. I don't like to leave him. My own room is at the other end of the house. Excuse me, sir, if I've asked what I shouldn't. But I don't like to sleep on the landing for fear he should look out and see me, and be displeased."

Of course I assented, almost eagerly, for I felt a strange dis-comfort and loneliness myself.

Parker went noiselessly downstairs and got a rug or two and a pillow, and then, with many apologies, lay down on the sofa near the window. My bed stood at the other end of the long narrow room under the sloping side of the roof. I blew the candles out presently, and the room was in darkness.

I could not sleep at first. I was anxious for my friend, and I lay and listened for the slightest sound from the landing. But Parker's face, as I had seen it as he had stood with the candle in his hand, reassured me that he too would be on the watch. The wind had half died down again. Only there came gusts from time to time that shook the leaded windows. Gradually I began to doze, then I sup-pose I dropped off to sleep, and I dreamed.

In my dream I knew that I was still in my room, lying on my bed, but the room seemed illuminated with a light whose source I could not imagine. The curtains, I thought, were no longer drawn over the windows, but looped back, and the light from my room fell distinctly upon the panes. I thought I was sitting up in bed watching for something at the window, something which would terrify me when it came. And then as I watched there came a gust of wind, and lashed, to judge by the sound, a big spray of ivy across the outside. Then again it came, and again, but the sound grew more distinct. I could see nothing at the window, but there came that ceaseless patter and tap, like a thousand fingers. Then a dead

leaf or two was whirled up, stuck for a moment on the glass, and
whirled away again. It seemed to me that the ivy-spray and the
leaves were clamouring to be admitted into shelter from that wild
wind outside. I grew terrified at their insistence, and tried in my
dream to call to Parker, whom I fancied to be still in the room, and
in the struggle awoke, and the room was dark. No; as I looked about
me it was not quite dark. There lay across the floor an oblong patch
of light from the door. I gradually realised that the door was open;
there came a draught round the corner at the foot of my bed. I sat
up and called gently to Parker. But there was no answer. I got out
of bed noiselessly, and went across the floor to where I saw the
dim outlines of the sofa. As I drew near I stumbled over a rug, and
then felt the pillow, also on the floor. I put my hands almost instinctively down, and felt that the sofa was still warm, but Parker
was gone. Then I looked out of the door. The landing was lit by an
oil-lamp, and its light fell upon the priest's door. It was almost
closed, but I could hear a faint murmur of voices.

I put on my dressing-gown and slippers and went out. Almost
simultaneously the door opposite opened a little wider, and
Parker's face looked out, white and scared. When he saw me, he
came swiftly out and down the stairs, beckoning to me; but as we
met, a loud high voice came from the priest's room.

"Parker, Parker! tell him to come in—at once—at once. Don't
leave me."

"Go in, sir: go in," Parker said, in a loud whisper to me, pushing
me towards the door. I went quickly up the two steep steps and
entered, Parker close behind me, and I heard him close the door
softly.

There was a tall screen on my left, and behind it was the bed,
with the head in the corner of the room: a fire was burning near
the bed. I came round the screen quickly, and saw the priest sitting up in bed. He wore a tippet over his shoulders and a small
skull-cap on his head. His eyes were large and bright, and looked
at me almost unintelligently. His hands were hidden by the bed-
clothes. There was a little round table by the head of the bed, on

which stood two burning candles in silver candlesticks. I drew up
a chair by the table and sat down.

"My old friend," I said, "what is it? Cannot you sleep?"

He made no answer to me directly, but stared past me round
the room, and then fixed his eyes at the foot of the bed.

"The sorrows of the world," he said, "and the sorrows under
the earth. They come to me now, because I have not understood
them, nor wept for them."

And then he drew out his old, thin, knotted hands, and clasped
them outside the rug that lay on the outside of the bed. I laid my
own hand upon them.

"You have had a greater gift than that," I said. "You have known
instead the joys of the world."

He paid no attention to me, but stared mournfully before him,
but he did not withdraw his hands.

There came a sudden gust of wind outside; and even in that
corner away from the window the candle flames leant over to one
side, and then the chimney behind me sighed suddenly.

The priest unclasped his hands, and my own hand fell suddenly
on the coverlet. He stretched out his left hand to the window as it
still shook, and pointed at it in silence, glaring over my head as he
did so.

Almost instinctively I turned to the long low window and looked.
But the curtains were drawn over it: they were just stirring and
heaving in the draught, but there was nothing to be seen. I could
hear the pines tossing and sighing like a troubled sea outside.

Then he broke out into a long wild talk, now in a whisper, and
now breaking into something like a scream.

Parker came quickly round from the doorway, where he had
been waiting out of sight, and stood behind me, anxious and scared.
Sometimes I could not hear what the priest said: he muttered to
himself: much of it I could not understand: and some of it I cannot
bring myself to write down—so sacred was it—so revealing of his
soul's inner life hidden with Christ in God.

"The sorrows of the world," he cried again; "they are crying at
my window, at the window of a hard old man and a traitorous priest

. . . betrayed them with a kiss. . . . Ah! the Holy Innocents who have suffered! Innocents of man and bird and beast and flower; and I went my way or sat at home in the sunshine; and now they come crying to me to pray for them. How little I have prayed!" Then he broke into a torrent of tender prayer for all suffering things. It seemed to me as he prayed as if the wind and the pines were silent. Then he began again:

"Their pale faces look through the glass; no curtains can shut them out. Their thin fingers tap and entreat. . . . And I have closed my heart at that door and cannot open it to let them in. . . . There is the face of a dog who has suffered—his teeth are white, but his eyes are glazed and his tongue hangs out. . . . There is a rose with drenched petals—a rose whom I forgot. See how the wind has battered it. . . . The sorrows of the world! . . . There come the souls from under the earth, crying for one to release them and let them go—souls that all men have forgotten, and I, the chief of sinners. . . . I have lived too much in the sweetness of God and forgotten His sorrows."

Then he turned to a crucifix of ebony and silver that hung on the wall at his side, and looked on it silently. And then again he broke into compassionate prayer to the Saviour of the world, entreating Him by His Agony and Bloody Sweat, by His Cross and Passion, to remember all suffering things. That prayer that I heard gave me a glimpse into mysteries of which I had not dreamed; mysteries of the unity of Christ and His members, a unity of pain. These great facts, which I thank God I know more of now, stood out in fiery lines against the dark sorrow that seemed to have filled the room from this old man's heart.

Then suddenly he turned to me, and his eyes so searched my own that I looked down, while his words lashed me.

"You, my son," he said, "what have you done to help our Lord and His children? Have you watched or slept? Couldst thou not watch with me one hour? What share have you borne in the Incarnation? Have you believed for those who could not believe, hoped for the despairing, loved and adored for the cold? And if you could not understand nor do this, have you at least welcomed pain that would have made you one with them? Have you even pitied them? Or have you hidden your face for fear you should grieve too much? But what am I that I should find fault?" Then he broke off again into self-reproach.

At this point Parker bent over me and whispered:

"He will die, sir, I think, unless you can get him to be quiet."

The old man overheard, and turned almost fiercely.

"Quiet?" he cried, "when the world is so unquiet! Can I rest, do you think, with those at my window?" Then, with a loud cry, "Ah! they are in the room! They look at me from the air! I cannot bear it." And he covered his face with his old thin hands, and shrank back against the wall.

I got up from my seat, and looked round as I did so. It seemed to my fancy as if there were some strange Presence filling the room. It seemed as I turned as if crowding faces swiftly withdrew themselves over and behind the screen. A picture on the wall overhead lifted and dropped again like a door as if to let something escape. The coverlet, which was a little disarranged by the old man's movement, rippled gently as if some one who had been seated on the bed had risen. I heard Parker, too, behind me draw his breath quickly through his teeth. All this I noticed in a moment; the next I had bent over the bed towards the priest and put my hand on his shoulder. Either he or I was trembling, I felt as I touched him.

"My dear old friend," I said, "cannot you lie down quietly a little? You cannot think how you are distressing us both."

Then I added a word or two, presumptuously, I felt, in the presence of this old man, who knew so much about the Love of God and the Compassion of our Saviour.

Presently he withdrew his hands and looked at me.

"Yes, yes," he said; "but you do not understand. I am a priest."

I sat down again. I tried hard to control a great trembling that had seized me. Still he watched me. Then he said more quietly:

"Is it nearly morning?"

"It is not yet twelve o'clock, sir," said Parker's voice steadily behind me.

"Then I must watch and pray a little longer," said the old man. "Joy cometh in the morning."

Then quite quietly he turned and lifted the crucifix from its nail, kissed it and replaced it. Then he put his hands over his face again and remained still.

The wind outside seemed quieter. But whenever it sighed in the chimney or at the window the priest winced a little, as if a sudden pain had touched him.

He was supported by pillows behind his back and head, against which he leaned easily. After a few minutes of silence his hands dropped and clasped themselves on his lap. His eyes were closed, and he seemed breathing steadily. I hoped that he would fall asleep so. But as I turned to whisper to Parker, I suppose I must have made a slight noise, for when I looked at the servant he paid no attention to me, but was looking at his master. I turned back again, and saw the old man's eyes gazing straight at me.

"Yes," he said; "go and sleep; why are you here? Parker, why did you allow him to come?"

"I woke up and came myself," I said. "Parker did not disturb me."

"Well, go back to bed now. You will serve me in the morning?"

I tried to say something about his not being fit to get up, but he waved it aside.

"You cannot understand," he said quietly. "That is my one hope and escape. Joy cometh in the morning. There are many souls here and elsewhere that are waiting for that joy, and I must not disappoint them. And I too," he added softly, "I too look for that joy. Go now, and we will meet in the morning." And he smiled at me so gently that I got up and went, feeling comforted.

After I had been in bed a little while, I heard the priest's door open and close again, and then Parker tapped at my open door and came in.

"I have left him quiet, sir. I do not think he will sleep, but he would not let me stay."

"Have you ever seen him like this before?" I asked.

"Never quite like this, sir," he said; and as I looked at the old servant I saw that his eyes were bright with tears, and his lips twitching.

"Well," I said, "we have both heard strange things to-night. Your master whom you love is in the hands of God."

The old servant's face broke into lines of sorrow; and then the tears ran down his face.

"Excuse me, sir," he said, "I am not quite myself. Shall I put the candle out, sir?" Then he lay down on the sofa.

"One word more, Parker. You will wake me if you hear anything more. And anyhow you will call me at seven if I should be asleep."

"Certainly, sir," answered Parker's voice from the darkness.

I slept and woke often that night. Each time I woke I went quietly to the door and looked across the landing and listened. Each time I was not so quiet but that Parker heard me and was by me as I looked, and each time there was a line of light under the priest's door; and once or twice a murmur of one voice at least from the room.

Towards morning I fell into a sound sleep, and awoke to find Parker arranging my clothes and setting ready my bath. The rugs and the pillow were gone from the sofa, and there was no sign on the servant's face that anything unusual had happened during the night.

"How is he?" I asked quickly. "Have you seen him?"

"Yes, sir," said Parker; "he is dressing now, and will be ready at half-past seven. It is a little before seven now, sir."

"But how is he?" I asked again.

"I scarcely know, sir," answered Parker. "He does not seem ill, but he is very silent again this morning, sir."

Then, after a pause, "Is there anything I can do for you, sir?"

"There is nothing more, thank you," I said, and he left the room.

I got up presently and dressed. The morning was still dark, and I dressed by candlelight. When I drew the curtains back the sky had just begun to glimmer in the reflected dawn from the other side of the house; but it was too dark to see to read except by artificial light.

I went out on to the landing, paused a moment, and heard a footstep in the priest's room. Then I opened the door of the oratory and went in.

"At the end of woe suddenly our
eyes shall be opened, and in
clearness of light our sight shall
be full: which light is God, our
Maker and Holy Ghost, in Christ
Jesus our Saviour."

Mother Julian

The oratory is a little room, whitewashed, crossed by oaken beams on the walls. The window is opposite the door; and the altar stands to the left. There is a bench or two on the right.

When I entered on this morning the tapers were lighted, the vestments laid out upon the altar, and all prepared. I went across and knelt by the window. Presently I heard the priest's door open, and in a moment more he came in, followed by Parker, who closed the door behind him and came and knelt at the bench. I looked eagerly at the old man's face; it was white and tired-looking, and the eyebrows seemed to droop more than ever, but it was a quiet face. It was only for an instant that I saw it, for he turned to the altar and began to vest: and then when he was ready he began.

It was strange to hear that voice, which had rung with such intensity of pain so few hours before, now subdued and controlled; and to watch the orderly movements of those hands that had twisted and gesticulated with such terrible appeal. I felt that Parker too was watching with a close and awful interest what we both half

feared would be a shocking climax to the scenes of the night before, but which we half hoped too would recall and quiet that
troubled spirit.

Dawn was now beginning to shine on the western sky. There
was a tall holly tree that rose nearly to the level of the window. As
I looked out for a moment my eye was caught by the outline of a
bird, faintly seen, sitting among the upper branches.

Now I will only mention one incident that took place. I was in
such a strange and disordered state of mind that I scarcely now
can remember certainly anything but this. As the Priest's Communion drew near there came a sudden soft blow against the window
panes. . . .

When the priest began to unvest, I left the chapel and went
downstairs to await him in the breakfast room. But as he did not
come, I went outside the house for a few minutes, and presently
found myself below the chapel window. It seemed to me that I was
in a dream—the very earth I trod on seemed unreal. I was unable
to think connectedly. The scene in the chapel seemed to stand out
vividly. It seemed to me as if in some sense it were a climax, but of
what nature, whether triumphant or full of doom, I could not tell.

As I stood there, perplexed, downcast, in the growing glimmer
of the day, my eyes fell upon a small rumpled heap at my feet, and
looking closer I saw it was the body of a thrush; it was still limp
and warm, and as I lifted it I remembered the sudden blow against
the window panes. But as I still stood, utterly distracted, the chapel
window was thrown open, and Parker's face looked out as I gazed
up. He beckoned to me furiously and withdrew, leaving the window swinging.

I laid the thrush under a bush at the corner of the house as I
ran round, and came in quickly and up the stairs. Parker met me
on the landing.

"He just reeled and fell, sir," he said, "up the stairs into his
room. I've laid him on the bed, and must get down to the stables to
send for the doctor. Will you stay with him, sir, till I come back?"
And without waiting for an answer he was gone.

That evening I was still sitting by my friend's side. I had food brought up to my room during the day, but except for those short intervals was with him continually. The doctor had come and gone. All that he could tell us was that the old man had had a seizure of some kind, and he had looked grave when I told him of the events of the night before.

"His age is against him, too," the doctor had said; "I cannot say what will happen."

And then he had given directions, and had left, promising to return again, at any rate the next morning.

I had been trying to read with a shaded lamp, looking from time to time at the figure of the old man on the bed, as he lay white and quiet, with his eyes closed, as he had lain all day.

At about six o'clock, I had just glanced at my watch, when a slight movement made me turn to the bed again, and I could see in the dim light that his eyes were open and fixed upon me, but all the pain was gone out of them, and they were a child's eyes again. I rose and went to his side, and sat down in the same chair that I had occupied the night before. Immediately I had sat down he put out his hand, and I took it and held it. His eyes smiled at me, and then he spoke, very slowly, with long pauses.

"Well," he said, "you have been with me and have seen and heard, last night and this morning; but it is all ended, and the valley is lightening again at its eastern end where the sun rises. So it was not all dreams and fancies—those old stories that you bore with so patiently to please me. Now tell me what you heard and saw. Did you see them all in the room last night? and—and" —his eyes grew wide and insistent— "what did you see this morning?"

Now the doctor had told me that he must not be over-excited, but soothed; and honestly enough, though some who may read this may not agree with me, I thought it was better to speak plainly of those things so strange to you and me, but so dear and familiar to him. And so I told him all I had heard and seen.

"Ah!" he said when I had finished, "then we were not quite as one. But still you saw and heard more than most men. Now will you hear one more story? I will not tell you all I saw last night,

because the Lord has been gracious to me, and is rising with heal-
ing in His wings on me and on many other poor creatures. But the
wounds are aching still, and if you will spare me, I will not speak
much of the shadows of last night, but only of the joys that came in
the morning. Will you hear it?"

"My dear old friend," I said, "are you sure it will not be too
much for you?"

He shook his head; and then, still holding my hand in his, his
fingers tightening and relaxing as he told his tale, with many pauses
and efforts, he began:

"Last night the sorrows of death came to me," he said, "and all
the blood and agony and desolation of the whole world seemed to
be round me. And I have had so little sorrow in my life that I was
ill prepared to meet them. Our Lord has always shown me such
grace and given me so much joy. But He warned me again and again
this autumn. That was why I spoke to you as I did when you came
before Christmas.

"Well, last night, all this came to me. And it seemed as if I were
partly responsible. Years ago I was set apart as a priest to stand
between the dead and the living. It was meant that I should be the
meeting-place, as every priest must be, of creation's need and God's
grace—as every Christian must be in his station. That is what intercession and the Holy Sacrifice both signify and effect. The two tides
of need and fulfilment must meet in a priest's heart. But all my life
I have known much of fulfilment and little of need. Last night the
first was almost withdrawn, and the second deepened almost beyond bearing. But I knew, as I told you last night, that with the
morning would come peace—that I should be able to carry up the
burden laid on me, and make it one with Him on whom the iniqui-
ties of us all are laid. But I need not say more of that now. This
morning when I went to the altar a lull had come in the storm. But
it was all in my heart still. I felt sure that I should have the clear
vision once more: and as I lifted up the Body of our Lord, it came.

"As I lifted It up It disappeared; as those tell us who look in
crystals. And this is what I saw. I do not know how long I saw it, it

seemed as if time stood still, but you told me there was no perceptible pause. Well"—and the old man raised himself slightly in the
bed— "between my hands I saw a long slope running as it seemed
from me downhill. On the nearer higher end of the slope were men
going to and fro, and I knew they needed something—and yet many
of them did not seem to know it themselves—but they were all in
need. One there was who walked quickly, clenching and unclenching
his hands, and I knew he fought with sin. And there was a woman
with a dead child across her knees; and there was a blind child
crying in a corner.

"Then further down the slope were wounded creatures of all
kinds, and lonely beasts seeking a place to die, and the very grass
of the field seemed to be in sorrow, and there were blind sea-crea-
tures gasping. They were not small, as you might think, but I saw
them as if I looked through a hole in a wall.

"And they stretched down, rank on rank, heaving and striving,
men and beasts warring and trampling down the flowers. There
was a thrush I saw, too, shivering in a tree; and the thought of the
story I have told you came to my mind, and there were a thousand
things that I forget.

"Now when I saw all this my hands trembled, but what I saw
did not tremble, so I knew that it was real. And then very far away
and faint at the foot of the slope was a level silvery mist, like a sea-
fog, with delicate currents and lines, now swift and piercing, now
slow; and in the mist moved faces; but I could not distinguish the
features. And these were the souls that waited until their sins
should be done away.

"And then with something like terror I remembered that I held
in my hands the Body of the Lord. And I was puzzled and distracted,
but I knelt to adore, and as I lowered the Holy Thing, the clouds
closed and the light died out. And it may be that I was cowardly—
and I think God will pardon an old man for whom the light was too
strong—but when I consecrated the chalice, I dared not look at it.
At the Communion, too, I closed my eyes again." The old man
paused a moment and then continued. "I heard no sound such as

you describe. As I unvested and went to my room I was still perplexed at what I had seen, and could not understand it, and then on a sudden I understood it, and it was then I suppose that I fell down."

There was a silence for a moment: then I answered.

"I cannot understand even now."

The priest smiled at me, and his hand closed again on mine.

"I think there is no need for me to tell you that. It will be plain to you soon. Remember what it was that I saw, and where I saw it, and all will be easy.

"You can leave me now for a little," he went on. "I am perfectly free from pain, and I wish to think. Would you send Parker to me in about an hour's time?" And then, as I went towards the door, he added:

"One word more. I had forgotten something. I have yet one more clear vision to see before I die. I have seen, you remember, what you too have seen, how all things need God; but there is yet one more thing to see which will make all plain, and I think you can guess what that is. And I pray that you will be with me when I see it."

Then I turned and went quietly out.

"Jhesu! Jhesu! Esto michi, Jhesu!"
Old Prayer

As day after day went by and the old man seemed no worse, I began to have hopes that he might recover, but the doctor discouraged me.

"At the best," he said, "he may just linger on. But I do not think the end is far off. You must remember he is an old man." And so at last the end came.

During these days, since Parker was of course too much occupied with his master, a boy waited on me. On the last evening, as the boy came in for the second time at dinner, he looked white and frightened.

"What is it?" I asked.

"We don't like it, sir, in the servants' hall. Two children ran in just now and said they had seen something, and we are all upset, sir. The maids are crying."

"What was it the children thought they saw?" I asked. The boy hesitated.

"Tell me," I repeated.

The boy put down the dish he held and came closer to me.

"They say they saw the master himself, sir, on the front lawn, at the gate."

"Where were the children?" I asked.

"Passing round from the house, sir, in front, under the chest-nut. They had been sent by the Rector to inquire."

I got up from the table.

"Where are they?" I asked.

"In the servants' hall, sir."

"Bring them into the sitting-room." And I followed him out and waited. Presently the swing-door opened and the children looked in. Behind them were the pale faces of the servants, whispering and staring.

"Come in," I said to the children, "and sit down. Don't be afraid." They came timidly in, evidently very much frightened. The door closed behind them.

This was their story.

They had been to the house to inquire how the old man was, and were returning to the Rectory. But they had hardly started, in fact had only just reached the chestnut-tree in front of the house, when both of them, who were looking towards the lighted windows, had seen quite plainly the figure of the old priest standing just in-side the gate. He was bareheaded, they said, dressed in black, but they could only see his head and shoulders over the bank, as the road is a little lower than the grass which borders on it and runs up to the gate. He seemed, they said, to be looking out for some one. When I asked them how they could possibly see any one at that distance on such a dark night, they had no sort of explana-tion; they could only repeat that they did see him quite plainly At last I took them out myself, and made them point out to me the place where they had seen it; but, as I expected, all was dark, and we could not even make out the white balls on the pedestals. I took them on to the end of the drive, as they still seemed upset; and they told me there that they would not be frightened to go the rest of the way alone. Fortunately, however, as we waited a man passed in the direction of the village, and he consented to see them as far as the Rectory gate.

When I entered the house again the maids with the boy were standing in the hall. They looked eagerly towards the door as I opened it, and one of them cried out.

"What is it now?" I asked. One of the elder servants answered:

"Oh sir, the master's worse. Parker's afraid he's going. He's just run downstairs for you, sir; and now he's gone back."

I did not wait to hear any more, but pushed past them, through the sitting-room, and ran upstairs.

The door of the old man's room was open, and I heard faint sounds from within. I went straight in without knocking, and turned the corner of the screen.

Parker, who was kneeling by the bed, supporting his master in his arms, turned his head as I came in sight, and made a gesture with it. I came close up.

"He's going fast, sir, I'm afraid," he whispered.

The old man was sitting up in bed looking quite straight before him. His lips were slightly parted; and his eyes were full of expectancy. He kept lifting his hands gently, half opening them with a welcoming movement, and then letting them fall. Now he leaned gently forward, as if to meet something with his hands extended, then sinking a little back upon Parker's arm. He paid no attention to me, and it seemed as if his eyes were focused to an almost infinite distance.

I too knelt down by the bed and waited watching him. Then there came soft footsteps at the door, but it was not for that he waited. Then a whispering and a sobbing: and I knew that the servants were gathering outside.

Still he waited for that which he knew would come before he died. And the expectancy deepened in his eyes to an almost terrible intensity; and it was the expectancy that feared no disappointment. It was perfectly still outside, the servants were quiet now, and the old man's breathing was inaudible. Once I heard the far-off bark of a dog away somewhere in the village.

As I watched his face I saw how wrinkles covered it, the corners of his eyes and his forehead were deeply furrowed, and the lines deepened and shifted as his face worked. And then suddenly he cried out: "He is coming, my son, He is coming far away." And then silence.

I heard a sudden movement outside and then stillness again. Then a maid broke out into sobbing: and I heard footsteps, and then the door of my room across the landing open and shut: and the sobbing ceased. But the old man paid no heed. Then suddenly he cried out again:

"Behold He stands at the door and knocks."

He made an indescribable gesture with his hands. Then I was startled, for there came a loud pealing at the bell downstairs.

Parker whispered to me to send one of the servants downstairs: and I went to the door for an instant and told the boy to go: then I came back. The boy's footsteps died away down the staircase. I knelt down again by the bed.

Then once more the old man cried out:

"He is coming, my son. He is here:" and then, "Look!"

As he said this across his face there came an extraordinary smile; for one moment, as I started up and looked, his face was that of a child, the wrinkles seemed suddenly erased, and a great rosy flush swept from forehead to mouth, and his eyes shone like stars. I noticed too, even at this moment, for I was almost facing him as I sprang up, that the focus of his eyes was contracted to a point at the foot of his bed where the screen stood.

Then he fell back; and Parker laid him gently down.

A moment after footsteps came up the stairs: and the boy whispered from the doorway that the Rector had come.

A MIRROR OF SHALOTT

Being a Collection of Tales told at
an Unprofessional Symposium

"I maintain," said Monsignor with a brisk air of aggressiveness, and holding his pipe a moment from his mouth, "I maintain that agnosticism is the only reasonable position in these matters. Your common agnostic is no agnostic at all; he is the most dogmatic of sectarians. He declares that such things do not happen, or that they can be explained always on a materialistic basis. Now, your Catholic—"

Father Bianchi bristled and rolled his black eyes fiercely. If he had had a moustache he would have twirled it.

We were sitting in the upstairs *sala* of the presbytery attached to the Canadian Church of S. Filippo in Rome. It had been a large, comfortless room, stone floored, stone walled, and plaster ceilinged, but it had been made possible by numerous rugs, a number of armchairs, and an English fireplace. Above, in the cold plaster, dingy, flesh-colored gods and nymphs attempted to lounge on cotton clouds with studied ease, looking down dispiritedly upon seven priests and myself, a layman, who sat in a shallow semicircle round the red logs. In 1871 the house had fallen into secular hands, whence issued the gods and nymphs, but in 1897 the Church had come by her own again, and had not yet banished Olympus. There was no need to annihilate the conquered.

In the centre sat the Father Rector, a placid old man, and round about him were the rest of us—Monsignor Maxwell, a French priest, an English, an Italian, a Canadian, a German, and myself. This was five years ago. I do not know where these people are now—one I think is in heaven, two I should suppose in purgatory, four on earth. In spite of my feelings toward Padre Bianchi, I should assign him to purgatory. He made a good death two years later in the Naples epidemic.

We had begun at supper by discussing modern miracles. The second nocturn had furnished the text to the mouth of Monsignor, and we had passed on by natural channels to levitation, table-turning, family curses, ghosts, and banshees. The Italian was sceptical and scornful. Such things, in his opinion, did not take place; he excepted only the incidents recorded in the lives of the saints. I did not mind his scepticism (that, after all, injures no one but the sceptic), but scorn and contumely is another matter, and I was glad that Canon Maxwell had taken him in hand, for that priest has a shrewd and acrid tongue, and wears purple, besides, round his person and on his buttons, so he speaks with authority.

"You have some tale, then, no doubt, Monsignor?" sneered the Italian.

The Englishman smiled with tight lips.

"Every one has," he said briefly. "Even you, Padre Bianchi, if you will but tell it."

The other shook his head indulgently.

"I will swear," he said, "that none here has such a tale at first hand."

It was Father Meuron's turn to bristle.

"But yes!" he exclaimed.

Canon Maxwell drew on his pipe a moment or two and regarded the fire.

"I have a proposition to make," he said. "Father Bianchi is right. I have one tale, and Father Meuron has another. With the Father Rector's permission we will tell our tales, one each night. On Sunday two or three of us are supping at the French College, so that shall be a holiday, and by Monday night these other gentlemen will no doubt have remembered experiences—even Father Bianchi, I believe. And Mr. Benson shall write them all down, if he wishes to, and make an honest penny or two, if he can get any publisher to take the book."

I hastened to express my approval of the scheme.

The Father Rector moved in his chair.

"That will be very amusing, Monsignor. I am entirely in favor of it, though I doubt my own capacity. I propose that Canon Maxwell takes the chair."

"Then I understand that all will contribute one story," said Monsignor briskly, "on those terms—?"

There was a chorus of assent.

"One moment, Monsignor," interrupted Father Brent; "would it not be worth while to have a short discussion first as to the whole affair? I must confess that my own ideas are not clear."

"Well," said Monsignor shortly, "on what point?"

The younger priest mused a moment.

"It is like this," he said; "half at least of the stories one hears have no point—no reason. Take the ordinary haunted-house tale or the appearances at the time of death. Now, what is the good of all that? They tell us nothing; they don't generally ask for prayers. It is just a white woman wringing her hands, or a groaning or something. At the best one only finds a skeleton behind the panelling. Now, my story, if I tell it, has absolutely no point at all."

"No point?" said Monsignor; "you mean that you don't understand the point, or that no one does; is that it?"

"Well, yes; but there is more, too. How do you square these things with purgatory? How can spirits go wandering about, and be so futile at the end of it, too? Then why is everything so vague? Why don't they give us a hint? I'm not wanting precise information, but a kind of hint of the way things go. Then the whole thing is mixed up with such childish nonsense. Look at the spiritualists, and the tambourine business, and table-rapping. Either those things are true, even if they're diabolical—and in that case people in the spiritual world seem considerably sillier even than people in this—or they're not true; and in that case the whole thing is so fraudulent that it seems useless to inquire. Do you see my point?"

"I see about twenty," said Monsignor; "and it would take all night to answer them. But let me take two. Firstly, I am entirely willing to allow that half the stories one hears are fraudulent or hysterical—I'm quite ready to allow that. But it seems to me that there remain a good many others; and if one doesn't accept those to some extent, I don't know what becomes of the value of human evidence. Now, one of your points, I take it, is that even these seem generally quite pointless and useless; is that it?"

"More or less," said Father Brent.

"Well, first I would say this: It seems perfectly clear that these other stories aren't sent to help our faith, or anything like that. I don't believe that for one instant. We have got all we need in the Catholic Church, and the moral witness, and the rest. But what I don't understand in your position is this: What earthly right have you got to think that they're sent just for your benefit?"

The other demurred.

"I don't," he said; "but I suppose they're sent for somebody's benefit."

"Somebody still on earth, you mean?"

"Well—yes."

Monsignor leaned forward.

"My dear Father, how very provincial you are—if I may say so! Here is this exceedingly small earth, certainly with a very fair number of people living on it, but absolutely a mere fraction of the number of intelligences that are in existence. And all about us— since we must use that phrase—is a spiritual world compared with which the present generation is as a family of ants in the middle of London. Things happen; this spiritual world is crammed full of energy and movement and affairs. . . . We know practically nothing of it all, except those few main principles which are called the Catholic Faith—nothing else. What conceivable right have we to demand that the little glimpses that we seem to get sometimes of the spiritual world are given to us for our benefit or information?"

"Then why are they given?"

Monsignor made a disdainful sound with closed lips.

"My dear Father, a boy drops a piece of orange peel into the middle of the ants' nest one day. The ants summon a council at once and sit on it. They discuss the lesson that is to be learned from the orange peel; they come to the conclusion that Buckingham

Palace must be built entirely of orange peel, and that the reason why it was sent to them was that they were to learn that great and important lesson."

Father Brent sat up suddenly.

"My dear Monsignor, you seem to me to strike at the root of Revelation. If we aren't to deduce things from supernatural incidents, why should we believe in our religion?"

Monsignor lifted a hand.

"Next day there is slid into the ants' nest a box divided into compartments, containing exactly that which the ants need for the winter—food and so forth. The ants hold another Parliament. Two-thirds of them who have determined in the last hour or two to reject the Buckingham-Palace-orange-peel theory reject this, too. All is fortuitous, they say. The orange peel was, therefore the box is."

Father Brent relapsed, smiling.

"That is all right," he said; "I was a fool."

"One-third," continued the Canon severely, "come to the not unreasonable conclusion that a box which shows such evident signs of intelligence, and of knowledge and care for their circumstances, proceeds from an Intelligence which wishes them well. But there is a further schism. Half of those who accept Revelation remain agnostic about most other things, and say frankly that they don't know—especially as regards the orange peel. The other half rages on about the orange peel; some are inclined to think that there was no orange peel—it was no more than an hallucination; others think that there is some remarkable lesson to be learned from it, and these differ evidently as to what the lesson is. Others, again, regard it unintelligently and say to one another, 'Look, a piece of orange peel! How very beautiful and important!'"

I laughed softly to myself. Monsignor spoke with such earnestness. I would like him to be my advocate if I ever get into trouble.

"Now, my dear Father," he went on, "I take up the first position of those who accept Revelation, and I acknowledge the fact of the orange peel; but really nothing more. My religion teaches me that there is a spiritual world of indefinite size; and that things not only may, but must, go on there which have nothing particular to do with me. Every now and then I get a glimpse of some of these things—an orange pip at the very least. But I don't immediately demand an explanation. It probably isn't deliberately meant for me at all. It has something to do with affairs of which I know nothing, and which manage to get on quite well without me."

Father Brent, still smiling, protested once more.

"Very ingenious, Monsignor; but then why does it happen to happen to you?"

"I have not the slightest idea, any more than I have the slightest idea why Providence made me break a tooth this morning. I accept the fact; I believe that somehow it works into the scheme. But I do not for that reason desire to understand it. . . . And as for purgatory—well, I ask you, what in the world do we know about purgatory except that there is such a thing, and that the souls of the faithful detained there are assisted by our suffrages? What conceivable possibility is there that we should understand the details of its management? My dear Father, no one in this world has a greater respect for, or confidence in, dogmatic theology than myself; in fact, I may say that it is the only thing which I do have confidence in. But I respect the limits which it itself has laid down."

"Then you are an agnostic as regards everything but the Faith?"

"Certainly I am. Well, possibly, except mathematics, too. And so is every wise man. I have my ideas of, and I make guesses sometimes; but I really do not think that they have any value."

There was silence a moment.

"Then there is this, too," he continued; "it really is important to remember that the spiritual world exists in another mode from that in which the material world exists. That is where the ant simile breaks down. It is more as if an ant went to the Royal Academy. . . . Of course, in the Faith we have an adequate and guaranteed translation of the supernatural into the natural and *vice versa;* and in these ghost stories, or whatever we call them, we have a certain sort of translation, too. The real thing, whatever it is, expresses itself in material terms, more or less. But in these we have no sort of guarantee that the translation is adequate, or that we are adequate to understand it. We can try, of course; but we really don't know. Therefore it seems to me that in all ghost stories the best thing is to hear it, to satisfy ourselves that the evidence is good or bad—and then to hold our tongues. We don't want elaborate commentaries on what may be, after all, an utterly corrupt text."

"But some of them do support the Faith," put in Father Brent.

"So much the better, then. But it is much safer not to lean your weight on them. You never can tell. Now, with the Faith you can."

There was another silence.

Then the Rector stood up, smiling.

"Night prayers, reverend Fathers," he said.

I was still thinking over the Canon's remarks as I came up into the *sala* on the following evening. They seemed to me eminently sensible; or, in other words, they exactly represented what I had always held myself, though I had never so expressed them even to my own mind.

I felt some interest, therefore, in the question as to the class to which Monsignor's own story would be found to belong—whether to that which contains merely a series of phenomena or to that which appeared to corroborate the Christian Religion.

The rest of the company, with two or three strangers, were already in their places when I arrived, and Monsignor was enthroned in the centre chair, staring with a preoccupied look at the blazing fire. The Rector was on his right.

The conversation died away at last; there was a shifting of attitudes. Then the Canon looked at his watch, bending his sleek gray head sideways.

"We have twenty minutes," he said in his terse way. Then he crossed his buckled feet and began without any preliminary comment.

"This happened to me in England. Naturally I shall not mention where it took place, nor how long ago. I knew a man, a Catholic from birth, of a remarkable faith and piety. He had tried his vocation in Religion again and again, for he seemed a born Religious, but his health had always broken down, and he had finally married. He had been told by his Director that his vocation was evidently to live in the world and as a layman. Whether I agree or disagree with the latter part of his advice is not to the point, but there was no question as to the former part of it. The man's health simply could not stand it. But he led a most mortified and interior life with his wife in his London house, with a servant or two to look after them, and was present daily at mass at the church that I served then. His wife, too, was a very exceptional woman, utterly devoted to her husband, and I may say that I never paid them a visit without being very much the better for it.

"Now, he had a brother, a solicitor in a town in the North, also a Catholic, of course, whom I never saw, but who enters very materially into the story. We will call the brothers, if you please, Mr. James and Mr. Herbert, though I need not say that these were not their names.

"One morning after mass Mr. James came to me in the sacristy and said he wished to have a word with me, so I took him through into the presbytery and up into my own room. I could see that something was very much the matter with him.

"He took a letter out and gave it to me to read. It was from his brother, Mr. Herbert, and contained very sad news indeed—nothing else, in fact, than an announcement of his intention to secede from the Church. There was a story of a marriage difficulty, too, as there so often is in such cases. He had fallen in love with a woman of strong agnostic convictions, and nothing would induce her to marry him unless he conformed to her religion, such as it was. But, to do Mr. Herbert justice, I could see that there was a real loss of faith as well. There were two or three sheets filled with arguments that I could see were real to the man—or statements, perhaps, rather than arguments—against the Incarnation and the inspiration of the Scriptures and the authority of the Church, and so on, and I must confess that they were not mere clap-trap. The woman was plainly capable and shrewd, and had been talking to him, and both his heart and his head were seriously entangled.

"Well, I handed the letter back to Mr. James, and said what I could—recommended a book or two, promised to get him prayers, and so on, but the man waved it aside.

"'Yes, yes, Father,' he said; 'I know, and I thank you, but I must do more than that. You don't know what this means to me. I got the letter yesterday at midday, and I may say that I have done nothing but pray since, and this morning at mass I saw a light; at least, I think so, and I want your advice.'

"He was terribly excited, his eyes were bright and the lines in his face deeper than I had ever seen them, for he was only just entering middle age, and the papers shook in his hands. I did my best to quiet him, but it was no good. All his tranquility, which had been one of his most striking virtues, was gone, and I could see that his whole being was rent.

"'You don't know what this means to me,' he said again. 'There is only one thing to be done. I must offer myself for him.'

"Well, I didn't understand him at first, but we talked a little, and at last I found that the idea of mystical substitution had seized on his mind. He was persuaded that he must make an offering of himself to God, and ask to be allowed to bear the temptation instead of his brother. Of course, we know that that is one of the claims of the Contemplative, but, to tell the truth, I had never come across it before in my own experience.

"Well, he didn't want my opinion upon the doctrine, and, indeed, I was glad he didn't, for I knew nothing about it myself; but he wanted to know if I thought him justified in running the risk—for he seemed to take it as a matter of course that I believed it.

"'Am I strong enough, Father?' he asked. 'Can I bear it? I cannot imagine my losing my faith,' and a smile just flickered on his mouth and vanished again in trembling; 'but—but God knows how weak I am.'

"Well, I reassured him on that point, at any rate, and told him that so far as his faith was concerned I considered it robust enough. To tell the truth, I suppose I was a little careless, because—because"—and Monsignor shifted a little in his chair and looked around— "well it was all so bewildering.

"Well, he soon went after that, saying that he would tell his wife, and imploring me to get prayers for him in his struggle, and I was left alone to think it over.

"For the next day or two he appeared at mass as usual, and just waited for me one morning to tell me that he had made the offering of himself before God. Then I had to go into the country on some business or other and was away from Monday to Saturday.

"Now, to tell the truth, I did not think of him very much; I was harassed and bothered myself about my business, and scarcely did more than just mention his name at the altar, and I am ashamed to say I completely forgot to get prayers elsewhere for his brother or himself, and I was entirely unprepared for what was waiting for me when I reached home on the Saturday evening."

Monsignor paused a moment or two. He was evidently speaking with a certain difficulty. His brisk, business-like way of talking had just a tinge of feeling in it which it generally lacked, and he moved in his chair now and then with something almost like nervousness. The other priests were silent. The young Englishman was bending forward in the firelight with his chin on his hands, and old Father Stein had sat back in his chair very quiet and was shading his face from the candlelight.

"My housekeeper heard my key in the lock of the front door," went on Canon Maxwell, "and was waiting for me in the hall. She told me that Mr. James' wife had sent round four times for me that afternoon, saying she must have me at once on my return, and that any delay might be fatal. But it was not a case for the Last Sacraments, apparently. I was astonished by such phrases, but they were evidently word for word what she had said, for my housekeeper apologized for repeating them.

"'There is something terribly the matter, Father,' she said; 'the last time the servant was crying, and said that her master was out of his mind.'

"Well, I ran into church and told my penitents there that they must wait, or go to my colleague, and that I had had a sick call and did not know how long I should be away; and then I ran straight out of the church and down to the house, which was three or four streets off. (You must forgive my telling you this story with so many details; but somehow it is the only way I can do it; it is all as vivid and clear as if it had happened last week.) . . .

"It was a November evening; all the lamps were lit as I passed out of the thoroughfare down the side road where his house was; here the pavements were empty, and I ran again as fast as I could down the street and up the steps that led to his front door. Even as I stood there out of breath I knew that something was seriously wrong.

"Down in the kitchen below, as I could see plainly through the lighted windows, the Irish cook had been kneeling with her face hidden on the table; and she was now staring up at me with her eyes red and her hair disordered as the peal of the bell died away. Then she was out in the area almost screaming:

"'Oh, God bless you, Father!' and then the door opened and I was in the hall.

"'Where is he?' I asked the maid, all panting with my run; and she told me, 'In his study,' and then I was up at the door in a moment, knocking, and then, without waiting, I went in.

"It was one of those little back rooms that you see sometimes in London houses, just at the top of the stairs that lead down to the servants' quarters. There was a little garden at the back of the house and a side street beyond that. The curtains over the window had not been drawn, and a lamp shone into the room from the lane outside. But I did not understand that at the time. I was only aware that the room was dark, except for a pale light that lay across the floor and wall and on the door that I closed behind me.

"But the horror of the room was beyond anything that I have ever felt. It—it"—Monsignor hesitated— "it was almost physical, and yet I knew it was not, but it was the sense of some extraordinary influence, spiritual and on the point of—" He stopped again. "You must forgive me," he said, "but I can put it in no way but this—it seemed on the point of expressing itself visibly or tangibly; at any rate, I felt my hair rise slowly as I stood there, and then I leaned back against the door and groped for the handle."

Old Father Stein nodded gravely.

"I know, I know," he said in his heavy voice; "it was so with me at Benares."

"It was so dark at first," went on Monsignor, "that I could see nothing but the outlines of the furniture. There was the writing table, and so on, immediately on my left, the fireplace beyond it in the left-hand wall, a tall bureau beside the window opposite me. Then I felt my hand seized and gripped in the dark, and I looked down, horribly startled, and saw that his wife had been kneeling at his *prie-dieu* on the right, and had turned and clutched my hand as she saw me in the light of the street lamp, but she said nothing, and her silence was the worst of all.

"I looked again round the room and then suddenly gasped and, I must confess, nearly screamed, because quite close to me the man sat and stared up at me. I had been confused as I came in, and I believe now that I only had not seen him, because I had taken the dark outline of his body and the whiteness of his face to be a little side-table with papers upon it that often stood by his writing-place.

"Well, however that was, here was the man quite close to me, sitting bolt upright, with the lamplight falling on that deadly face, all lined as it was, with patches of dark beneath those awful, bright eyes."

Monsignor stopped again, and I could see that the hand on his chair arm twitched sharply once or twice.

"Well, two or three times, I should think, I opened my mouth to speak, and I have never known before or since what it was literally not to be able to do it. It was as if a hand gripped my throat each time. I suppose it was a kind of hysterical contraction of the muscles. I understood then why the wife could not speak. The only emotion I was conscious of was an insane desire to get out of the room and the house, away from that terrifying silence and oppressiveness; and, under God, I believe that the one thing that kept me there was that frightful grip on my fingers, that tightened as if the wife read my thoughts even as the desire surged up.

"I stood there, I suppose, half a minute more before I moved or spoke, and then I made a little motion, and drew my fingers out of hers, and made the sign of the cross, and even then I dared not speak. But the face remained still in that tense quietness and the bright, sunken eyes never flinched or stirred.

"Then I dropped on my knees; and at last with really an extra-ordinary effort, as if I was breaking something, I managed to speak and say a prayer or two—the *Our Father* and the *Hail, Mary*; I could remember nothing else. Then I glanced at him quickly, and he had not stirred, but was watching me with a kind of bitter indif-ference—that is all I can say of it. I went on with the creed, fin-ished it, said Amen, and then one loud, harsh bark of laughter broke from him, and—and—I could swear that something else laughed, too."

A sharp exclamation broke from Father Brent, and a kind of sigh from the French priest as Monsignor suddenly sat up and struck his hand on his knee at his last word, and my own heart leaped and stood still, while my nerves jangled like struck wires.

"There, there," said the Rector; "our nerves are out of order; be kind to us, Monsignor."

He shook his head.

"But I must tell you," he said, "though I hardly know what words to use. . . . This other laughter was not like his. I could not swear that—that there was a vibration of sound. It might have been inte-rior, but it was there; it was objective and external to me. . . . Only I was absolutely convinced that there was laughter, neither mine, nor the man's, nor his wife's. There; that is all I can say of it."

He paused a moment.

"Well," he went on, "we got him upstairs at last, and on his bed. I tell you it was a very odd relief to get out of the room down-stairs. He had not slept, his wife whispered to me as we went up, for four nights—not since the Monday, in fact, and had scarcely eaten, either. There was no time to hear more, for he turned round as he walked up and looked at us as we held him, and there was no more talking with that face before us. And there we sat beside him in his bedroom—he lay quiet with closed eyes—and I did not dare to leave him till three or four in the morning, when I was nearly dead with weariness. His wife made me go then, and promised to send again if there was any change.

"Well, during the sung mass, at which I was not officiating, the message came, and I was back at his house directly. There had been a change; he was now willing to talk. He looked ghastly, but his wife told me that she thought he had slept an hour or two after I had left.

"Well, we talked, and I found that the man's faith was gone—or perhaps it is safer to say completely obscured. I scarcely know how to express it, but it was as if he had practically no conception of what I was talking about.

"'I believed it once,' he said; 'yes, I am sure I did, but I can't imagine why or how.' "

"'Then what is all this trouble of mind about?' I asked.

"'Why,' he said, 'why, if it is not true, what is left?'

"I didn't quite see what he meant, and asked him.

"'You,' he said, and just touched me with his finger; 'you and I,' and he touched himself, 'and—and—all this,' and he tapped the table, 'and—all that,' and he flung his arm out toward the window and the chimney-pots and the bustling thoroughfare. 'All of it—all of it—what does it all mean; what is the good of it?'

"It was a piteous thing to see his face, the blackness and the misery of his despair at an empty, meaningless world and a self that could do nothing but writhe and cry in the dark.

"You see the whole thing for him stood or fell by God, lived and moved in Him; now God was gone, and what was left?

"Well, of course I reminded him of his offering of himself to God for his brother. God had accepted it, I told him; and he just laughed miserably in my face.

"'Do you think Herbert suffered like this?' he asked.

"Well, I was tired and bewildered, and this seemed to me an answer. Of course you all see the explanation."

"The other suffered less because his faith was less," put in Father Brent instantly.

"Exactly," said Monsignor. "Well, I am ashamed to say I didn't see that, at least not clearly enough to put it to him; but I did point out that it was of the very essence of his contract that he should suffer severely in the very manner in which he was suffering, and that the coincidence was remarkable; and, further, that the fact that he was in such distress showed that God was something to him after all. I don't know even then that I accepted the whole thing as being quite real. But what else could I say? . . . Well, he smiled again at that.

"'Have you never regretted a happy dream?' he said.

"Well, I am wearying you," said Monsignor, looking at his watch, "but I am just at the end. I went to that man every day for, I suppose, two or three hours for five or six weeks, and it seemed practically useless. I had never realized before so completely that faith was a gift which can be given or withdrawn; that it is something infused into us, not produced by us. Finally the man died of congestion of the brain."

"Good Lord!" said a voice.

"Yes," said Canon Maxwell, blowing down his pipe, "those—those were my sentiments."

"Monsignor! Do you mean he died without faith?"

"Father Jenks, I gave him the sacraments. He asked for them. I did not press too many questions; I thought it best to leave well alone."

"And the brother?"

"Oh, the brother—Mr. Herbert—was at the funeral, and informed me that the marriage was broken off, and I never heard of his apostasy. And there was one other person who contributed to the interest of the whole affair, and that was the wife."

"What happened to her?"

"She became a Poor Clare. She told me that self-immolation was the only possible act for her after what she had seen and known."

There was a long silence.

"Well, well, well," said Father Bianchi.

Father Meuron was very voluble at supper on the Saturday. He exclaimed; he threw out his hands; his bright black eyes shone above his rosy cheeks, and his hair appeared to stand more on end than I had ever known it.

He sat at the further side of the horse-shoe table from myself, and I was able to remark on his gaiety to the English priest who sat beside me without fear of being overheard.

Father Brent smiled.

"He is drunk with *la gloire*," he said. "He is to tell the story to-night."

N.B. This explained everything.

I did not look forward, however, to his recital. I was confident that it would be full of tinsel and swooning maidens who ended their days in convents under Father Meuron's spiritual direction; and when we came upstairs I found a shadowy corner, a little back from the semicircle, where I could fall asleep if I wished without provoking remark.

In fact, I was totally unprepared for the character of his narrative.

When we had all taken our places, and Monsignor's pipe was properly alight, and himself at full length in his deck chair, the Frenchman began. He told his story in his own language; but I am venturing to render it in English as nearly as I am able.

"My contribution to the histories," he began, seated in his up-right arm-chair in the centre of the circle, a little turned away from

129

me— "my contribution to the histories which these good priests are to recite is an affair of exorcism. That is a matter with which we who live in Europe are not familiar in these days. It would seem, I suppose, that grace has a certain power, accumulating through the centuries, of saturating even physical objects with its force. However, men may rebel, yet the sacrifices offered and the prayers poured out have a faculty of holding Satan in check and preventing his more formidable manifestations. Even in my own poor country at this hour, in spite of widespread apostasy, in spite even of the deliberate worship of Satan, yet grace is in the air; and it is seldom indeed that a priest has to deal with a case of possession. In your respectable England, too, it is the same; the simple piety of Protestants has kept alive to some extent the force of the Gospel. Here in this country of Italy it is somewhat different. The old powers have survived the Christian assault, and while they cannot live in Holy Rome, there are corners where they do so."

From my place I saw Padre Bianchi turn a furtive eye upon the speaker, and I thought I read in it an unwilling assent.

"However," went on the Frenchman with a superb dismissory gesture, "my recital does not concern this continent, but the little island of La Souffrière. These circumstances are other than here. It was a stronghold of darkness when I was there in 1891. Grace, while laying hold of men's hearts, had not yet penetrated the lower creation. Do you understand me? There were many holy persons whom I knew, who frequented the Sacraments and lived devoutly, but there were many of another manner. The ancient rites survived secretly among the negroes, and darkness—how shall I say it?— dimness made itself visible.

"However, to our history."

The priest resettled himself in his chair and laid his fingers together like precious instruments. He was enjoying himself vastly, and I could see that he was preparing himself for a revelation.

"It was in 1891," he repeated, "that I went there with another of our Fathers to the mission-house. I will not trouble you, gentlemen, with recounting the tale of our arrival, nor of the months that followed it, except perhaps to tell you that I was astonished by much that I saw. Never until that time had I seen the power of the Sacraments so evident. In civilized lands, as I have suggested to you, the air is charged with grace. Each is no more than a wave in the deep sea. He who is without God's favor is not without His grace at each breath he draws. There are churches, religions, pious persons about him; there are centuries of prayers behind him. The very buildings he enters, as M. Huysmann has explained to us, are browned by prayer. Though a wicked child, he is yet in his father's house: and the return from death to life is not such a crossing of the abyss, after all. But there in La Souffrière all is either divine or Satanic, black or white, Christian or devilish. One stands, as it were, on the seashore to watch the breakers of grace, and each is a miracle. I tell you I have seen holy Catechumens foam at the mouth and roll their eyes in pain, as the saving water fell on them, and that which was within went out. As the Gospel relates, '*Spiritus conturbavit ilium: et elisus in terram, volutabatur spumans.*'"

Father Meuron paused again.

I was interested to hear this corroboration of evidence that had come before me on other occasions. More than one missionary had told me the same thing; and I had found in their tales a parallel to those related by the first preachers of the Christian religion in the early days of the Church.

"I was incredulous at first," continued the priest, "until I saw these things for myself. An old father of our mission rebuked me for it. 'You are an ignorant fellow,' he said; 'your airs are still of the seminary.' And what he said was just, my friends.

"On one Monday morning as we met for our council I could see that this old priest had somewhat to say. M. Lasserre was his name. He kept very silent until the little businesses had been accomplished, and then he turned to the Father Rector.

"'Monseigneur has written,' he said, 'and given me the necessary permission for the matter you know, my father. And he bids me take another priest with me. I ask that Father Meuron may accompany me. He needs a lesson, this zealous young missionary.'

"The Father Rector smiled at me as I sat astonished, and nodded at Father Lasserre to give permission.

"'Father Lasserre will explain all to you,' he said as he stood up for the prayer.

"The good priest explained all to me as the Father Rector had directed."

N.B. It appeared that there was a matter of exorcism on hand. A woman who lived with her mother and husband had been affected by the devil, Father Lasserre said. She was a Catechumen, and had been devout for several months, and all seemed well until this—this assault had been made on her soul. Father Lasserre had visited the woman and examined her, and had made his report to the Bishop, asking permission to exorcise the creature, and it was this permission that had been sent on that morning.

"I did not venture to tell the priest that he was mistaken and that the affair was one of epilepsy. I had studied a little in books for my medical training, and all that I heard now seemed to confirm me in the diagnosis. There were the symptoms, easy to read. What would you have?"—the priest again made his little gesture—"I knew more in my youth than all the Fathers of the Church. Their affairs of devils were nothing but an affection of the brain—dreams and fancies! And if the exorcisms had appeared to be of direct service, it was from the effect of the solemnity upon the mind. It was no more."

He laughed with a fierce irony.

"You know it all, gentlemen!"

I had lost all desire to sleep now. The French priest was more interesting than I had thought. His elaborateness seemed dissipated; his voice trembled a little as he arraigned his own conceit, and I began to wonder how his change of mind had been wrought.

"We set out that afternoon," he continued. "The woman lived on the further side of the island, perhaps a couple of hours' travel, for it was rough going; and as we went up over the path Father Lasserre told me more.

"It seemed that the woman blasphemed. (The subconscious self, said I to myself, as M. Charcot has explained. It is her old habit reasserting itself.)

"She foamed and rolled her eyes. (An affection of the brain, said I.)

"She feared holy water; they dared not throw it on her, her struggles were so fierce. (Because she has been taught to fear it, said I.)

"And so the good father talked, eyeing me now and again, and I smiled in my heart, knowing that he was a simple old fellow who had not studied the new books.

"She was quieter after sunset, he told me, and would take a little food then. Her fits came on her for the most part at midday. And I smiled again at that. Why it should be so I knew. The heat affected her. She would be quieter, science would tell us, when evening fell. If it were the power of Satan that held her she would surely rage more in the darkness than in the light. The Scriptures tell us so.

"I said something of this to Father Lasserre, as if it were a question, and he looked at me.

"'Perhaps, brother,' he said, 'she is more at ease in the darkness and fears the light, and that she is quieter therefore when the sun sets.'

"Again I smiled to myself. What piety, said I, and what foolishness!

"The house where the three lived stood apart from any others. It was an old shed into which they had moved a week before, for the neighbors could no longer bear the woman's screaming. And we came to it towards a sunset.

"It was a heavy evening, dull and thick, and as we pushed down the path I saw the smoking mountain high on the left hand between the tangled trees. There was a great silence round us, and no wind, and every leaf against the rosy sky was as if cut of steel.

"We saw the roof below us presently, and a little smoke escaped from a hole, for there was no chimney.

"'We will sit here a little, brother,' said my friend. 'We will not enter till sunset.'

"And he took out his office book and began to say his Matins and Lauds, sitting on a fallen tree-trunk by the side of the path.

"All was very silent about us. I suffered terrible distractions, for I was a young man and excited; and though I knew it was no more than epilepsy that I was to see, yet epilepsy is not a good sight to regard. But I was finishing the first Nocturn when I saw that Father Lasserre was looking off his book.

"We were sitting thirty yards from the roof of the hut, which was built in a scoop of the ground, so that the roof was level with the ground on which we sat. Below it was a little open space, flat, perhaps twenty yards across, and below that yet further was the wood again, and far over that was the smoke of the village against the sea. There was the mouth of a well with a bucket beside it; and by this was standing a man, a negro, very upright, with a vessel in his hand.

"This fellow turned as I looked, and saw us there, and he dropped the vessel, and I could see his white teeth. Father Lasserre stood up and laid his finger on his lips, nodded once or twice, pointed to the west, where the sun was just above the horizon, and the fellow nodded to us again and stooped for his vessel.

"He filled it from the bucket and went back into the house.

"I looked at Father Lasserre and he looked at me.

"'In five minutes,' he said; 'that is the husband. Did you not see his wounds?'

"I had seen no more than his teeth, I said, and my friend nodded again and proceeded to finish his Nocturn."

Again Father Meuron paused dramatically. His ruddy face seemed a little pale in the candle-light, and yet he had told us nothing yet that could account for his apparent horror. Plainly, something was coming soon.

The Rector leaned back to me and whispered behind his hand in reference to what the Frenchman had related a few minutes before, that no priest was allowed to use exorcism without the special leave of the Bishop. I nodded and thanked him.

Father Meuron flashed his eyes dreadfully round the circle, clasped his hands and continued:

"When the sun showed only a red rim above the sea we went down to the house. The path ran on high ground to the roof and then dipped down the edge of the cutting past the window to the front of the shed.

"I looked through this window sideways as I went after Father Lasserre, who was carrying his bag with the book and the holy water, but I could see nothing but the light of the fire. And there was no sound. That was terrible to me!

"The door was closed as we came to it, and as Father Lasserre lifted his hand to knock there was a howl of a beast from within.

"He knocked and looked at me.

"'It is but epilepsy!' he said, and his lips wrinkled as he said it."

The priest stopped again, and smiled ironically at us all. Then he clasped his hands beneath his chin like a man in terror.

"I will not tell you all that I saw," he went on, "when the candle was lighted and set on the table, but only a little. You would not dream well, my friends—as I did not that night.

"But the woman sat in a corner by the fireplace, bound with cords by her arms to the back of the chair and her feet to the legs of it.

"Gentlemen, she was like no woman at all. . . . The howl of a wolf came from her lips, but there were words in the howl. At first I could not understand till she began in French, and then I understood. My God!

"The foam dripped from her mouth like water, and her eyes— but there! I began to shake when I saw them until the holy water was spilled on the floor, and I set it down on the table by the candle. There was a plate of meat on the table, roasted mutton, I think, and a loaf of bread beside it. Remember that, gentlemen—that mutton and bread! And as I stood there I told myself, like making acts of faith, that it was but epilepsy, or at the most madness.

"My friends, it is probable that few of you know the form of exorcism. It is neither in the Ritual or the Pontifical, and I cannot remember it all myself. But it began thus:"

The Frenchman sprang up and stood with his back to the fire, with his face in the shadow.

"Father Lasserre was here where I stand, in his cotta and stole, and I beside him. There where my chair stands was the square table, as near as that, with the bread and meat and the holy water and the candle. Beyond the table was the woman; her husband stood beside her on the left hand, and the old mother was there"—he flung out a hand to the right, "on the floor telling her beads and weeping—but weeping.

"When the Father was ready and had said a word to the others, he signed to me to lift the holy water again—she was quiet at the moment—and then he sprinkled her.

"As he lifted his hand she raised her eyes, and there was a look in them of terror, as if at a blow, and as the drops fell she leaped forward in the chair, and the chair leaped with her. Her husband was at her and dragged the chair back. But my God! it was terrible to see him; his teeth shone as if he smiled, but the tears ran down his face.

"Then she moaned like a child in pain. It was as if the holy water burned her; she lifted her face to her man as if she begged him to wipe off the drops.

"And all the while I still told myself that it was the terror of her mind only at the holy water—that it could not be that she was possessed by Satan—it was but madness—madness and epilepsy!

"Father Lasserre went on with the prayers, and I said Amen, and there was a psalm—*Deus in nomine tuo salvum me fac*—and then came the first bidding to the unclean spirit to go out, in the name of the Mysteries of the Incarnation and Passion.

"Gentlemen, I swear to you that something happened then, but I do not know what. A confusion fell on me and a kind of darkness. I saw nothing—it was as if I were dead."

The priest lifted a shaking hand to wipe off the sweat from his forehead. There was a profound silence in the room. I looked once at Monsignor, and he was holding his pipe an inch off his mouth, and his lips were slack and open as he stared.

"Then when I knew where I was, Father Lasserre was reading out of the Gospels; how Our Lord gave authority to his Church to cast out unclean spirits, and all this while his voice never trembled."

"And the woman?" said a voice hoarsely from Father Brent's chair.

"Ah! the woman! My God! I do not know. I did not look at her. I stared at the plate on the table; but at least she was not crying out now.

"When the Scripture was finished Father Lasserre gave me the book.

"'Bah, Father!' he said; 'it is but epilepsy, is it not?'

"Then he beckoned me, and I went with him, holding the book till we were within a yard of the woman. But I could not hold the book still, it shook, it shook—"

Father Meuron thrust out his hand. "It shook like that, gentlemen.

"He took the book from me, sharply and angrily. 'Go back, sir,' he said, and he thrust the book into the husband's hand.

"'There,' he said.

"I went back behind the table and leaned on it.

"Then Father Lasserre—my God! the courage of this man!—he set his hands on the woman's head. She writhed up her teeth to bite, but he was too strong for her, and then he cried out from the book the second bidding to the unclean spirit.

"*Ecce crucem Domini!* Behold the Cross of the Lord! Flee ye adverse hosts! The lion of the tribe of Judah hath prevailed!'

"Gentlemen"—the Frenchman flung out his hands— "I who stand here tell you that something happened. God knows what. I only know this, that as the woman cried out and scrambled with her feet on the floor, the flame of the candle became smoke-coloured for one instant. I told myself it was the dust of her struggling and her foul breath. . . . Yes, gentlemen, as you tell yourselves now. . . . Bah! it is but epilepsy, is it not so, sir?"

The old Rector leaned forward with a deprecating hand, but the Frenchman glared and gesticulated; there was a murmur from the room, and the old priest leaned back again and propped his head on his hand.

"Then there was a prayer. I heard *Oremus*, but I did not dare to look at the woman. I fixed my eyes so on the bread and meat; it was the one clean thing in that terrible room. I whispered to myself, 'Bread and mutton, bread and mutton.' I thought of the refectory at home—anything. You understand me, gentlemen—anything familiar to quiet myself.

"Then there was the third exorcism. . . ."

I saw the Frenchman's hands rise and fall, clenched, and his teeth close on his lip to stay its trembling. He swallowed in his throat once or twice. Then he went on in a very low, hissing voice.

"Gentlemen, I swear to you by God Almighty that this was what I saw. I kept my eyes on the bread and meat. It lay there beneath my eyes, and yet I saw, too, the good Father Lasserre lean forward to the woman again, and heard him begin, '*Exorcizo te . . .*'

"And then this happened—this happened . . .

"The bread and the meat corrupted themselves to worms before my eyes . . ."

Father Meuron dashed forward, turned round and dropped into his chair as the two English priests on either side sprang to their feet.

In a few minutes he was able to tell us that all had ended well; that the woman had been presently found in her right mind, after an incident or two that I will take leave to omit; and that the apparent paroxysm of nature that had accompanied the words of the third exorcism had passed away as suddenly as it had come.

Then we went to night-prayers and fortified ourselves against the dark.

Father Brent's Tale

It was universally voted on Monday that the Englishman should follow Father Meuron, and we looked with some satisfaction on his wholesome face and steady blue eyes as he took up his tale after supper.

"Mine is a very poor story," he began, "after the one we heard on Saturday and, what is worse, there is no explanation that I have ever heard that seemed to me adequate. Perhaps some one will supply one this evening. I feel very much like the ant in London whom Monsignor has such sympathy with."

He drew at his cigarette, smiling, and we settled ourselves down with looks of resolute science on our features. I at least was conscious of wishing to wear one.

"After my ordination to the sub-diaconate I was in England for the summer, and went down to stay with a friend on the Fal at the beginning of October.

"My friend's house stood on a spot of land running out into the estuary; there was a beech wood behind it and on either side. There was a small embankment on which the building actually stood, of which the sea-wall ran straight down on to the rocks, so that at high tide the water came half way up the stone-work. There was a large smoking-room looking the same way and a little paved path separated its windows from the low wall.

"We had a series of very warm days when I was there, and after dinner we would sit outside in the dark and listen to the water lapping below. There was another house on the further side of the river about half a mile away, and we could see its lights sometimes. About three miles upstream—that is, on our right—lay Truro; and Falmouth, as far as I remember, about four miles to the left. But we were entirely cut off from our neighbors by the beechwoods all round us, and, except for the house opposite, might have been clean out of civilization."

Father Brent tossed away his cigarette and lit another.

He seemed a very sensible person, I thought, unlike the excitable Frenchman, and his manner of speaking was serene and practical.

"My friend was a widower," he went on, "but had one boy, about eleven years old, who, I remember, was to go to school after Christmas. I asked Franklyn, my friend, why Jack had not gone before, and he told me, as parents will, that he was a peculiarly sensitive boy, a little hysterical at times and very nervous, but he was less so than he used to be, and probably, his father said, if he was allowed time, school would be the best thing for him. Up to the present, however, he had shrunk from sending him.

"'He has extraordinary fancies,' he said, 'and thinks he sees things. The other day—' and then Jack came in, and he stopped, and I clean forgot to ask him afterward what he was going to say.

"Now, if any one here has ever been to Cornwall they will know what a queer county it is. It is cram full of legends and so on. Every one who has ever been there seems to have left their mark. You get the Phoenicians in goodness knows what century; they came there for tin, and some of the mines still in work are supposed to have been opened by them. Cornish cream, too, seems to have been brought there by them, for I need not tell you, perhaps, that the stuff is originally Cornish and not Devon. Then Solomon, some think, sent ships there, though personally I believe that is nonsense; but you get some curious names—Marazion, for instance, which means the bitterness of Zion. That has made some believe that the Cornish are the lost tribes. Then you get a connection with both Ireland and Brittany in names, language, and beliefs, and so on. I could go on forever. They still talk of 'going to England' when they cross the border into Devonshire.

"Then the people are very odd—real Celts—with a genius for religion and the supernatural generally. They believe in pixies; they have got a hundred saints and holy wells and holy trees that no one else has ever heard of. They have the most astonishing old churches. There is one convent—at Lanherne, I think—where the Blessed Sacrament has remained with its light burning right up to the present. And lastly, all the people are furious Wesleyans.

"So the whole place is a confusion of history, of a sort of palimpsest, as the Father Rector here would tell us. A cross you find in the moor may be pagan, or Catholic, or Anglican, or most likely all three together. And that is what makes an explanation of what I am going to tell you such a difficult thing.

"I did not know much about this when I went there on October 3d, but Franklyn told me a lot, and he took me about to one or two places here and there—to Truro to see the new Cathedral, to Perranzabuloe, where there is an old mystery theatre and a church in the sands, and so on. And one day we rowed down to Falmouth.

"The Fal is a lovely place when the tide is in. You find the odd combination of seaweed and beech trees growing almost together. The trees stand with their roots in saltish water, and the creeks run right up into the woods. But it is terrible when the tide is out— great sheets of mud, with wreckage sticking up, and draggled weed, and mussels, and so on.

"About the end of my first week it was high tide after dinner, and we sat out on the terrace looking across the water. We could hear it lapping below, and the moon was just coming up behind the house. I tossed over my cigarette end and heard it fizz in the water, and then I put out my hand to the box for another. There wasn't one, and Franklyn said he would go indoors to find some. He thought he had some Nestors in his bedroom.

"So Franklyn went in and I was left alone.

"It was perfectly quiet; there was not a ripple on the water, which was about eight feet below me, as I got up from my chair and sat on the low wall. There was a sort of glimmer on the water from the moon behind, and I could see a yellow streak clean across the surface from the house opposite among the black woods. It was as warm as summer, too."

Father Brent threw his cigarette away and sat a little forward in his chair. I began to feel more interested. He was plainly interested himself, for he clasped his hands round a knee and gave a quick look into our faces. Then he looked back again at the fire as he went on.

"Then across the streak of yellow light, and where the moon glimmered, I saw a kind of black line moving. It was coming toward me, and there seemed to be a sort of disturbance behind. I stood up and waited, wondering what it was. I could hear Franklyn pulling out a drawer in the bedroom overhead, but everything else was deadly still.

"As I stood it came nearer swiftly; it was just a high ripple in the water, and a moment later the flat surface below heaved up, and I could hear it lapping and splashing on the face of the wall.

"It was exactly as if some big ship had gone up the estuary. I strained my eyes out, but there was nothing to be seen. There was the glimmer of the moon on the water, the house lights burning half a mile away, and the black woods beyond. There was a beach, rocks, and shingle on my right, curving along toward a place called Meopas; and I could hear the wave hiss and clatter all along it as it went upstream.

"Then I sat down again.

"I cannot say I was exactly frightened; but I was very much puzzled. It surely could not be a tidal wave; there was certainly no ship; it could not be anything swimming, for the wave was like the wave of a really large vessel.

"In a minute or two Franklyn came down with the Nestors, and I told him. He laughed at me. He said it must have been a breeze, or the turn of the tide, or something. Then he said he had been in to look for Jack, and had found him in a sort of nightmare, tossing and moaning; he had not wakened him, he said, but just touched him and said a word or two, and the boy had turned over and gone to sleep.

"But I would not let him change the subject. I persisted it had been a really big wash of some kind.

"He stared at me.

"'Take a cigarette,' he said; 'I found them at last under a hat.'

"But I went on at him. It had made an impression on me, and I was a little uncomfortable.

"'It is bosh,' he said; 'but we will go and see if you like. The wall will be wet if there was a big wave.'

"He fetched a lantern, and we went down the steps that led round the side of the embankment into the water. I went first, until my feet were on the last step above the water. He carried the lantern.

"Then I heard him exclaim.

"'You are standing in a pool,' he said.

"I looked down and saw that it was so; the steps, three of them, at least, were shining with water in the light of the lantern.

"I put out my hand for the lantern, held on to a ring by my left hand, and leaned out as far as I could, looking at the face of the wall. It was wet and dripping for at least four feet above the mark of the high tide.

"I told him, and he came down and looked, too, and then we went up again to the house.

"We neither of us said very much more that evening. The only suggestion that Franklyn could make was that it must have been a very odd kind of tidal wave. For myself, I knew nothing about tidal waves; but I gathered from his tone that this certainly could not have been one.

"We sat about half an hour more, but there was no sound again.

"When we went up to bed we peeped into Jack's room. He was lying perfectly quiet on his right side, turned away from the window, which was open, but there was a little frown, I thought, on his forehead, and his eyes seemed screwed up."

The priest stopped again.

We were all very quiet. The story was not exciting, but it was distinctly interesting, and I could see the others were puzzled. Perhaps what impressed us most was the very matter-of-fact tone in which the story was told.

The Rector put in a word during the silence.

"How do you know it was not a tidal wave?" he asked.

"It may have been, Father," said the young priest; "but that is not the end."

He filled his lungs with smoke, blew it out, and went on.

"Nothing whatever happened of any interest for the next day or two, except that Franklyn asked a boatman at Meopas whether he had heard anything of a wave on the Monday night. The man looked at us and shook his head, still looking at us oddly.

"'I was in bed early,' he said.

"On the Thursday afternoon Franklyn got a note asking him to dine in Truro, to meet some one who had come down from town. I told him to go, of course, and he went off in his dog-cart about half-past six.

"Jack and I dined together at half-past seven, and I may say we made friends. He was less shy when his father was away. I think Franklyn laughed at him a little too much, hoping to cure him of his fancies.

"The boy told me some of them, though, that night. I don't remember any of them particularly, but I do remember the general effect, and I was really impressed by the sort of insight he seemed to have into things. He said some curious things about trees and their characters. Perhaps you remember Macdonald's 'Phantastes.' It was rather like that. He was fond of beeches, I gathered, and thought himself safe in them; he liked to climb them and to think the house was surrounded by them. And there was a lot of things like that he said. I remember, too, that he hated cypresses and cats and the twilight.

"'But I am not afraid of the dark,' he said. 'I like the dark as much as the light, and I always sleep with my windows open and no curtains.'"

Monsignor Maxwell nodded abruptly. I could see he was watching.

"I know," he said— "I knew another child like that."

"Well," went on Father Brent, "the boy said good-night and went to bed about nine. I sat in the smoking-room a bit, for it had turned a little cold, and about ten stepped out on to the terrace.

"It was perfectly still and cloudy. I forget whether there was a moon. At any rate, I did not see it. There was just the black gulf of water, with the line of light across it from the house opposite. Then I went indoors and shut the windows.

"I read again for a while, and finished my book. I had said my office, so I looked about for another novel. Then I remembered there had been one I wanted to read in Franklyn's room overhead, so I took a candle and went up. Jack's room was over the smoking-room, and his father's was beyond it on the right, and there was a door between them. Both faced the front, remember.

"Franklyn's room had three windows, two looking on to the river and one upstream toward Truro, over the beach I spoke of before. I went in there, and saw that the door was open between the two rooms, so I slipped off my shoes for fear of disturbing the boy and went across to the book-shelf that stood between the two front windows. All three windows were open. Franklyn was mad about fresh air.

"I was bending down to look at the backs of the books, and had my finger on the one I wanted when I heard a kind of moan from the boy's room.

"I stood up, startled, and it came again. Why, he had had a nightmare only three days before, I remembered. As I stood there wondering whether it would be kind to wake him, I heard another sound.

"It was a noise that came through the side window that looked up the beach, and it was the noise of a breaking wave."

The priest made a momentary pause, and as he flicked the end of his cigarette I saw his fingers tremble very slightly.

"I didn't hesitate then, but went straight into the room next door, and as I went across the floor heard the boy moaning and tossing. It was pitch dark, and I could see nothing. I was thinking that tidal waves don't come downstream. Then my knee struck the edge of the bed.

"'Jack,' I said, 'Jack.'

"There was a rustle from the bed-clothes, and (I should have thought) long before he could have awakened I heard his feet on the floor, and then felt him brush past me. Then I saw him out-lined against the pale window, with his hands on the glass over his head. Then I was by him, taking care not to touch him.

"All this took about five seconds, I suppose, from the time when I heard the wave on the beach. I stared out now over the boy's head, but there was nothing in the world to be seen but the black water and the glimmer of the light across it.

"Jack was perfectly silent, but I could see that he was watch-ing. He didn't seem to know I was there.

"Then I whispered to him rather sharply.

"'What is it, Jack? What do you see?'

"He said nothing, and I repeated my question.

"Then he answered, almost as if talking to himself.

"'Ships,' he said; 'three ships.'

"Now I swear there was nothing there. I thought it was a night-mare.

"'Nonsense,' I said; 'how can you see them? It's too dark.'

"'A light in each,' he said; 'in the bows—blazing!'

"As he said it I saw his head turning slowly to the left as if he was following them. Then there came the sound of the wave break-ing on the stone-work just below the windows.

"'Are you frightened?' I said suddenly.

"'Yes,' said the boy.

"'Why?'

"'I don't know.'

"Then I saw his hands come down from the window and cover his face, and he began to moan again.

"'Come back to bed,' I said; but I daren't touch him. I could see he was sleep walking.

"Then he turned, went straight across the room, still making an odd sound, and I heard him climb into bed.

"I covered him up and went out."

Father Brent stopped again. He had rather a curious look in his face, and I saw that his cigarette had gone out. None of us spoke or moved.

Then he went on again abruptly.

"Well, you know, I didn't know I was frightened exactly until I came out on to the landing. There was a tall glass there on the right hand of the staircase, and just as I came opposite I thought I heard the hiss of the wave again, and I nearly screamed. It was only the wheels of Franklyn's dog-cart coming up the drive, but as I looked in the glass I saw that my face was like paper. . . . We had a long talk about the Phoenicians that evening. Franklyn looked them out in the Encyclopaedia; but there was nothing particularly interesting.

"Well, that's all. Give me a match, Father. This beastly thing's gone out. It's a *spaghetto*."

We had no theories to suggest. Monsignor alone was temerarious enough to remark that the story was an excellent illustration of his own views.

THE FATHER RECTOR'S TALE

The Father-Rector of San Filippo was an old man, a Canadian by birth, who had been educated in England, but he had worked in many parts of the world since receiving the priesthood nearly fifty years ago, and for my part I certainly expected that he would have many experiences to relate.

At first, however, he entirely refused to tell a story. He said he had had an uneventful life, that he could not compete with the tales he had heard. But persuasion proved too strong, and on going in to see him on another matter one morning I found him at his tin despatch-box with a diary in his hand.

"I have found something that I think may do," he said, "if no one else has promised for this evening. It is really the only thing approaching the preternatural I have ever experienced."

I congratulated him and ourselves; and the same evening after supper he told his story, with the diary beside him, to which he referred now and then. (I shall omit his irrelevancies, of which there were a good many.)

"This happened to me," he said, "nearly thirty years ago. I had been twenty years a priest, and was working in a town mission in the south of England. I made the acquaintance of a Catholic family who had a large country house about ten miles away. They were not very fervent people, but they had a chapel in the house, where I would say mass sometimes on Sundays, when I could get away from my own church on Saturday night.

148

"On one of these occasions I met for the first time an artist, whose name you would all know if I mentioned it, but it will be convenient to call him Mr. Farquharson. He made an extremely unpleasant impression on me, and yet there was no reason for it that I could see. He was a big man, palish, with curling brown hair. He was always very well dressed, with a suspicion of scent about him; he talked extremely wittily and would say the most surprising things that were at once brilliant and dangerous; and yet in his talk he never transgressed good manners. In fact, he was very cordial always to me; he seemed to go out of his way to be courteous and friendly, and yet I could not bear the fellow. However, I tried to conceal that, and with some success, as you will see.

"I was astonished that he asked me no questions about our beliefs or practices. Such people generally do, you know; and they profess to admire our worship and its dignity. In the evening he played and sang magnificently—very touching and pathetic songs, as a rule.

"On the following morning he attended mass, but I did not think much of that. Guests generally do, I have found, in Catholic houses. Then I went off in the afternoon back to my mission.

"I suppose it was six weeks before I met him again, and then it was at the same place. My hostess gave me tea alone, for I arrived late, and as we sat in the hall, told me that Mr. Farquharson was there again. Then she added, to my surprise, that he had expressed a great liking for me, and had come down from town partly with the hope of meeting me. She went on talking about him for a while; told me that three of his pictures had been taken again by the French Salon, and at last told me that he had been baptized and educated as a Catholic, but had for many years ceased to practise his religion. She had only learned this recently.

"Well, that explained a good deal; and I was a good deal taken aback. I did not quite know how to act. But she talked on about him a little, and I became sorry for the man and determined that I would make no difference in my behavior toward him. From what she said, I gathered that it might be in my power to win him back. He had everything against him, she told me.

"Now, let me tell you a word about his pictures. I had seen them here and there, as well as reproductions of them, as all the world had at that time, and they were very remarkable. They were on extraordinarily simple and innocent subjects, and often religious— a child going to first Communion; a knight riding on a lonely road; a boy warming his hands at the fire; a woman praying. There was not a line or a color in them that any one could dislike, and yet— yet they were corrupt. I know nothing about art; but it needed no art to see that these were corrupt. I did not understand it then, and I do not now; but—well, there it is. I cannot describe their effect on me; but I know that many others felt the same, and I believe that kind of painting is not uncommon in the French school."

The priest paused a moment.

"As I went down the long passage to the smoking-room I declare that I was not thinking of this side of the man. I was only wondering whether I could do anything, but the moment I came in and found him standing alone on the hearth-rug all this leaped back into my mind.

"His personality was exactly like his own pictures. There was nothing that one could point to in his face and say that it revealed his character. It did not. It was a clean-shaven, clever face, strong and artistic; his hand as he took mine was firm and slender and strong, too. And yet—yet my flesh crept at him. It seemed to me he was a kind of devil.

"Again I did my utmost to hide all this as we sat and talked that evening till the dressing gong rang; and again I succeeded, but it was a sore effort. Once when he put his hand on my arm I nearly jerked it off, so great was the horror it gave me.

"I did not sit near him at dinner; there were several people dining there that night, but our host was unwell and went to bed early, and this man and myself, after he had played and sung an hour or so in the drawing-room, talked till late in the smoking-room, and all the while the horror grew; I have never felt anything like it. I am generally fairly placid; but it was all I could do to keep quiet. I even wondered once or twice whether it was not my duty to tell him plainly what I felt, to—to—well, really, this sounds absurd—

but to curse him as an unclean and corrupt creature who had lost faith and grace and everything, and was on the very brink of eternal fire."

The old man's voice rang with emotion. I had never seen him so much moved, and was astonished at his vehemence.

"Well, thank God, I did not!

"At last it came out that I knew about his having been a Catholic. I did not tell him where I had learned it, but perhaps he suspected. Of course, though, I might have learned it in a hundred ways.

"He seemed very much surprised—not at my knowing, but at my treating him as I had. It seemed that he had met with unpleasantness more than once at the hands of priests who knew.

"Well, to cut it short, before I went away next day he asked me to call upon him some time at his house in London, and he asked me in such a way that I knew he meant it."

The priest stopped and referred to his diary. Then he went on.

"It was in the following May, six months later, that I fulfilled my promise.

"It may have been association, and what I suspected of the man, but the house almost terrified me by its beauty and its simplicity and its air of corruption. And yet there was nothing to account for it. There was not a picture in it, as far as I could see, that had anything in it to which even a priest could object. There was a long gallery leading from the front door, floored, ceiled, and walled with oak in little panels, with pictures in each along the two sides, chiefly, I should suppose now, of that same French school of which I have spoken. There was an exquisite crucifix at the end, and yet, in some strange way, even that seemed to be tainted. I felt, I suppose, in the manner that Father Stein described to us when he mentioned Benares; and yet there, I have heard, the pictures and carving correspond with the sensation, and here they did not.

"He received me in his studio at the end of the passage. There was a great painting on an easel, on which he was working, a painting of Our Lady going to the well at Nazareth—most exquisite and yet terrible. I could hardly keep my eyes off it. It was nearly finished, he told me. And there was his grand piano against the wall.

"Well, we sat and talked; and before I left that evening I knew everything. He did not tell me in confession, and the story became notorious after his death five years later; but yet I can tell you no more now than that all I had felt about him was justified by what I heard. Part of what the world did not hear would not have seemed important to any but a priest; it was just the history of his own soul, apart from his deeds, the history of his wanton contempt of light and warnings. And I heard more besides, too, that I cannot bear to think of even now."

The priest stooped again; and I could see his lips were trembling with emotion. We were all very quiet ourselves; the effect on my mind, at least, was extraordinary. Presently he went on:

"Before I left I persuaded him to go to confession. The man had not really lost faith for a moment, so far as I could gather. I learned from details that I cannot even hint at that he had known it all to be true, pitilessly clear in his worst moments. Grace had been prevailing especially of late, and he was sick of his life. Of course, he had tried to stifle conscience, but by the mercy of God he had failed. I cannot imagine why, except that there is no end to the loving kindness of God; but I have known many souls, not half so evil as his, lose their faith and their whole spiritual sense beyond all human hope of recovery."

The priest stopped again, turned over several pages of his diary, and as he did so I saw him stop once or twice and read silently to himself, his lips moving.

"I must miss out a great deal here. He did not come to confession to me, but to a Carthusian, after a retreat. I need not go into all the details of that, so far as I knew them, and I will skip another six months.

"During that time I wrote to him more than once, and just got a line or two back. Then I was ordered abroad, and when we touched at Brindisi I received a letter from him."

The priest lifted his diary again near his eyes.

"Here is one sentence," he said; "listen.

"'I know I am forgiven; but the punishment is driving me mad. What would you say if you knew all! I cannot write it. I wonder if we shall meet again. I wonder what you would say.'

"There was more that I cannot read; but it offers no explanation of this sentence. I wrote, of course, at once, and said I would be home in four months, and asked for an explanation. I did not hear again, though I wrote three or four times; and after three or four months in Malta I went back to England.

"My first visit was to Mr. Farquharson, when I had written to prepare him for my coming."

The old man stopped again, and I could see he was finding it more and more difficult to speak. He looked at the diary again once or twice, but I could see that it was only to give himself time to recover. Then he lowered it once more, leaned his elbow on the chair arm and his head on his hand, and went on in a slow voice full of effort.

"The first change was in the gallery; its pictures were all gone, and in their place hung others—engravings and portraits of no interest or beauty that I could see. The crucifix was gone, and in its place stood another very simple and common—a plaster figure on a black cross. It was all very commonplace—such a room as you might see in any house. The man took me through as before, but instead of opening the studio door as I expected, turned up the stairs on the right, and I followed. He stopped at a little door at the end of a short passage, tapped, and threw it open. He announced my name and I went in."

He paused once more.

"There was a Japanese screen in front of me, and I went round it, wondering what I should find. I caught a sight of a simple, commonplace room with a window looking out on my left, and then I saw an old man sitting in a high chair over the fire, on which boiled a saucepan, warming his hands, with a rug over his knees. His face was turned to me, but it was that of a stranger.

"There was a table between us, and I stood hesitating, on the point of apologizing, and the old man looked at me, smiling.

"'You do not know me,' he said.

"Then I saw he bore an odd sort of resemblance to Mr. Farquharson; and I supposed it was his father. That would account for the mistake, too, I thought in a moment. My letter must have been delivered to him instead.

"'I came to see Mr. Farquharson,' I said. 'I beg your pardon if—' Then he interrupted me. Well, you will guess—this was the man I had come to see.

"It took a minute or two before I could realize it. I swear to you that the man looked not ten, nor twenty, nor thirty, but fifty years older.

"I went and took his hand and sat down, but I could not say a word. Then he told me his story; and as he told it I watched him. I looked at his face; it had been full and generous in its lines, now the skin was drawn tightly over his cheeks and great square jaw. His hair, so much of it as escaped under his stuff cap, was snow white and like silk. His hands, stretched over the fire, were gnarled and veined and tremulous. And all this had come to him in less than one year.

"Well, this was his story: His health had failed abruptly within a month of my last sight of him. He had noticed weakness coming on soon after his reconciliation, and the failure of his powers had increased like lightning.

"I will tell you what first flashed into my mind—that it was merely a sudden, unprecedented breakdown that had first given room for grace to reassert itself, and had then normally gone forward. The life he had led—well, you understand.

"Then he told me a few more facts that soon put that thought out of my head. All his artistic powers had gone, too. He gave me an example.

"'Look round this room,' he said in his old man's voice, 'and tell me frankly what you think of it—the pictures, the furniture.'

"I did so, and was astonished at their ugliness. There were a couple of hideous oleographs on the wall opposite the window; perhaps you know them—of the tombs of our Lord and His Blessed Mother, with yellow candlesticks standing upon them. There were green baize curtains by the windows; an Axminster carpet of vivid colors on the floor; a mahogany table in the centre with a breviary upon it and a portfolio open. It was the kind of a room that you might find in twenty houses in a row on the outskirts of a colliery town.

"I supposed, of course, that he had furnished his room like this out of a morbid kind of mortification, and I hinted this to him.

"He smiled again, but he looked puzzled.

"'No,' he said; 'indeed not. Then you do think them ugly, too? Well, well; it is that I do not care. Will you believe me when I tell you that? There is no asceticism in the matter. Those pictures seem to me as good as any others. I have sold the others.'

"'But you know they are not good,' I said.

"'My friends tell me so, and I remember I used to think so once, too. But that has all gone. Besides, I like them.'

"He turned in his chair and opened the portfolio that lay by him.

"'Look,' he said, and pushed it over to me, watching my face as I took it.

"It was full of sheets of paper scrawled with such pictures as a stupid child might draw. There was not the faintest trace of any power in them. Here is one of them that he gave me." (He drew out a paper from his diary and held it up.) "I will show it you presently.

"As I looked at them it suddenly struck me that all this was an elaborate pose. I suppose I showed the thought in the way I glanced up at him. At any rate, he knew it. He smiled again pitifully.

"'No,' he said; 'it is not a pose. I have posed for forty years, but I have forgotten how to do it now. It does not seem to me worth while, either.'

"'Are you happy?' I asked.

"'Oh, I suppose so,' he said.

"I sat there bewildered.

"'And music?' I said.

"He made a little gesture with his old hands.

"'Tell Jackson to let you see the piano in the studio,' he said, 'as you go downstairs. And you might look at the picture of Our Lady at Nazareth at the same time. You will see how I tried to go on with it. My friends tell me it is all wrong, and asked me to stop. I supposed they knew, so I have stopped.'

"Well, we talked a while, and I learned how all was with him. He believed with his whole being, and that was all. He received the sacraments once a week, and he was happy in a subdued kind of way. There was no ecstasy of happiness; there was no torment from the imagination, such as is usual in these cases of conversion. He had suffered agonies at first from the loss of his powers, as he realized that his natural perceptions were gone, and it was then that he had written to me."

The Rector stopped again a moment, fingering the paper.

"I saw his doctor, of course, and—"

Monsignor broke in. I noticed that he had been listening intently.

"The piano and the picture," he said.

"Ah, yes. Well, the piano was just a box of strings; many of the notes were broken, and the other wires were hopelessly out of tune. They were broken, the man told me, within a week or two of his master's change of life. He spoke quite frankly to me. Mr. Farquharson had tried to play, it seemed, and could scarcely play a right note, and in a passion of anger it was supposed he had smashed the notes with his fists. And the picture—well, it was a miserable sight. There was a tawdry sort of crown, ill drawn and ill colored, on her head, and a terrible sort of cherub was painted all across the sky. Some one else, it seemed, had tried to paint these out, which increased the confusion.

"The doctor told me it was softening of the brain. I asked him honestly to tell me whether he had ever come across such a case before, and he confessed he had not.

"It took me a week or two, and another conversation with Mr. Farquharson, before I understood what it all meant. It was not natural, the doctor assured me, and it could scarcely be that Almighty God had arbitrarily inflicted such a punishment. And then I thought I understood, as no doubt you have all done before this."

The old priest's voice had an air of finality in his last sentence, and he handed the scrap of paper to Father Bianchi, who sat beside him.

"One moment, Father," I said; "I do not understand at all."

The priest turned to me, and his eyes were full of tears.

"Why, this is my reading of it," he said; "the man had been one mass of corruption, body, mind, and soul. Every power of his had

been nurtured on evil for thirty years. Then he made his effort and
the evil was withdrawn, and—and—well, he fell to pieces. The only
thing that was alive in him was the life of grace. There was nothing
else to live. He died, too, three months later, tolerably happy, I
think."

As I pondered this the paper was handed to me, and I looked at
it in bewildered silence. It was a head grotesque in its feebleness
and lack of art. There was a crown of thorns about it, and an in-
scription in a child's handwriting below:

Deus in virtute tua salvum me fac!

Then my own eyes were full of tears, too.

I

"I have found another *raconteur* for this evening," said Monsignor as he came in to dinner on the following day, "but he cannot be here till late."

The Rector looked up questioningly.

"Yes, I know," said Monsignor unfolding his napkin. "But it is a long story; it will take at least two nights; but—but it is a beauty, reverend Fathers."

We murmured appreciatively.

"I heard him tell it twenty years ago," proceeded the priest. "I was a boy then. . . . I had a bad night after it, I remember. But the first part is rather dull."

The appreciative murmur was even louder.

"Well, then, is that settled?"

We assented.

The entrance of Father Girdlestone that evening was somewhat dramatic. We were all talking briskly together in our wide semi-circle when Father Brent uttered an exclamation. The talk died, and I, turning from my corner, saw a very little old man standing behind the Rector's chair, motionless and smiling. He was one of the smallest men, not actually deformed, I have ever seen; small and very delicate looking. His white, silky hair was thin on his head, but abundant over his ears; his face was like thin ivory, transparent and exquisitely carved; his eyes so overhung that I could see nothing of them but two patches of shadow with a diamond in each. And there he stood, as if materialized from air, beneath the folds of his ample Roman cloak.

"I beg your pardon, reverend Fathers," he said, and his voice was as delicate as his complexion. "I tapped, but no one seemed to hear me."

The Rector bustled up from his chair. "My dear Father," he began; but Monsignor interrupted.

"A most appropriate entry, Father Girdlestone," he said. "You could not have made a more effective beginning." He waved his hand— "Father Girdlestone," he said, introducing us. "And this is the Father Rector."

We were all standing up by now, looking at this tranquil little old man, and we bowed and murmured deferentially. There was something very dignified about this priest.

Then chairs were re-sorted. I got my own again, moving it against the wall, watching him as with almost foreign manners he bowed this way and that before seating himself in the centre. Then we all sat down; and after a word or two of talk he began.

"I understand from my friend, Monsignor Maxwell," he said, "that you gentlemen would like to hear my story. I am very willing indeed to tell it. No possible harm can follow from it, and, per-haps, even good may be the result, if ever any one who shall hear it is afflicted with the same visitation. But it is a long story, gentle-men, and I am an old man and shall no doubt make it longer."

He was reassured, I think, by our faces, and without further apology he began his tale.

"My first and only curacy," he said, "was in the town of Cardiff. I was sent there after my ordination, four years before the re-es-tablishment of the hierarchy in England; and the year after our bishops were given us I was sent to found a mission inland. Now, gentlemen, I shall not tell you where that was, though no doubt you will be able to find out if you desire to do so. It will be enough now to describe to you the circumstances and the place.

"It was a little colliery village to which I went—we will call it Abergwyll. There was a number of Irish Catholics there, who are, as you know, the most devout persons on the face of the earth. They begged very hard for a priest, and I expect, gentlemen, there was collusion in the matter. The Bishop's chaplain had Irish blood in his veins."

He smiled pleasantly.

"At least, there I was sent, with a stipend of £40 and a letter of commendation and permission to beg. My parishioners set at my disposal a four-roomed house standing at the outskirts of the village, removed, I should say, forty yards from any other house. Behind my house was open country—a kind of moor—stretching over hill and dale to the mountains of Brecon. The colliery itself stood on the further side of the village and beneath it, half a mile away. Of the four rooms, I used one as a chapel on the ground floor; that at the back was the kitchen. I slept over the kitchen, and used as my sitting-room and sacristy that over the chapel.

"I will not detain you with my first experiences. They were most edifying. I have never seen such devotion and fervor. My own devotion was sensibly increased by all that I heard and saw. The shepherd in this case, at least, was taught many lessons by his sheep.

"Now, the first ambition of every young priest who is worthy of the name is to build a great church to God's glory. Even I had this ambition. I had not a great deal of work to do—in fact, I may say that there was really nothing to do except to say mass and office and to conduct evening devotions, as I did every night in the chapel; and that little chapel, gentlemen, was full every night.

"Much of the day, therefore, I spent in walking and dreaming. In the morning, as summer came on, I was accustomed to take my office-book out with me and to go over the moor, perhaps three hundred yards away, to a little ravine where a stream went down into the valley. There I would sit in the shade of a rock, listening to the voice of the water and saying my prayers. When I had done I would lie on my back, looking up at the rock and the sky, and dreaming—well, as every young priest dreams.

"I do not know when it was that I first understood what God intended me to do. I began by thinking of a great town where my church should stand—Cardiff, or perhaps Newport. I even arranged its architecture; it was to be a primitive Roman basilica, large and plain, with a great apse with a Christ in glory frescoed there. On His right were to be the redeemed, on His left the lost—no, more than that, with a pair of great angels behind the throne. That, gentlemen, without text or comment, has always seemed to me the greatest sermon on earth."

He paused and looked round at us an instant.

"Well, gentlemen, you know what day-dreaming is. I even occupied my time—I, with £40 a year and twenty colliery parishioners—in drawing designs for my church. And then suddenly on a summer's day a new thought came to me, and something else with it.

"I was lying on my back on the short grass, looking up at the rock against the sky, when the thought came to me that here my basilica should stand. The rock should be levelled, I thought, to a platform. The foundations should be blasted out, and here my church should stand, alone on the moor, to witness that the demands of God's glory were dominant and sovereign. . . . Yes, gentlemen, most unpractical and fantastic. . . .

"I sat up at the thought. It came to me as a revelation. In that instant I no more doubted that it should be accomplished than that God reigned. I looked below me at the stream. Yes; I saw it all; there the stream should dash and chatter; all about me were the solemn moors; and here on the rock behind me should stand my basilica, and the Blessed Sacrament within it.

"I was just about to turn to look at my rock again when something happened."

The old man stopped dead.

"Now, gentlemen, I do not know if I can make this plain to you. What happened to me happened only interiorly; but it was as real as a thunderclap or a vision. It was this: It was an absolute conviction that something was looking at me from over the top of the rock behind.

"My first thought was that I had heard a sound. Then simultaneously the horn blew from the colliery a mile away, and—and"—he hesitated— "I was aware that this external sound was on a different plane. I do not know how to make that plain to you; but it was as when one's imagination is full of some remembered melody and a real sound breaks upon it. The horn ceased and there was silence again. Then after a moment my interior experience ceased, too, as abruptly as it had begun.

"All that time, three or four seconds, at least, I had sat still and rigid without turning my head. I must describe to you as well as I can my sensations during those seconds. You must forgive me for being verbose about it.

"Those who have attained to Saint Teresa's Prayer of Quiet tell us that it is a new world into which they consciously penetrate—a world with objects, sounds and all the rest—but that these are almost incommunicable even to the brain of the percipient. No adequate image or analogy can be found for those intentions; still less can they be expressed in words. I suppose that this is an illustration of the truth that the Kingdom of Heaven is within us. . . .

"Well, gentlemen, I was aware during those seconds that I was in that state that I had, as it were, slipped through the crust of the world of sense and even of intellectual thought. What I perceived of a person watching me was not on this plane at all. It was not One who in any sense had a human existence, who had ever had one, or ever would. It did not in the least resemble, therefore, an apparition of the dead. But the perception of this was gradual, as also of the nature of the visitation, of which I shall speak in a moment. At first there was only the act of the entrance into my neighborhood, as of one entering a room; then gradually, although with great speed, I perceived the nature of the visitation and the character of the visitant.

"And again that sound, if I may call it so, was not that of a material object; it was not a cry or a word or a movement. Yet it was in some way the expression of a personality. Shall we say"—he stopped again— "well, do you know what the sound of a flame is? There is not exactly a vibration—not a note—not a roar nor a—nor anything.

Well, I do not think I can express it more clearly than by saying that that is the nearest analogy I can name in the world of sense. It was as the note of a vivid and intense personality, and it continued during that period and died noiselessly at the end like a sudden singing in the ears.

"Now, I have taken the sense of hearing as the one which best expresses my experience; but it was not really hearing any more than seeing or tasting or feeling. It seemed to me that if it was true, as scientists tell us, that we have but one common sense expressing itself in five ways, that common sense was indirectly affected in this intense and piercing way only beneath its own plane, if I may say so.

"And one thing more. Although this presence seemed to bring on me a kind of paralysis, so that I did not move or even objectively think, yet beneath, my soul was aware of a repulsion and a hatred that I am entirely unable to describe. As God is Absolute Goodness and Love, so this presence affected me with precisely the opposite instinct. . . . There, I must leave it at that. I must just ask you to take my word for it that there was present to me during those few seconds a kind of distilled quintessence of all that is not God, under the aspect of a person, and of a person, as I have said, quite apart from human existence."

The priest's quiet little voice, speaking now even lower than when he began, yet perfectly articulate and unmoved, ceased, and I leaned back in my chair, drawing a long breath. Again I will speak only for myself, and say that he had seemed to be putting into words for the first time in my experience something which I had never undergone and which yet I recognized as simply true. I doubted it no more than if he had described a walk he had taken in Rome.

He looked round at the motionless faces; then he lifted one knee on to the other and began to nurse it.

"Well, gentlemen, it would be about ten minutes, I suppose, before I stood up. I looked over my shoulder before that, yet knowing I should see nothing; and, indeed, there was nothing to see but the old rock and the sky and the silhouette of the grasses against it. I continued to sit there, because I felt too tired to move. It was a kind of complete languor that took possession of me. I had no actual fear now; I knew that the thing, whatever it was, had withdrawn itself—it had whisked, if I may say so, out of my range as swift as a lizard who knows himself observed. I knew perfectly well that it would approach more cautiously if it should ever approach me again, but that for the present I need not fear.

"There was another curious detail, too. I had—and have now—no reflex horror when I think of it. You see that it had not taken place before my senses; not even, indeed, before my intellect or my conscious powers. It was completely in the transcendent sphere, and, therefore—at least I can only suppose that this is the reason—therefore when the door was shut and I was returned to my human existence, I had no associations or even direct memory of the horror. I knew that it had taken place, but my objective imagination was not tarnished by it. Later it was different; but I shall come to that presently. There was the languor, taking its rise, I suppose, in the very essence of my being where I had experienced and resisted the assault, and this languor communicated itself to my mind, just as weariness of mind communicates itself to the body. Then, after a little rest, I got up and went home. It was curious also that after dining the languor had risen even higher; I felt intolerably tired, and slept dreamlessly in my chair the whole afternoon.

"That, then, gentlemen, was the beginning of my visitation. It was only the beginning, and to some degree differed from its continuation. It seemed to me later when I looked back upon it that the personality had changed its assault somewhat, that at first it had rushed upon me unthinking, impelled by its own passion, and that afterward it laid siege with skill and deliberation. . . . But are you sure, gentlemen, that I am not boring you with all this?"

Monsignor answered for us. I noticed that he cleared his throat slightly before speaking.

"No, no, Father. . . . Please go on."

The old priest paused a moment as if to recollect himself, then still nursing his knee, he began again in his quiet little voice.

"I do not know exactly how long it was before I began to understand my danger; but I think the thought first occurred to me one

day during my meditation. Soon after my ordination I had read
Mme. Guyon's book on prayer in order to understand exactly what
it was that had been condemned in Quietism, and I suppose it had
affected me to some extent. It is indeed a very subtle book and
extremely beautiful. At any rate, I had long been accustomed to
close my meditation with what she calls the 'awful silence' in the
Presence of God. I do not think that, normally speaking, there is
any harm in this; on the contrary, for active-minded people in danger of intellectualism I think it a very useful exercise. Well, it was
one day I should think within a fortnight of my experience by the
rock that I first understood that for me there was danger. I was in
my little chapel before the Blessed Sacrament. Everything was quite
quiet; the men were at work and the women in their houses; it was
a hot, sunny morning, I remember, breathlessly still. I had finished my formal meditation and was sitting back in my chair.

"You all know, gentlemen, of course, the way in which one can
approach the Silence before God. Of course, the simplest can do it
if they will take pains."

Monsignor Maxwell interrupted, still in that slightly strained
voice in which he had spoken just now.

"Please describe it," he said.

The priest looked up deprecatingly.

"Well, then, first I had withdrawn myself from the world of
sense. That takes, as you know, sometimes several minutes; it is
necessary to sink down in thought in such a manner that sounds
no longer distract the attention, even though they may be heard
and even considered and reflected upon. Then the second step is
to leave behind all intellectual considerations and images, and that,
too, sometimes is troublesome, especially if the mind is naturally
active. Well, this day I found an extraordinary ease in both the acts."

Father Brent leaned forward.

"May I interrupt, Father? But I am not sure that I understand."

The old man pursed his lips. Then he glanced up at the rest of
us almost apologetically.

"Well, it is this, my dear Father. . . . How can I put it? . . . It is
the introversion of the soul. Instead of considering this object or

that, either by looking upon it or reflecting upon it, the soul turns inward. There are the two distinct planes on which many men, especially those who pay little or no attention to the soul, live continually. Either they continually seek distractions—they cannot be devout except in company or before an image—or else—as, indeed, many do who have even the gift of recollection—they dwell entirely upon considerations and mental images. Now the true introversion is beneath all this. The soul sinks, turning inward upon itself . . . there are no actual considerations at all; these become in their turn as much distractions to the energy of the soul as external objects to the energy of the mind. . . . Is that clearer, my dear Father?"

It was all said with a kind of patient and apologetic simplicity. Father Brent nodded pensively two or three times, and dropped his chin again upon his hand. The old priest went on.

"Well, gentlemen, as I said just now, on this morning I came into the Silence without an effort. First the sensible world dropped away; I heard a woman open and shut her door fifty yards away down the street, but it was no more than a sound. Then almost immediately the world of images and considerations went past me and vanished, and I found myself in perfect stillness.

"For an instant it seemed to me that all was well. There was that strange tranquility all about me. . . . I cannot put it into words except by saying, as all do who practise that method, that it is a living tranquility full of a very vital energy. This is not, of course, that to which contemplatives penetrate; St. John of the Cross makes that very plain; it is no more than that in which we ought always to live. It is that Kingdom of God within of which our Blessed Lord tells us, but it is not the Palace itself. . . . However, as I have said, when one has but learned the way there—and the difficulty of doing so lies only in its extreme and singular simplicity—when one has learned the way there it is full of pleasure and consolation.

"I remained there, as my manner was, drawing a long breath or two, as one is obliged to do. I do not know why—and at first all seemed well. There was that peace about me which may be described under the image of any one of the five senses. I prefer to speak of it now as under the image of light—a very radiant, mellow light full of warmth and sweetness. There was, too, just at first, that sense of profound abasement and adoration which is so familiar. . . . As I said, gentlemen, I do not, of course, for an instant pretend to the gift of pure contemplation; that is something far beyond.

"Then all in instant that sense of adoration vanished.

"Now, it was not that I had risen back again to meditation; there were no images before my attention, no reflections of any formulated kind. It was still the pure perception, and yet all sense of adoration and of God's majesty was gone. The light and the peace were there still, but—but not God. . . .

"Then I perceived, if I may say so, that something was on the point of disclosure. It was as if something was about to manifest itself. I perceived that the light was not as it had been. It was like that strange, vivid sunlight that we see sometimes when a heavy cloud is overhead. That is the only way in which I can express it. It is for that reason that I called it *light* rather than sound or touch. For an instant still I hesitated. The thought of what had happened to me by the rock never came to my mind, and with inconceivable swiftness the process passed on. To use an auditory metaphor for a moment it was like the change of an orchestra. The minor note steals in; a light passes over the character of the sound, and simultaneously the volume increases, the chords expand, tearing the heart with them, and the listener perceives that a moment later the climax will break in thunder."

He had raised his voice a little by now; his eyes glanced this way and that, though still without a trace of self-consciousness. Then again his voice dropped.

"Well, gentlemen, before that final moment came I had remembered; the vision of the rock and the chatter of the stream was before me sharp as a landscape under lightning. . . . I do not know what I did, but I was aware of making a kind of terrified effort. My soul sprang up as a diver who chokes under water, and in an instant the whole thing was gone. Then I became aware that my eyes were open and that I was standing up. I was still terrified by the suddenness of the experience, and stood there, saying something aloud to Our Lord in the Tabernacle. Then I heard the door open behind me.

"'Did you cry out, Father?' said Bridget. 'Why, Mother of Mercy—'

"I felt myself beginning to sway on my feet. Well, gentlemen, I need not trouble you with all that. The truth was that Bridget, who was washing up my breakfast things in the kitchen, heard me cry out. She told me afterward that when she saw my face she thought that I was dying. . . . I sat down a little then, and she fetched me something, and presently I was able to walk out.

"Well, gentlemen, that is enough for this evening."

He stopped abruptly.

We got up and went to night-prayers.

II

"Well, so far," began Father Girdlestone on the following evening— "so far you see two things had happened to me. First there seems to have been a kind of unpremeditated assault that affected my body, mind, and soul. That was the attack by the rock. Then he began to lay siege more deliberately, and attacked me in my meditation, in what I may call the innermost chamber, that anteroom of the transcendent world. Now, I have to tell you of his next assault."

There was a rustle of expectation as we settled ourselves to listen. I had found on questioning the others in the morning that they were in the same attitude as myself, impressed, but not convinced— indeed, strangely impressed by the extreme subtlety of the experience related to us. Yet there had been no proof, no tangible evidence, such as we are accustomed to demand, that the incidents had been anything more than subjective. At the same time there had been something remarkable in the priest's assurance as well as in the precise particularity of his narrative. It seemed now, however, from what he said, that perhaps we were to have more materialistic elements presented to us.

"The result, of course," continued Father Girdlestone, "of the attack upon my soul was that I became terrified at the thought of any further act of introversion. It seemed to me on reflection that I had probably overstrained my faculties a little and that I had better be more distinctly meditative in devotion.

"I fetched down, therefore, from my shelves a copy of the 'Spiritual Exercises,' and set to work. I began with a carefully objective act of the Presence of God, dwelling chiefly upon the Blessed Sacrament, and then pursued carefully the lines laid down. Two or three times every day, I should say, I was tempted to fall back upon the Prayer of Quiet, and each time I resisted it. It was a kind of frightened fascination that I felt for it. It was as if it had been a cupboard where something terrible lurked in silence and darkness, ready to tear me if I opened the door. Of course I should have opened it boldly; any priest of experience would have told me so at once; but I did not fully understand what was wrong. The result was as you shall hear.

"All went well for several days. I meditated with care, making the prescribed considerations—the preludes, the pictures, and all the rest, observing to go straight from the intellectual act to the voluntary. I became soothed and content again. Then, without any warning, the new assault was made. It came about in this fashion:

"I was meditating upon the Particular Judgment, and had formed the picture as vividly as possible of my soul before the Judge. I saw the wounds and the stains on one side, the ineffably piercing grace and holiness on the other. I saw the reproach in the Judge's face. I seized my soul by the neck, as it were, and crushed it down in humility and penitence. And then suddenly it seemed to me that my hold relaxed, and all faded. Now this assault came to me in intellectual form, yet I cannot remember the arguments. It began, if I may say so, as a blot upon the subject of my meditation, effacing the image of my Judge and of myself, and it spread with inconceivable swiftness over the whole of my faith. . . ."

The priest paused, smiling steadily at the fire.

"How shall I put it?" he said. . . . "Well, in a word, it was intellectual doubt of the whole thing. A kind of cloud of infidelity seemed to envelop me. I beat against it, but it passed on, thick and black. There seemed to me no Person behind it; it was the very negation of Personality that surrounded me. 'After all,' it seemed to say to me, yet without words or intellect, you understand— 'after all, this is a pretty picture, but where is the proof? What shadow of a proof is there that the whole thing is not a dream? If there were objective proof, how could any man doubt? If there is not objective proof, what reason have you to trust in religion at all—far more, to sacrifice your life to it? . . . Death, too, what is that but the resolving of the elements that issue in what you call the soul? And when the elements resolve the soul disperses.' . . . And so on, and so on. You know it, gentlemen. . . . It suggested horrible things against Our Lord when I turned to the Tabernacle. And then, on a sudden, as it had done in the deeper plane, it spread upward to an intolerable climax. I began to see myself as a dying spark in a burning-out world, and there was no escape, for there was nothing but empty space about me—no God, no heaven, not even a devil to hint at life in some form at least after death. I looked during those seconds into the gulf of annihilation. . . . I cried out in my heart that I would sooner live in hell than die there . . . and the vision, if I may call it so, of ultimate eternal blackness cleared every instant before my intellect until it was imminent upon me as a demonstrable certainty; and then, once more, before that loomed out as actually intellectually certain, I struggled and stood up, saying something aloud, the name of God, I think, while the sweat poured down my face.

"It passed then—at least, in its acuteness. There was the little domed tabernacle before me with its white curtains, and the altar-cards and the gilt candlesticks, and a woman went past the window in clogs, and I heard a bird twitter beneath the eaves, and it was all, for a while, natural and peaceful again."

The priest stopped.

"Now, gentlemen," he said very slowly, "intellectual difficulties have occurred to most people, I imagine. How should it not be so? If religion were small enough for our intellects it could not be great enough for our soul's requirements. But this was not just that fleeting transient obscurity that we call intellectual difficulty. It was to ordinary darkness what substance is to imagination, what a visible concrete scene is to a fancy, what life is to dreaming. I know I cannot express what I mean; but I want you to take it on my word that this visitation in the realm of the intellect was a solid blackness,

compared with which all other difficulties that I have ever heard
of or experienced are as a mere lowering of intellectual lights. It
was paralleled only by my experience in introversion. That, too,
had not been an emotional withdrawal, or a spiritual dryness, as
we commonly use those words. It had been a solid, unutterably
heavy burden—real beyond description. . . . And further, I want
you to consider my dilemma. I had been routed in my soul and
dared not take refuge there; I had been overwhelmed, too, in my
intellect, and even when the first misery had passed it seemed to
me that the arguments against the Faith were stronger than those
for it. I did not dare to pit one against the other. A heavy deposit
had been left upon my understanding. I did not dare to sit down
and argue; I did not dare to run for refuge to the Silence of God. I
was driven out into the sole thing that was left—the world of sense."

Again he stopped, still with that tranquil smile. I hardly understood him, though I think I saw very dimly what he had called his
dilemma. Yet I did not understand what he meant by the "world of
sense."

After a little pause he went on.

"To the world of sense," he repeated. "It seemed to me now
that this was all that was left. I determined then and there to drop
my meditation and to confine myself to mass, office and rosary. I
would say the words with my lips, quickly and steadily, keeping
my mind fixed upon them rather than upon their meaning, and I
would trust that presently the clouds would pass.

"Well, gentlemen, for about two months I continued this. The
misery I suffered is simply indescribable. You can imagine all the
suggestions I made to myself when I was off my guard. I told myself that I was a coward and a sham—that I had lost my faith and
that I continued to act as a priest! What was especially hard to
bear was the devotion of my parishioners. As I knelt in front saying the rosary and they responded I could hear the thrill of conviction in every word they uttered. Oh, those Irish! The things they
said to me sometimes were like swords for pain . . . the masses
they asked me to say . . !

"I went to a priest at a distance once or twice and told him the bare outline—not as I have told it to you. He laughed at me, kindly, of course. He told me that it was the effect of loneliness, while I knew that at the best it was the work of One who bore me continual company now and who was stronger than I. He told me that all young priests had to win the victory in some form or other; that every priest thought his own case the most desperate. . . . Yet I knew from every word that he said that he did not understand, and that I could never make him understand. Yet, somehow, I set my teeth; I told God that I was willing to bear this dereliction for as long as He willed—so paradoxical and mysterious is the gift of Faith—if He would but save my soul, and at last, in a kind of defiance, I began to look once more at my designs for the church I was to build.

"You see, gentlemen, what I meant by taking refuge in the world of sense. I deliberately contemplated never daring to face God again interiorly, or even my own soul. I would do my duty as a priest; I would say my mass and office; I would preach strictly what the Church enjoined; I would live and die like that, with my teeth set. Better God beaten and denied than all the world beside in prosperity!"

For the first time in the whole of his narrative Father Girdlestone's voice trembled a little. He passed his thin old hand over his mouth once or twice, shifted his position and began again.

"It was on the first of October that I took down my plans again. I had not looked at them for two months; I had not the heart to do so.

"Now let me describe to you exactly the room in which I sat, and the other necessary circumstances.

"In the centre of my room stood my table, with two windows on my left, the fire in front, and the door behind me to the right. The windows were hung with serge curtains. I had no carpet, but a little mat only beneath my table and another before the fire.

"It was in the beginning of October—to be accurate, the third of the month—that this thing happened that I am about to tell you.

"I awoke early that morning, said my mass as usual, with attention and care, but no sensible devotion, and after my thanksgiving sat down to breakfast. It was then that I first had any uneasiness.

"I was breakfasting at my table, and beyond me, in front and to the right, stood a large basket-chair. I was reading some book or other, and can honestly say that nothing was further from my mind than my experiences in the summer. Remember, during two months nothing had happened—nothing, at least, beyond that intolerable intellectual darkness. Then the basket-chair suddenly clicked in the way in which they do half an hour after one has sat in them. It distracted my attention for an instant—it was just enough for that; no more. I went on with my book.

"Then it clicked again three or four times, and I looked up, rather annoyed. . . . Well, to be brief, this went on and on. After breakfast, when Bridget came to fetch the tray, I asked whether she had touched the chair that morning. She told me No. All this time, remember, no thought of anything odd had entered my head. I supposed it was the damp and said so.

"Well, she was still in the room. I went out to fetch my breviary from the chapel, and as I set foot on the stairs, leaving the door open behind me, I heard her, as I thought, come out after me with the tray and follow me, three or four steps behind, all down the staircase. I had no more doubt of that than of the fact that I myself was going downstairs. At the turn of the stairs I did not even look behind. By the sounds—not clear footfalls, you understand, but a kind of shuffling and breathing, and still more by the consciousness that there she was—I judged she was in a hurry, as she often was. At the foot of the stairs I turned to say something, and as I began to turn I will swear that I saw a figure out of the corner of my eye; but when I looked it was simply not there. There was nothing there. . . . Do you understand, gentlemen? Nothing at all.

"I called up to her, and heard her come across the floor. Then she looked over the banister.

"'Did you come out of the room just now?' I said.

"'No, your reverence.'

"Well, I made my theory, of course. It was to the effect that she had moved in the room as I came out; that I therefore thought she was following me, and that the rest was simply self-suggestion.

"I got my breviary and came out. As I came into the little lobby again there occurred to the impression that some one was there, waiting in the corner. I looked round me; there was nothing, and I went upstairs.

"Gentlemen, do you know that nervous condition when one feels there is some one in the room? It is generally dissipated by ten minutes' conversation. Well, I was in that condition all the morning. But there was more than that.

"It was not only that sense of some one there; there were sounds now and then, very faint, but absolutely distinct, coming from all quarters—sounds so minute and unimportant in themselves that I might have heard them a hundred times without giving them another thought if they had not been accompanied by that sense of a presence with me. They were of all kinds. Once or twice a piece of woodwork somewhere in the room clicked, as my basket-chair had done—a sharp, minute rap, such as one hears in damp weather. Once the door became unlatched and slid very softly with the sound of a hush over a piece of matting that lay there. I got up and shut the door again, looking, I must confess, for an instant on to the landing, and as I came back to my chair that clicked twice.

"Gentlemen, I know this sounds absurd. You will be saying, as I said, that I was simply in a nervous condition. Very well, perhaps I was; but please wait. Once, as I sat in my chair drawn sideways near the fireplace, a very slight movement caught my eye. I turned sharply; it was no more than the fringe of the mat under the table lifting in the draught. As I looked it ceased.

"Well, my nerves got worse and worse. I stared every now and then round the room. There was nothing to be seen but the boards, the mats, the familiar furniture, the black and white crucifix over the mantle-shelf, my few books, and the vestment-chest near the door. There were the curtains, too, hanging at the windows. That was all. It was a cloudy October day, and rained a little about half-past twelve. I remember starting suddenly as a gust came and dashed the drops against the glass.

"At about a quarter to one Bridget came in to lay dinner. ... I am ashamed to say it, but I was extraordinarily relieved when I heard her open the downstairs door. She came in, you remember, three or four times a day to see after me; otherwise I was alone in the house.

"When she came into the room I looked up at her. . . . She smiled at me, and then it seemed to me that her face took on it rather an odd expression. She stopped smiling, and before she set down the tablecloth and knives she looked round the room rather curiously, I thought.

"'Well, Bridget,' I said, 'what is it?'

"There was just a moment before she answered.

"'It is nothing, your reverence,' she said.

"Then she laid dinner. I dined, reading all the while, and she brought in the dishes one by one. I am afraid I hurried rather over dinner. I made up my mind to go out for a long walk; there was something else in my mind, too—well, I may as well tell you; it seemed to me that I should rather like to be out of the house before she was. Yes; it was cowardly; but remember that all this while I was telling myself that I had an attack of the nerves, and that I had better not be alone except in the fresh air.

"Well, nothing at all happened that afternoon. It seemed to me as I went over the moors that all sense of haunting had ceased; I noticed first consciously that it had gone soon after leaving the outskirts of the village; I was entirely happy and serene.

"As I came back into sight of the village at dusk and saw the lights shining over the hill the uneasiness came on me again. It struck me vividly for the first time that a night spent alone in that house would be slightly uncomfortable. By this time, of course, too, the possibility of a connection between my present state and my previous experiences had occurred to my mind; but I had striven to resist this idea as merely one more nervous suggestion.

"My uneasiness grew greater still as I came up the street. I am ashamed to say that I stopped to talk three or four times to my parishioners simply out of that unaccountably strong terror of my own house. I noticed, too, across the street that a face peeped from Bridget's window and drew back on seeing me. A moment later her door opened and she came out.

"I did not turn or wait for her, but as I reached my door I was conscious of a very distinct relief that she was behind me, and as I went in she came immediately after me.

"'I am very sorry, Father,' she said, 'I haven't your tea ready yet.'

"I told her to bring it as soon as she could, and went slowly upstairs with the horror deepening at every step. I knew perfectly well now why she had waited; it was that she did not like to enter the empty house alone. . . . Yet I did not feel that I could ask her what it was she feared. That would be a kind of surrender on my part—an allowing to myself that there was something to fear, and you must remember that I still was trying to tell myself that it was all nerves."

The Rector leaned forward.

"I am very sorry, Father Girdlestone," he said softly, "but it is past time for night prayers." He paused. "But may we make an exception to-night and hear the rest afterward?"

The old man stood up and motioned with a little smile toward the chapel gallery.

III

"As I went forward into the room," began the old man again as soon as we had taken our seats in silence, "I knew beyond doubt that I was accompanied. I heard Bridget moving about downstairs, but it was as sound heard through the roar of a train. There went with me something resembling a loud noise—interior, you understand, yet on the brink of manifestation in the world of sense; or you may call it a blackness, or a vast weight, as heavy as heaven and earth, and it was all centred round a personality. It was of such a nature that I should have been surprised at nothing. It appeared to me that all that I looked upon—the serge curtains, my table, my chair, the glow of the fire on the hearth, and the glimmer on the bare boards—all these were but as melting shreds and rays hanging upon some monstrous reality. They were there, they were just in existence, but they were as accidents without substance.

"I do not know if there were definite sounds or not, or even definite appearances, beyond the normal, material sounds and sights. There may have been, but I do not think so.

"I went across the room, walking, it seemed to me, on nothingness. My body was still in sensible relations with matter, but it seemed to me that I was not. I found my chair and sat down in it to wait. I was nerveless now, sunk in a kind of despair that I cannot hope to make plain to you. I imagine that a lost soul on the edge of death must be in that state.

"I looked almost vacantly round the room once or twice; but there was nothing. I understood without consideration what was happening, and the general course of events. It was all one, I perceived now. That which had started up at the rock, which had invaded first the innermost chamber of my soul, and then the intellectual plane, and had established itself there, had now taken its frail step forward, and was claiming the world of sense as well. I felt entirely powerless. You will wonder why I did not go downstairs to the Blessed Sacrament. I do not know, but it was impossible. Here was the battlefield, I knew very well.

"I perceived something else, too. It was the reason of the assaults. I did not fully understand it, but I knew that the object was to drive me from the place—to make the village and the neighborhood detestable to me. I knew that I could escape by going away, yet it was not exactly a temptation. I had no interior desire to escape. It was merely a question as to which force would prevail in my soul—that which impelled me away and grace which held me there. I was as a passive dummy between them. . . .

"I do not know how long it was before Bridget pushed open the door. I saw her with the tray come across the room and set it down upon my table. Then I saw her looking at me.

"'Bridget,' I said, 'I shall want no supper to-night. And tell the people that I am unwell and that there will be no night-prayers. There will be mass, I hope, as usual in the morning.'

"I said those words, I believe; but the voice was not as my own. It was as if another spoke. I saw her looking at me across the dusk with an extraordinary terror in her face.

"'Come away, Father,' she whispered.

"I shook my head.

"'Come away,' she whispered again. 'This is not a good house to be in.'

"I said nothing.

"'Shall I fetch Father Donovan to you, Father,' she whispered, 'or the doctor?'

"'Fetch no one,' I said to her. 'Tell no one. Ask for prayers, if you will. Go and leave me to myself, Bridget.'

"I think I understood even then what the struggle was she was going through. I do not know if she perceived all that I perceived, but even from her face, without her words, I knew that she was conscious of something. Yet she did not like to leave me alone. She stood perfectly still, looking first at me, then slowly round the room, then back at me again. And as she looked the dusk fell veil on veil.

"Then something happened, I do not know what; I never questioned her afterward, but she was gone. I heard her stumbling and moaning down the stairs. An instant later the street door opened and banged, and I was left alone.

"I cannot tell you what I felt. I knew only that the crisis was come, and that the result was out of my hands. I closed my eyes, I think, and lay right back in my chair. It was as if I were submitting myself to an operation; I wondered vaguely as to what shape it would take.

"All about the room I felt the force gathering. There was no oscillation, no vibration, but a steady, continuous stream concentrating itself within the four walls. With this the sense of the central personality grew every moment more and more intense and vivid. It seemed to me as if I were some tiny, conscious speck of matter in the midst of a life whose vastness and malignance was beyond conception. At times it was this; at other times it was as if I looked within and saw a space full of some indescribable blackness—a space of such a nature that I could not tell whether it was as tiny as a pinhole or as vast as infinity. It was spaceless space, sheer emptiness, but with an emptiness that was a horror, and it was within me.

"Yet it was not simple spirit—it was not the correlative of matter. It was rather spirit in the very throes of manifestation in matter. . . .

"Sometimes then I attended to this; sometimes I lay with every sense at full stretch—at a tenseness that seemed impossible, directed outward. I cannot tell even now whether the room was poised in deathly silence or in an indescribable clamor and roar of tongues. It was one or the other, or it was both at once.

"Or, to take the sense of sight. . . . Although my eyes were closed, every detail of the room was before me. Sometimes I saw it as rigid as a man at grips with death, in a kind of pallor—the table, the dying fire, the uncurtained windows—all in the pallor—the very names of the books visible—all, as it were, striving to hold themselves in material being under the stress of some enormous destructive force with which they were charged—as rigid and as silent and as significant as an electric wire—and as full of power. Or at times all seemed to me to have gone, simply to have dissolved into nothingness, as a breath fades on a window—to retain but a phantom of themselves. . . .

"Well, well . . . words are very useless, gentlemen; . . . they are poor things—"

The old priest paused a moment, leaning forward in his chair with his thin, veined hands together. For myself I cannot say what I felt. I seemed to be in somewhat of the same state as that which he was describing; all my senses, too, were stretched to the full by the intensity of my attention. Yet the narrator seemed little affected; he leaned and looked peacefully into the fire, and I caught the glint of light on his deep eyes.

Then he leaned back and went on.

"Now you must picture to yourselves, gentlemen, that this state grew steadily in its energy. I did not know before—and I can scarcely believe it now—that human nature could bear so much. Yet I seemed to myself to be observing my strained faculties from a plane apart from them. It was as the owner of a besieged castle might stand on a keep and watch the figures of his men staring out over the battlements at a sight he could not see. There were my eyes looking, my ears listening, even the touch of my fingers on the chair-arms questioning what it was that they held; and there was I—my very self—far within waiting for communications.

"I suppose that I knew there was no escape. I could not descend into the sphere of reason, for another Power held the keys; I could not sink again to the inner Presence of God, for that chamber, too, was occupied; there was this last stand to be made—the world of sense. If that was lost, all was lost; and I could not lift a finger to help. And, as I said, the strain grew greater each instant, as the opening swell of an organ waxes with a long, steady crescendo to its final roar. . . .

"I do not know at exactly what point I understood the assault, but it became known to me presently that what was intended was to merge the world of sense, so far as I was concerned, into this mighty essence of evil—to burst through, or, rather, to transcend the material. Then I knew I should be wholly lost. I remember, too, that I perceived soon after this that this was what the world calls madness . . . and I understood at this moment as never before how that process consummates itself. It begins, as mine did, with the carrying of the inner life by storm; that may come about by deliberate acquiescence in sin. I should suppose that it always does in some degree. Then the intellect is attacked—it may only be in one point—a 'delusion' it is called, and with many persons regarded only as eccentric—the process goes no further. But when the triumph is complete the world of sense, too, is lost, and the man raves. I knew at that time for absolute fact that this is the process. The 'delusions' of the mad are not non-existent—they are glimpses, horrible or foul or fantastic, of that strange world that we take so quietly for granted, that at this moment and at every moment is perpetually about us, foaming out its waters in lust or violence or mad irresponsible blasphemy against the Most High.

"Well, I saw that this was what threatened, yet I could not move a finger. No thought of flight entered my mind. All had gone too far by now. . . .

"Then, gentlemen, the climax came."

Again the old priest was silent.

I heard Monsignor's pipe drop with a clatter, and my nerves thrilled like a struck harp. He made no movement to pick it up. He stared only at the old man.

Then the quiet voice went on.

"This was the climax, gentlemen. . . . The intensity swelled and swelled; . . . each moment I thought must be the last—the utmost effort of hell. Then with a crash the full close sounded; and through the rending tear, through the veil of matter that whirled away and was gone, I caught one swift glimpse of all that lay beneath. It was not through one sense that I perceived it; it was through perception pure and simple. . . . Well, how can I say it? It was this. . . .

"I perceived two vast forces pressed one against the other, as silent and as rigid as . . . as the glass of a diver's helmet against the huge, incumbent, glittering water. It is a wretched simile. . . . Let us say that the appearance was as the meeting of fire and water without mist or tumult. The forces were absolutely opposed, absolutely alien, yet absolutely one in the plane of being. They could meet as the created and uncreated could not—as flesh and spirit cannot. They met, level, coincident, each rigid to breaking point—each full of an energy to which there is no parallel in this world.

"It seemed to me that all had waited for this. The enemy had been permitted to enter the gate; and at the instant of his triumph the fire of God was upon him, locked in the embrace of utter repulsion. . . .

"And it was given to me to watch that, gentlemen. . . . On the edge of what the world labels as madness, at the very instant that I hung balanced on that line, I saw that endless war of spirit and spirit, which has been waging since Michael drove Satan from heaven—that ceaseless, writhing conflict in which all that is not for God is against Him, seeking to dethrone and annihilate Him who gave it being. Ah, words . . . words . . . but I saw it . . . !"

There was a dead silence in the room. The priest drew one breath.

"Then I saw no more. I was in my chair as before, holding the arms; and the room round me stole back into being—through the pallor of a phantom to the dusk of earthly twilight; and I perceived that my eyes were closed and not open.

"There then I stayed, knowing that the war still waged beneath, yet fainter every moment as the tide crawled back, contesting inch by inch, rolled back by that remorseless power. Twice or three times I heard the murmur of sound in the room; the serge curtains swayed. I could hear them. I heard the door vibrating softly; then once more the quiet silence was there, and I heard the ashes slip by their weight from grate to fender. Nature at least was itself again.

Then once more, as into my intellect, the light stole back, and I
knew that God reigned and that His Son was Incarnate, crucified
and risen by many irrefragable proofs, round the house I could
hear the murmuring of voices, and saw through closed eyelids of
utter repose the glimmer of lanterns on the ceiling.

"Within myself, too, I watched the roar of evil; I drew breath
after breath, deep and life-giving, as far down within the secret
chambers of my soul the foul filth ebbed and sank, and that spring
raising into life everlasting, of which our Saviour spoke, welled up
in its stead, filling every cranny and corner of my soul with that
strange sweetness, so sweet and so dear that we forget it as the
very air we breathe.

"The murmur of conflict was infinitely far away; and it seemed
to me that once more I went down, down, in that introversion of
which I spoke just now, seeing all clear and sweet about me, down
into the Presence of the Lord who rules heaven and earth at His
will. Then a door closed, deep, deep below, and I knew that the
enemy was gone. . . .

"Well, gentlemen," said the priest after a pause, leaning back,
"that is really the story. But there are a few details to add.

"When the men that Bridget had fetched came upstairs they
found me asleep, but they told me afterward there were streaks of
foam at the corners of my mouth. Yet she was not gone three minutes.

"I never spoke a word to them of what happened. They knew
quite enough for laymen. . . . We had night-prayers as usual that
evening. I said the *Visita quæsumus Domine* at the end. . . .

"I slept like a child, and I said a mass of thanksgiving next day."

Father Brent broke the silence that followed. His voice seemed
strange.

"And the church, Father?"

The old priest smiled at him full.

"You have guessed it," he said. "Yes, the church was built thirty
years later. It is a basilica, as I said; it presents Our Lord in glory
in an apse. It stands, curiously enough, on the rock; but it is in the
middle of a huge colliery town, and—well, I may as well say it—

there is a grated tribune above the high altar at one side through which a convent of Poor Clares can assist at the holy sacrifice. Poor Clares!

"I ceased to wonder at the assault as soon as the convent was built."

He stood up, smiling.

Father Bianchi, as the days went on, seemed a little less dog-matic on the theory that miracles (except, of course, those of the saints) did not happen. He was warned by Monsignor Maxwell that his turn was approaching to contribute a story, and suddenly at supper announced that he would prefer to get it over at once that evening.

"But I have nothing to tell," he cried, expostulating with hands and shoulders, "nothing to tell but the nonsense of an old peasant woman."

When we had taken our places upstairs, and the Italian had again apologized and remonstrated with raised eyebrows, he be-gan at last, and I noticed that he spoke with a seriousness that I should not have expected.

"When I was first a priest," he said, "I was in the south of Italy, and said my first mass in a church in the hills. The village was called Arripezza."

"Is that true?" said Monsignor suddenly, smiling.

The Italian grinned brilliantly. "Well, no," he said, "but it is near enough, and I swear to you that the rest is true. It was a vil-lage in the hills, ten miles from Naples. They have many strange beliefs there; it is like Father Brent's Cornwall. All along the coast, as you know, they set lights in the windows on one night of the year, because they relate that our Lady once came walking on the water with her divine Child, and found none to give her shelter.

186

Well, this village that we will call Arripezza was not on the coast. It was inland, but it had its own superstitions to compensate it— superstitions cursed by the Church.

"I knew little of all this when I went there. I had been in the seminary until then.

"The *parrocho* was an old man, but old! He could say mass sometimes on Sundays and feasts, but that was all, and I went to help him. There were many at my first mass as the custom is, and they all came up to kiss my hands when it was done.

"When I came back from the sacristy again there was an old woman waiting for me, who told me that her name was Giovannina. I had seen her before as she kissed my hands. She was as old as the *parrocho* himself—I cannot tell how old—yellow and wrinkled as a monkey.

"She put five loie into my hands.

"'Five masses, Father,' she said, 'for a soul in purgatory.'

"'And the name?'

"'That does not matter,' she said. 'And will you say them, my Father, at the altar of S. Espedito?'

"I took the money and went off, and as I went down the church, I saw her looking after me, as if she wished to speak, but she made no sign, and I went home; and I had a dozen other masses to say, some for my friends, and a couple that the *parrocho* gave me, and those, therefore, I began to say first. When I had said the fifth of the twelve, Giovannina waited for me again at the door of the sacristy. I could see that she was troubled.

"'Have you not said them, my Father?' she asked. 'He is here still.'

"I did not notice what she said, except the question, and I said no; I had had others to say first. She blinked at me with her old eyes a moment, and I was going on, but she stopped me again.

"'Ah! Say them at once, my Father,' she said; 'he is waiting.'

"Then I remembered what she had said before and I was angry.

"'Waiting!' I said; 'and so are thousands of poor souls.'

"'Ah, but he is so patient,' she said; 'he has waited so long.'

"I said something sharp, I forget what, but the *parrocho* had told me not to hang about and talk nonsense to women, and I was going on, but she took me by the arm.

"'Have you not seen him too, my Father?' she said.

"'I looked at her, thinking she was mad, but she held me by the arm and blinked up at me, and seemed in her senses. I told her to tell me what she meant, but she would not. At last I promised to say the masses at once. The next morning I began the masses, and said four of them, and at each the old woman was there close to me, for I said them at the altar of S. Espedito that was in the nave, as she had asked me, and I had a great devotion to him as well, and she was always at her chair just outside the altar-rails. I scarcely saw her, of course, for I was a young priest and had been taught not to lift my eyes when I turned round, but on the fourth day I looked at her at the *Orate fratres* and she was staring not at me or the altar, but at the corner on the left. I looked there when I turned, but there was nothing but the glass case with the silver hearts in it to S. Espedito.

"That was on a Friday, and in the evening I went to the church again to hear confessions, and when I was done, the old woman was there again.

"'They are nearly done, my Father?' she said, 'and you will finish them to-morrow?'

"I told her Yes; but she made me promise that whatever happened I would do so.

"Then she went on, 'Then I will tell you, my Father, what I would not before. I do not know the man's name, but I see him each day during mass at that altar. He is in the corner. I have seen him there ever since the church was built.'

"Well, I knew she was mad then, but I was curious about it, and asked her to describe him to me; and she did so. I expected a man in a sheet or in flames or something of the kind, but it was not so. She described to me a man in a dress she did not know—a tunic to the knees, bareheaded, with a short sword in his hand. Well, then I saw what she meant, she was thinking of S. Espedito himself. He was a Roman soldier, you remember, gentlemen?

"'And a curiass?' I said. 'A steel breastplate and helmet?'

"Then she surprised me.

"'Why, no, Father; he has nothing on his head or breast, and there is a bull beside him.'

"Well, gentlemen, I was taken aback by that. I did not know what to say."

Monsignor leant swiftly forward.

"Mithras," he said abruptly.

The Italian smiled.

"Monsignor knows everything," he said.

Then I broke in, because I was more interested than I knew.

"Tell me, Monsignor, what was Mithras?"

The priest explained shortly. It was an Eastern worship, extra-ordinarily pure, introduced into Italy a little after the beginning of the Christian era. Mithras was a god, filling a position not un-like that of the Second Person of the Blessed Trinity. He offered a perpetual sacrifice, and through that sacrifice souls were enabled to rise from earthly things to heavenly, if they relied upon it and accompanied that faith by works of discipline and prayer.

"I beg your pardon, Father Bianchi," he ended.

The Italian smiled again.

"Yes, Monsignor," he said, "I know that now, but I did not know it for many years afterwards, and I know something else now that I did not know then. Well, to return.

"I told my old woman that she was dreaming, that it could not be so, that there was no room for a bull in the corner, that it was a picture of S. Espedito that she was thinking of.

"'And why did you not get the masses said before?' I asked.

"She smiled rather slyly at me then.

"'I did get five said once before,' she said, 'in Naples, but they did him no good. And when once again I told the *parrocho* here, he told me to be off; he would not say them.'

"And she had waited for a young priest, it seemed, and had determined not to tell him the story till the masses were said, and had saved up her money meanwhile.

"Well, I went home, and got to talking with the old priest, and led him on, so that he thought that he had introduced the subject, and presently he told me that when the foundation of the church had been laid forty years before, they had found an old cave in the hill, with heathen things in it. He knew no more than that about it, but he told me to fetch a bit of pottery from a cupboard, and showed it me, and there was just the tail of a bull upon it, and an eagle."

Monsignor leaned forward again.

"Just so," he said, "and the bull was lying down?"

The Italian nodded, and was silent.

We all looked at him. It seemed a tame ending, I thought. Then Father Brent put our thoughts into words.

"That is not all?" he said.

Father Bianchi looked at him sharply, and at all of us, but said nothing.

"Ah! that is not all," said the other again persistently.

"Bah!" cried the Italian suddenly. "It was not all, if you will have it so. But the rest is madness, as mad as Giovannina herself. What I saw, I saw because she made me expect it. It was nothing but the shadow, or the light in the glass case."

A perceptible thrill ran through us all. The abrupt change from contempt to seriousness was very startling.

"Tell us, Father," said the English priest; "we shall think no worse of you for it. If it was only the shadow, what harm is there in telling it?"

"Indeed you must finish," went on Monsignor; "it is in the contract."

The Italian looked round again, frowned, smiled and laughed uneasily.

"I have told it to no one till to-day," he said, "but you shall hear it. But it was only the shadow—you understand that?"

A chorus, obviously insincere, broke out from the room.

"It was only the shadow, Padre Bianchi."

Again the priest laughed shortly; then the smile faded, and he went on.

"I went down early the next morning, before dawn, and I made my meditation before the Blessed Sacrament; but I could not help looking across once or twice at the corner by S. Espedito's altar; it was too dark to see anything clearly; but I could make out the silver hearts in the glass case. When I had finished Giovannina came in.

"I could not help stopping by her chair as I went to rest.

"'Is there anything there?' I asked.

"She shook her head at me.

"'He is never there till mass begins,' she said.

"The sacristy door that opens out of doors was set wide as I came past it in my vestments; and the dawn was coming up across the hills, all purple."

Monsignor murmured something, and the priest stopped.

"I beg your pardon," said Monsignor; "but that was the time the sacrifice of Mithras was offered."

"When I came out into the church," went on the priest, "it was all gray in the light of the dawn, but the chapels were still dark. I went up the steps, not daring to look in the corner, and set the vessels down. As I was spreading the corporal the server came up and lighted the candles. And still I dared not look. I turned by the right and came down, and stood waiting till he knelt beside me.

"Then I found I could not begin. I knew what folly it was, but I was terribly frightened. I heard the server whisper, *In nomine Patris* . . .

"Then I shut my eyes tight, and began.

"Well, by the time I had finished the preparation, I felt certain that something was watching me from the corner. I told myself, as I tell myself now," snapped the Italian fiercely— "I told myself it was but what the woman had told me. And then at last I opened my eyes to go up the steps, but I kept them down, and only saw the dark corner out of the side of my eyes.

"Then I kissed the altar and began.

"Well, it was not until the Epistle that I understood that I should have to face the corner at the reading of the Gospel; but by then I do not think I could have faced it directly, even if I had wished.

"So when I was saying the *Munda cor* in the centre, I thought of a plan, and as I went to read the Gospel I put my left hand over my eyes, as if I were in pain, and read the Gospel like that. And so all through the mass I went on; I always dropped my eyes when I had to turn that way at all, and I finished everything and gave the blessing.

"As I gave it, I looked at the old woman, and she was kneeling there, staring across at the corner; so I knew that she was still dreaming she saw something.

"Then I went to read the last Gospel."

The priest was plainly speaking with great difficulty; he passed his hands over his lips once or twice. We were all quiet.

"Well, gentlemen, courage came to me then; and as I signed the altar I looked straight into the corner."

He stopped again, and began resolutely once more; but his voice rang with hysteria.

"Well, gentlemen, you understand that my head was full of it now, and that the corner was dark, and that the shadows were very odd."

"Yes, yes, Padre Bianchi," said Monsignor easily, "and what did the shadows look like?"

The Italian gripped the arms of the chair, and screamed his answer.

"I will not tell you, I will not tell you. It was but the shadow. My God, why have I told you the tale at all?"

Father Jenks' Tale

I have not yet had occasion to describe Father Jenks, the Ontario priest; partly, I think, because he had not previously distinguished himself by anything but silence, and partly because he was so true to his type that I had scarcely noticed even that.

It was not until the following evening, when he was seated in the central chair of the group, that I really observed him sufficiently to take in his characteristics with any definiteness and to see how wholly he was American. He was clean-shaven, with a heavy mouth, square jaw, and an air of something that I must call dulness, relieved only by a spark of alertness in each of his eyes, as he leaned back and began his story. He spoke deliberately, in an even voice, and as he spoke looked steadily a little above the fire; his hands lay together on his right knee, which was crossed over his left, and I noticed a large, elastic-sided boot cocked toward the warmth. I knew that he had passed a great part of his early life in England, and I was not surprised to observe that he spoke with hardly a trace of American accent or phraseology.

"I, too, am a man of one story," he said, "and I dare say you may think it not worth the telling. But it impressed me."

He looked round with heavy, amused eyes as if to apologize.

"It was when I was in England, in the eighties. I was in the Cotswolds. You know them, perhaps?"

Again he looked round. Monsignor Maxwell jerked the ash off his cigarette impatiently. This American's air of leisure was a little tiresome.

"I lived in a cottage," went on the other, "at the edge of Minchester, not two hundred yards from the old church. My own schism shop, as the parson called it once or twice in the local paper, was a tin building behind my house; it was not beautiful. It was a kind of outlandish stranger beside the church, and the parson made the most of that. I never was able to understand."

He broke off again and pressed his lips in a reminiscent smile.

"Now, all that part of the Cotswolds is like a table; it is flat at the top, with steep sides sloping down into the valleys. The great houses stand mostly half way down these slopes. It is too windy on the top for their trees and gardens. The Dominicans have a house a few miles from Minchester up one of the opposite hills; and I would go over there to my confession on Saturdays and stay an hour or two over tea, talking to one of them. It was there that I heard the tale of the house I am going to speak about.

"This was a house that stood not two miles from my own village —a great place, built half way down one of the slopes. It had been a Benedictine house once, though there was little enough of that part left; most of it was red brick with twisted chimneys; but on the lawn that sloped down toward the wood and the stream at the bottom of the valley there was the west arch of the nave still standing, with the doorway beneath and a couple of chapels on either side. Mrs.—er—Arbuthnot we will call her, if you please—had laid it out with a rockery beneath; and once I saw her from the hill behind drinking tea with her friends in one of the chapels.

"Then the dining-room, I heard from the Dominicans, had been the abbot's chapel. This, too, was what they told me. The house had been shut up for forty years and had a bad name. It had once been a farm, but things had happened there—the sons had died, a famous horse bred there had broken its neck somehow on the lawn. Then another family had taken it from the owner, and the only son of the lot, too, had died; and then folks began to talk about a curse; and the oldest inhabitant was trotted out as usual to make mischief and gossip; and the end was, the house was shut up.

"Then the owner had built on to it. He pulled down a bit more of the ruins, meaning to live in it himself, and then his son went up."

The Canadian smiled with one corner of his mouth.

"This is what I heard from the Dominicans, you know."

Father Brent looked up swiftly.

"They are right, though," he said. "I know the house and others like it."

"Yes, Father," said the other priest; "your island has its points." He recrossed his legs and drew out his pipe and pouch.

"Well, as this priest says, there are other houses like it. Otherwise I could scarcely tell this tale. It's too ancient and feudal to happen in my country."

He paused so long to fill his pipe that Father Maxwell sighed aloud.

"Yes, Monsignor," said the priest without looking up, "I am going on immediately." He put his pipe into the corner of his mouth, took out his matches and went on.

"Well, Mrs. Arbuthnot had taken the house a year before I came to Minchester. She was what the Dominicans called a frivolous woman; but I called her real solid before the end. What they meant was that she had parties down there, and tea in the chapel, and a dresser with blue plates where the altar used to stand in the abbot's place, and a vestment for her fire-screen, and all that; and a couple of chestnuts that she used to drive about the country with, and a groom in boots, and a couple of fellows with powdered hair to help her in and out.

"Well, I saw all that at a garden-party she gave, and I must say we got on very well. I had seen her before once or twice out of my window on Sunday morning going along with a morocco prayer-book with a cross on it, and a bonnet on the back of her head. Then I showed her round the old church one day with some visitors of hers, and she left a card on me next day.

"On the day of the garden-party I saw the house, and the blue china and the rest, and she asked me what I thought of it all, and I said it was very nice; and she asked me whether I thought it wrong, with a sort of cackle; and I told her she had better follow her own religious principles and let me follow mine, and not have any exchanges. She told me then I was a sensible man, and called up her son to introduce us. He was a fellow of twenty or so, a bright lad, up at Oxford. He was just engaged to be married, too—that was why they had the party—and when I saw his girl, too, I thought things looked pretty unwholesome for the old curse, and I think I said so to the lady. She thought me more sensible than ever after that, and I heard her telling another old body what I had said."

The Canadian paused again to strike a match, and I saw the corners of his mouth twitching either with the effort to draw or with amusement; I scarcely knew which. When the pipe was well alight he went on.

"It was on the last Sunday of September that year that I heard the young man was ill, and that the marriage was put off. I remember it well, partly because they were having a high time at the church, decorating it all for Michaelmas, which was next day, with the parson pretending it was for Harvest Festival, as they always do. I had seen the pumpkins go in the day before, and wondered where they put them all. I went up to the churchyard after mass to have a look, and was nearly knocked down by the parson. I began to say something or other, but he ran past me, through from the vicarage, with his coat-tails flying and his man after him. But I stopped the man, and got out of him that Archie was ill, and that the parson was sent for.

"Well, then I went back home and sat down."

The priest drew upon his pipe in silence a moment or two.

I felt rather impressed. His airy manner of talking was shot now with a kind of seriousness, and I wondered what was coming next.

He went on almost immediately.

"I heard a bit more as the day wore on. One of my people stayed after Catechism to tell me that the young man was worse, that a doctor had come from Stroud, and another wired for from London.

"Well, I waited. I thought I knew what would happen. I thought I had seen a bit more in the old lady than the Dominicans had seen, but what I was going to say to her I knew no more than the dead.

"Then that night as I was going to bed—I had just said Matins and Lauds for Michaelmas day—the message came.

"I was half way upstairs when I heard a knocking at the door, and I went down again and opened it. There stood one of the fellows I had seen on the box of the carriage, and he was out of breath with running. He had a lantern in his hand, because there was a thick mist that night up from the valley.

"He gave me the lady's compliments, and would I step down? Master Archie was ill. That was all."

"Well, in a minute we were off into the thick of the mist. I took nothing with me but my stole, for it was not a proper sick call. We said little or nothing to each other. He just told me that Master Archie had been taken ill about ten o'clock, quite suddenly. He didn't know what it was."

The priest paused again for a moment.

Then he went on almost apologetically.

"You know how it is, gentlemen, when something runs in your head. It may be a tune or a sentence. And I don't know if you've noticed how strong it is sometimes when you have something on your mind.

"Well, what ran in my head was a bit of the office I had just said. It was this. I have never forgotten it since:

"*Stetit Angelus juxta oram templi habens thuribulum aureum in manu sua.*"

He said it again, and then added:

"It comes frequently in the office, you remember. It was very natural to remember it.

"Well, in half an hour we were at the top of the hill above the house. I think there must have been a moon, because we could see the mist round us like smoke, but nothing of the house, not even the lights in the top floors below us. It was all white and misty.

"Then we started down through the iron gate and the plantation. I could have lost my way again and again but for the fellow with me, and still we saw nothing of the house till we were close to it on one side; and then I looked up and saw a window like a great yellow door overhead.

"We came round to the front of the house, and there was a carriage there drawn up, with the lamps smoking in the mist, and as we came up I saw that the horses were steaming and blowing. The driver had just brought the London doctor from Stroud and was waiting for orders, I suppose."

The Canadian paused again.

I was more interested than ever. His descriptions had become queerly particular, and I wondered why. I did not understand yet. The rest, too, were very quiet.

"We went in through the hall past the stuffed bear that held the calling cards and all that, you know, and then turned in to the left to the big dining-room that had been the Abbot's chapel. Some fool had left the window open. I suppose they were too flurried to think of it. At any rate, the mist had got in, and made the gas-jets overhead look high up like great stars.

"There was a door open upstairs somewhere, and I could hear whispering.

"Well, we went up the staircase that opened on one side below the gallery, that they had put up above the eastern end. The foot-pad was still there, you know, below the gallery, and the sideboard stood there.

"We came out on to the gallery presently, and my man stopped.

"Then some one came out with Mrs. Arbuthnot and the door closed. She saw me standing there, and I thought she was going to scream; but the fellow with her in the fur coat—he was the London doctor I heard afterward—took her by the arm.

"Well, she was quiet enough then, but as white as death. She had her bonnet on still, just as she must have put it on to go to church with in the morning, when the young man was taken ill. She beckoned me along, and I went.

"As I was going past the doctor he first shook his head at me, and then whispered as I went on to keep her quiet. I knew there was no hope then for Archie, and I was sorry, very sorry, gentlemen."

The priest shook his own head meditatively once or twice, leaned forward and spat accurately into the heart of the fire.

"Well, it was a big room that I went into, and to tell the truth, I left the door open this time, because I was startled by the screen at the bed and all that.

"The screen stood in the corner by the window to keep off the draught; and the bed to one side of it. I could just catch a glimpse of the lad's face on the pillow and the local doctor close by him. There was a woman or two there as well.

"But the worst was that the lad was talking and moaning out loud, but I didn't attend to him then, and besides, Mrs. Arbuthnot had gone through by another door, and I went after her.

"It was a kind of dressing-room—Archie's perhaps. There was a tall glass and silver things on the table by the window, and a candle or two burning. She turned round there and faced me, and she looked so deadly that I forgot all about the lad for the present. I just looked out to catch her when she fell. I had seen a woman like that once or twice before.

"Well, she said all that I expected—all about the curse and that, and the sins of the fathers; and it was all her fault for taking the beastly place, and how she would swear to clear out—I couldn't get a word in—and at last she said she'd become a Catholic if the boy lived.

"I did get a word in then, and told her not to talk nonsense. The Church didn't want people like that. They must believe first and so on, and all the while I was looking out to catch her.

"Well, she didn't hear a word I said, but she sat down all on a sudden, and I sat down, too, opposite her, and all the while the boy's voice grew louder and louder from the next room.

"Then she started again, but she hadn't been under way a minute before I had given over attending to her. I was listening to the lad."

The priest stopped again abruptly. His pipe had gone out, but he sucked at it hard and seemed not to notice it. His eyes were oddly alert.

"As I listened I looked toward the door into the next room. Both that and the one with the gallery over the hall were open, and I saw the mist coming in like smoke.

"I couldn't catch every word the lad said. He was talking in a high, droning voice, but I caught enough. It was about a face looking at him through smoke.

"'His eyes are like flames,' he said, 'smoky flames—yellow hair—are you a priest? . . . What is that red dress?' . . . Things like that. Well, it seemed pretty tolerable nonsense, and then I—"

Monsignor Maxwell sat up suddenly.

"Good Lord!" he said.

"Yes," drawled the Canadian, "*Stetit Angelus habens thuribulum aureum.*"

He spoke so placidly that I was almost shocked. It seemed astonishing that a man— Then he went on again.

"Well, I stood up when I heard that, and I faced the old lady.

"'What's the dedication of the chapel?' I said; 'what's the saint? Tell me, woman, tell me!' There! I said it like that.

"Well, she didn't know what I meant, of course, but I got it out of her at last. Of course, it was St. Michael's.

"I sat down then and let her chatter on. I suppose I must have looked a fool, because she took me by the shoulder directly.

"'You aren't listening, Father Jenks,' she said.

"I attended to her then. It seemed as if she wanted me to do something to save him, but I don't think she knew what it was herself, and I'm sure I didn't, not at first, at least.

"Then she began again, and all the while the boy was crying out. She wanted to know if her becoming a Catholic would do any good, and to tell the truth I wasn't so sure then myself as I had been before. Then she said she'd give up the house to Catholics, and then at last she said this:

"'Will you take it off, Father? I know you can. Priests can do anything.'

"Well, I stiffened myself up at that. I was sensible enough not to make a fool of myself, and I said something like this."

He stopped again; sucked vigorously at his cold pipe.

"I said something like this: 'Mind you keep your promise,' I said, 'but as far as I am concerned, I'd let him off.'"

A curious rustle passed round the room, and the priest caught the sound.

"Yes, gentlemen, I said that. I did, indeed, and I guess most of you gentlemen would have done the same in my circumstances.

"And this is what happened.

"First the lad's voice stopped, then there was a whispering, then a footstep in the other room, and the next moment Mrs. Arbuthnot was on her feet, with her mouth opened to scream. I had her down again though in time, and when I turned a woman was at the door, and I could see she had closed the outer door through which the mist came.

"Well, her face told us. The lad had taken the right turn. It was something on the brain, I think, that had dispersed or broken or something—I forget now—but it seemed to come in pat enough, didn't it, gentlemen?"

The Canadian stopped and leaned back. "Was that the end then?"

Father Brent put my question into words:

"And what happened?"

"Well," added the other, drawling more than ever, "Mrs. Arbuthnot did not keep her promise. She's there still, for all I know, and attends the Harvest Festivals as regularly as ever. That spoils the story, doesn't it?"

"And the son?" put in the English priest swiftly.

"Well, the son was a bit better. That marriage did not take place. The girl broke it off."

"Well?"

"And Archie's at the English College at this moment studying for the priesthood. I had tea with him at Aragno's yesterday."

The Father Rector announced to us one day at dinner that a friend of his from England had called upon him a day or two before, and that he had asked him to supper that evening.

"There is a story I heard him tell," he said, "some years ago that I think he would contribute if you cared to ask him, Monsignor. It is remarkable; I remember thinking so."

"To-night?" said Monsignor.

"Yes; he is coming to-night."

"That will do very well," said the other; "we have no story for to-night."

Father Martin appeared at supper, a gray-haired old man with a face like a mouse and large brown eyes that were generally cast down. He had a way at table of holding his hands together with his elbows at his side, that bore out the impression of his face.

He looked up deprecatingly and gave a little nervous laugh as Monsignor put his request.

"It is a long time since I have told it, Monsignor," he said.

"That is the more reason for telling it again," said the other priest with his sharp geniality, "or it may be lost to humanity."

"It has met with incredulity," said the old man.

"It will not meet with it here, then," remarked Monsignor. "We have been practising ourselves in the art of believing. Another act of faith will do us no harm."

He explained the circumstances.

Father Martin looked round, and I could see that he was pleased.

"Very well, Monsignor," he said; "I will do my best to make it easy."

When we had reached the room upstairs the old priest was put into the arm-chair in the centre, drawn back a little so that all might see him; he refused tobacco, propped his chin on his two hands, looking more than ever like a venerable mouse, and began his story. I sat at the end of the semicircle, near the fire, and watched him as he talked.

"I regret I have not heard the other tales," he said; "it would encourage me in my own. But perhaps it is better so. I have told this so often that I can only tell it in one way, and you must forgive me, gentlemen, if my way is not yours.

"About twenty years ago I had charge of a mission in Lancashire, some fourteen miles from Blackburn, among the hills. The name of the place is Monkswell; it was a little village then, but I think it is a town now. In those days there was only one street, of perhaps a dozen houses on each side. My little church stood at the head of the street, with the presbytery beside it. The house had a garden at the back, with a path running through it to the gate; and beyond the gate was a path leading on to the moor.

"Nearly all the village was Catholic, and had always been so, and I had perhaps a hundred more of my folk scattered about the moor. Their occupation was weaving; that was before the coal was found at Monkswell. Now they have a great church there, with a parish of over a thousand.

"Of course I knew all my people well enough; they are wonderful folk, those Lancashire folk! I could tell you a score of tales of their devotion and faith. There was one woman that I could make nothing of. She lived with her two brothers in a little cottage a couple of miles away from Monkswell; and the three kept themselves by weaving. The two men were fine lads, regular at their religious duties, and at mass every Sunday. But the woman would

not come near the church. I went to her again and again, and before any Easter, but it was of no use. She would not even tell me
why she would not come; but I knew the reason. The poor creature
had been ruined in Blackburn, and could not hold up her head
again. Her brothers took her back, and she had lived with them for
ten years, and never once during that time, so far as I knew, had
set foot outside her little place. She could not bear to be seen, you
see."

The little pointed face looked very tender and compassionate
now, and the brown, beady eyes ran round the circle deprecatingly.

"Well, it was one Sunday in January that Alfred told me that
his sister was unwell. It seemed to be nothing serious, he said, and
of course he promised to let me know if she should become worse.
But I made up my mind that I would go in any case during that
week and see if sickness had softened her at all. Alfred told me,
too, that another brother of his, Patrick, on whom, let it be remembered"—and he held up an admonitory hand— "I had never set eyes,
was coming up to them on the next day from London for a week's
holiday. He promised he would bring him to see me later on in the
week.

"There was a fall of snow that afternoon, not very deep, and
another next day, and I thought I would put off my walk across the
hills until it melted, unless I heard that Sarah was worse.

"It was on the Wednesday evening about six o'clock that I was
sent for.

"I was sitting in my study on the ground floor with the curtains
drawn when I heard the garden gate open and close, and I ran out
into the hall just as the knock came at the back door. I knew that it
was unlikely that any one should come at that hour and in such
weather except for a sick call, and I opened the door almost before
the knocking had ended.

"The candle was blown out by the draught, but I knew Alfred's
voice at once.

"'She is worse, Father,' he said; 'for God's sake come at once. I think she wishes for the sacraments. I am going on for the doctor.'

"I knew by his voice that it was serious, though I could not see his face; I could only see his figure against the snow outside, and before I could say more than that I would come at once he was gone again, and I heard the garden door open and shut. He was gone down to the doctor's house, I knew, a mile further down the valley.

"I shut the hall door without bolting it and went to the kitchen and told my housekeeper to grease my boots well and set them in my room with my cloak and hat and muffler and my lantern. I told her I had had a sick call and did not know when I should be back; she had better put the pot on the fire, and I would help myself when I came home.

"Then I ran into the church through the sacristy to fetch the holy oils and the Blessed Sacrament.

"When I came back I noticed that one of the strings of the purse that held the pyx was frayed, and I set it down on the table to knot it properly. Then again I heard the garden gate open and shut."

The priest lifted his eyes and looked round again; there was something odd in his look.

"Gentlemen, we are getting near the point of the story. I will ask you to listen very carefully and to give me your conclusions afterward. I am relating to you only events as they happened historically. I give you my word as to their truth."

There was a murmur of assent.

"Well, then," he went on, "at first I supposed it was Alfred come back again for some reason. I put down the string and went to the door without a light. As I reached the threshold there came a knocking.

"I turned the handle and a gust of wind burst in as it had done five minutes before. There was a figure standing there, muffled up as the other had been.

"'What is it?' I said. 'I am just coming. Is it you, Alfred?'

"'No, Father,' said a voice—the man was on the steps a yard from me— 'I came to say that Sarah is better and does not wish for the sacraments.'

"Of course I was startled at that.

"'Why, who are you?' I said. 'Are you Patrick?'

"'Yes, Father,' said the man; 'I am Patrick.'

"I cannot describe his voice, but it was not extraordinary in any way; it was a little muffled; I supposed he had a comforter over his mouth. I could not see his face at all. I could not even see if he was stout or thin, the wind blew about his cloak so much.

"As I hesitated the door from the kitchen behind me was flung open, and I heard a very much frightened voice calling:

"'Who's that, Father?' said Hannah.

"I turned round.

"'It is Patrick Oldroyd,' I said; 'he is come from his sister.'

"I could see the woman standing in the light from the kitchen door; she had her hands out before her as if she were frightened at something.

"'Go out of the draught,' I said.

"She went back at that, but she did not close the door, and I knew she was listening to every word.

"'Come in, Patrick,' I said, turning round again.

"I could see he had moved down a step, and was standing on the gravel now.

"He came up again then, and I stood aside to let him go past me into my study. But he stopped at the door. Still I could not see his face; it was dark in the hall, you remember.

"'No, Father,' he said; 'I cannot wait. I must go after Alfred.'

"I put out my hand toward him, but he slipped past me quickly and was out again on the gravel before I could speak.

"'Nonsense!' I said. 'She will be none the worse for a doctor, and if you will wait a minute I will come with you.'

"'You are not wanted,' he said rather offensively, I thought. 'I tell you she is better, Father; she will not see you.'

"I was a little angry at that. I was not accustomed to be spoken to in that way.

"'That is very well,' I said; 'but I shall come for all that, and if you do not wish to walk with me I shall walk alone.'

"He was turning to go, but he faced me again then.

"'Do not come, Father,' he said; 'come tomorrow. I tell you she will not see you. You know what Sarah is.'

"'I know very well,' I said; 'she is out of grace, and I know what will be the end of her if I do not come. I tell you I am coming, Patrick Oldroyd. So you can do as you please.'

"I shut the door and went back into my room, and as I went the garden gate opened and shut once more.

"My hands trembled a little as I began to knot the string of the pyx; I supposed then that I had been more angered than I had known"—the old priest looked round again swiftly and dropped his eyes— "but I do not now think that it was only anger. However, you shall hear."

He had moved himself by now to the very edge of his chair, where he sat crouched up with his hands together. The listeners were all very quiet.

"I had hardly begun to knot the string before Hannah came in. She bobbed at the door when she saw what I was holding, and then came forward. I could see that she was very much upset by something.

"'Father,' she said, 'for the love of God do not go with that man.'

"'I am ashamed of you, Hannah,' I told her. 'What do you mean?'

"'Father,' she said, 'I am afraid. I do not like that man. There is something the matter.'

"I rose, laid the pyx down, and went to my boots without saying anything.

"'Father,' she said again, 'for the love of God do not go. I tell you I was frightened when I heard his knock.'

"Still I said nothing, but put on my boots and went to the table where the pyx lay and the case of oils.

"She came right up to me, and I could see that she was as white as death as she stared at me.

"I finished putting on my cloak, wrapped the comforter round my neck, put on my hat and took up the lantern.

"'Father,' she said again.

"I looked her full in the face then as she knelt down.

"'Hannah,' I said, 'I am going. Patrick has gone after his brother.'

"'It is not Patrick,' she cried after me; 'I tell you, Father—'

"Then I shut the door and left her kneeling there.

"It was very dark when I got down the steps, and I hadn't gone a yard along the path before I stepped over my knee into a drift of snow. It had banked up against a gooseberry bush. Well, I saw that I must go carefully, so I stepped back on to the middle of the path, and held my lantern low.

"I could see the marks of the two men plain enough; it was a path that I had made broad on purpose so that I could walk up and down to say my office without thinking much of where I stepped.

"There was one track on this side and one on that.

"Have you ever noticed, gentlemen, that a man in snow will nearly always go back over his own traces in preference to any one else's? Well, that is so, and it was so in this case.

"When I got to the garden gate I saw that Alfred had turned off to the right on his way to the doctor; his marks were quite plain in the light of the lantern, going down the hill. But I was astonished to see that the other man had not gone after him as he said he would, for there was only one pair of footmarks going down the hill, and the other track was plain enough, coming and going. The man must have gone straight home, I thought.

"Now—"

"One moment, Father Martin," said Monsignor, leaning forward; "draw the two lines of tracks here."

He put a pencil and paper into the priest's hands.

Father Martin scribbled for a moment or two and then held up the paper so that we could all see it.

As he explained I understood. He had drawn a square for the house, a line for the garden wall, and through the gap ran four lines, marked with arrows. Two ran to the house and two back as far as the gate; at this point one curved sharply round to the right and one straight across the paper beside that which marked the coming.

"I noticed all this," said the old priest emphatically, "because I determined to follow along the double track so far as Sarah

Oldroyd's house, and I kept the light turned on to it. I did not wish to slip into a snowdrift.

"Now, I was very much puzzled. I had been thinking it over, of course, ever since the man had gone, and I could not understand it. I must confess that my housekeeper's words had not made it clearer. I knew she did not know Patrick; he had never been home since she had come to me. I was surprised, too, at his behavior, for I knew from his brother that he was a good Catholic; and—well, you understand, gentlemen, it was very puzzling. But Hannah was Irish, and I knew they had strange fancies sometimes.

"Then there was something else, which I had better mention before I go any further. Although I had not been frightened when the man came, yet when Hannah had said that she was frightened I knew what she meant. It had seemed to me natural that she should be frightened. I can say no more than that."

He threw out his hands deprecatingly, and then folded them again sedately on his hunched knees.

"Well, I set out across the moor, following carefully in the double track of—of the man who called himself Patrick. I could see Alfred's single track a yard to my right; sometimes the tracks crossed.

"I had no time to look about me much, but I saw now and again the slopes to the north, and once when I turned I saw the lights of the village behind me, perhaps a quarter of a mile away. Then I went on again, and I wondered as I went.

"I will tell you one thing that crossed my mind, gentlemen. I did wonder whether Hannah had not been right, and if this was Patrick after all. I thought it possible—though I must say I thought it very unlikely—that it might be some enemy of Sarah's, some one she had offended, an infidel, perhaps, but who wished her to die without the sacraments that she wanted. I thought that, but I never dreamed of—of what I thought afterward and think now."

He looked round again, clasped his hands more tightly and went on.

"It was very rough going, and as I climbed up at last on to the little shoulder of hill that was the horizon from my house, I stopped to get my breath, and turned round again to look behind me.

"I could see my house lights at the end of the village, and the church beside it, and I wondered that I could see the lights so plainly. Then I understood that Hannah must be in my study, and that she had drawn the blind up to watch my lantern going across the snow.

"I am ashamed to tell you, gentlemen, that that cheered me a little; I do not quite know why, but I must confess that I was uncomfortable. I know that I should not have been, carrying what I did, and on such an errand, but I was uneasy. It seemed very lonely out there, and the white sheets of snow made it worse. I do not think that I should have minded the dark so much. There was not much wind and everything was very quiet. I could just hear the stream running down in the valley behind me. The clouds had gone, and there was a clear night of stars overhead."

The old priest stopped; his lips worked a little as I had seen them before two or three times during his story. Then he sighed, looked at us and went on.

"Now, gentlemen, I entreat you to believe me. This is what happened next. You remember that this point at which I stopped to take breath was the horizon from my house. Notice that.

"Well, I turned round and lowered my lantern again to look at the tracks, and a yard in front of me they ceased. They ceased!"

He paused again, and there was not a sound from the circle.

"They ceased, gentlemen; I swear it to you, and I cannot describe what I felt. At first I thought it was a mistake; that he had leaped a yard or two; that the snow was frozen. It was not so.

"There a yard to the right were Alfred's tracks, perfectly distinct, with the toes pointing the way from which I had come. There was no confusion, no hard or broken ground; there was just the soft surface of the snow, the trampled path of—of the man's footsteps and mine and Alfred's a yard or two away."

The old man did not look like a mouse now; his eyes were large and bright, his mouth severe, and his hands hung in the air in a petrified gesture.

"If he had leaped," he said, "he did not alight again."

He passed his hand over his mouth once or twice.

"Well, gentlemen, I confess that I hesitated. I looked back at the lights and then on again at the slopes in front, and then I was ashamed of myself. I did not hesitate long, for any place was better than that. I went on; I dared not run, for I think I should have gone mad if I had lost self-control; but I walked, and not too fast, either; I put my hand on the pyx as it lay on my breast, but I dared not turn my head to right or left. I just stared at Alfred's tracks in front of me and trod in them.

"Well, gentlemen, I did run the last hundred yards; the door of the Oldroyds' cottage was open, and they were looking out for me, and I gave Sarah the last sacraments, and heard her confession. She died before morning.

"And I have one confession to make myself—I did not go home that night. They were very courteous to me when I told them the story, and made out that they did not wish me to leave their sister; so the doctor and Alfred walked back over the moor together to tell Hannah I should not be back, and that all was well with me.

"There, gentlemen."

"And Patrick?" said a voice.

"Patrick, of course, had not been out that night."

Mr. Bosanquet's Tale

I think that it was on the second Sunday evening that Father Brent brought in his guest. There was a function of some kind at S. Silvestro—I forget the occasion; a Cardinal had given Benediction, and a reception was to follow. At any rate, there were only three of us at home, the German, Father Brent, and myself.

Of course, we talked of our symposium, and the guest, a middle-aged layman, seemed to listen with interest, but he did not say very much. He was a brown-bearded man; he ate slowly and deliberately, and I must confess that I was not particularly impressed with him. Neither did Father Brent try to draw him out. I noticed that he looked at him questioningly once or twice, but he did not actually express his thought till after a little speech from Father Stein.

"But it is a little tiresome to me," said the German, "this talk of footsteps and voices and visions. If that world in which we believe is spiritual, as we know it is, how is it that it presents itself to us under material images? These things are but appearances, but what is the reality?"

Father Brent turned to his friend.

"Well," he said, "what now?"

Mr. Bosanquet smiled and became grave again over his pastry.

"You will repeat it then?" persisted the priest.

The Englishman looked up for an instant, and I met his grave eyes.

"If these gentlemen really wish it," he said briefly.

Father Brent sighed with satisfaction.

"That is excellent," he said.

Then he explained.

Mr. Bosanquet had a story, it seemed, but had entirely refused to relate it to a mixed company. He had had a certain experience once which had changed his life, and it was not an experience to be described at random. There was no ghost in it; it was wholly unsensational, but it had, Father Brent thought, a peculiar interest of its own. He had persuaded his friend to sup with us, knowing that we should be but few, and hoping that the atmosphere might be found favorable. This was the gist of what he was saying, but he was interrupted by the entrance of Beppo with the coffee.

"Shall we have coffee upstairs?" he said.

Then we rose and went upstairs.

It was a few minutes before we settled down, and Mr. Bosanquet seemed in no hurry to begin. But a silence fell presently, and finally the young priest leaned forward.

"Now, Bosanquet," he said.

Mr. Bosanquet set his cup down, crossed his legs, and began. He spoke in a very quiet, unemotional voice.

"My friend has told you that this experience of mine is unsensational. In a manner of speaking he is right. It is unsensational, since it deals with nothing other than that which we must all go through sooner or later; but I think it has a certain interest from the fact that it is an experience of which, except under very peculiar circumstances, none of us will ever be able to give an account. It concerns the act of dying. . . ."

He paused for a moment.

"Yes; the act of dying," he repeated; "for I firmly believe that that is precisely what I did. I passed the point at which death is dogmatically declared by the doctors to have taken place. I underwent, that is, what is called 'legal death,' but I did not, of course, reach that further state called 'somatic death.'"

Father Brent voiced my question.

"Please explain," he said.

"Oh, well, the body, as we know, consists of cells; but there is a certain unity, usually identified with the vital principle, which merges these into one entity, so that if one member suffer, all the members suffer with it. Legal death is when this vital principle leaves the body. The lungs cease to act; the heart is motionless. But when this has taken place there yet remains a further stage. The cells, for a certain period, have a kind of life of their own. There is no vital union between them; the nerve system is suspended; and somatic death, marked by the *rigor mortis*, the stiffening of the cells, indicates the moment when the cells, too, even individually, cease to live. But the man is dead, doctors tell us, sometimes many hours before *rigor mortis* sets in. In fact, in the case of some of the saints, *rigor mortis* appears never to have set in at all; their limbs, we are told, retain softness and elasticity. There is no corruption, at least in the ordinary 'sense.'"

Father Brent grunted and nodded.

"In my case," pursued the Englishman, "I was declared dead, and, as I learned afterward, remained in that state about half an hour. It was after my body had been washed and the face bound up that I returned to life."

I sat up in my chair at that. At least he was explicit enough. He glanced at me.

"I can show you my death certificate if you care to come to my hotel to-morrow," he said. "I obtained it from the doctor—cancelled, however, you understand.

"Well, this is what took place.

"The cause of death was exhaustion, following upon angina pectoris, with other complications. I will spare you the details and begin at once at the point at which I was declared to be dying. Up to that point I had suffered extraordinary agony, tempered by morphia. I did not know that such pain was possible. . . . At the moments of the spasms, before each injection took effect, it seemed to me that I did not suffer pain so much as became pain. There was no room for anything else but pain. Then there came the beginning of the dulness of it; it retired and stood off from me. I was still conscious of it, as of a storm passing away, till all sank into a kind of peace. Then, after a long while as it seemed, the dulness lifted, and I came up again to the surface, becoming aware of the world, though of course this bore a certain aspect of unreality, owing to the effects of the drug. . . .

"Well, I said I would leave all that out. . . .

"The last time I came up I knew I was dying. It was all quite different. Things no longer bore that close relation to me that they had had before. I opened my eyes just enough to let me see my hands lying out on the counterpane, and the hillock of my feet, and even the lower part of the brass supports at the end of my bed; but I could not raise my eyelids higher, and almost immediately I closed them again.

"The sense of touch, too, was changed. . . . Once or twice when I have been falling asleep in my chair I have noticed the same phenomenon. I could not tell by feeling, unless I moved them, whether my fingers rested on the counterpane or not. I did move them, with that curious clawing motion that dying people use, simply in order to realize my relations with material surroundings. That, of course, as I know now, is the reason of those motions. It is not an involuntary contraction of the muscles; it is the will trying to get back into touch with the world.

"But the sense of hearing, oddly enough, was almost preternaturally acute. Others undergoing anaesthetics have told me the same. It is the last sense to leave them and the first to return. I could hear a continual minute series of sounds, not at all painfully loud, but absolutely distinct. There was my sister's breathing, irregular and uneven, beside me. I knew by it that she was trying not to break down. I could hear four timepieces ticking—her watch and the doctor's and that of the traveling-clock over the fire and the Dutch clock in the hall below. Then there were the country sounds in the distance and the breeze in the creepers outside my window.

"With regard to taste and smell, they were there, a kind of sour sweetness, if I may say so; but they did not interest me; they were below my level, if I may express it like that. . . .

"Well, I said just now that I knew I was dying. It was as if through all my being there was a steady, smooth retirement from the world. I was perfectly able to reflect—in fact, I reflected as I have never been able to before or since. Do you know the sensation of coming down from town and sitting out in the darkness after dinner in the garden? The silence, after the clatter and glare of London, makes it possible, seems to let the mind free. One is both alert and reflective—both at once. It was rather like that, only far more pronounced. And in that freedom from the pressure of matter I realized perfectly what was happening.

"Now, I must tell you at once that I was not at all frightened. My religion seemed to stand off from me with the rest of the world. I had been up to that time what may be called a 'conventional believer.' I had never doubted exactly, for I always realized that it was absurd for me to criticise what was so obviously the highest standard of morality and faith—I mean Christianity. But neither was I particularly interested. I had lived like other people. I attended church, I repeated my prayers, and I had conventional views of heaven, with which was mixed up a good deal of agnosticism. In a word, I think I may say that I had hope, but not faith, that is, as you Catholics seem to have it."

This was the first hint I had had that Mr. Bosanquet was not a Catholic, and I glanced up at Father Brent. He, too, glanced at me in a half-warning, half-suggestive look. I understood.

"I was not frightened, then," continued the other tranquilly. "My religion, as I see now, was altogether bound up with the world. Even my thoughts went no further than images. I conceived of heaven as in a picture, of Our Lord as a superhuman Man, of death as of a swift passage through the air. . . . We are all bound, of course, by our limitations to do that; but I had not realized the inadequacy of such images. I conceived of eternity and spiritual existence in terms of time and space, and I had not really even as much faith as that of the agnostic who recognizes that these are inadequate, and therefore foolishly believes that the reality is unknowable—as in one sense indeed it is."

Once more the German priest murmured, and I saw now why this man had been encouraged to tell his story.

"Well, then," he continued, "when the world retired from me with the approach of death, my religion retired naturally with it (that seems to me so obvious now!), and I was left, moving swiftly *inward*, if I may express it so, toward a state of which I was completely ignorant. I was dying as I suppose animals die. I never lost self-consciousness for a moment. As a rule, of course, one realizes self-consciousness, as philosophers tell us, by self-differentiation from what is not self. The baby learns it gradually by touching and looking. The dying lose it by ceasing to touch and see, or, rather, they lose that mode of realizing, and enter into themselves instead. . . .

"I had then a vague kind of animosity, but I was perfectly peaceful. I had no particular remembrance of sins, no faith or love or hope; nothing but a sense of extreme *naturalness*, if I may express it so. It seemed as if I had known all this all along, as a stone thrown into the air would, if it had consciousness, realize the inevitability of its curve as it neared the earth. I was to die; well, that was the corollary of having lived!

"Well, this inevitable movement inward went on, as it seemed to me, very swiftly. Each instant that I applied my consciousness it seemed to me as if I had gone a great way since the previous instant; the only thing that astonished me was the distance there was to travel. It was a sensation—how shall I express it?—a sensation of sinking swiftly into an inner depth of which I had not guessed the extent. I wondered in a complacent, half-curious kind of way as to what exactly would be the end, how things would be visualized when I passed finally from the body, and such things as I pictured, I pictured, of course, in terms of time and space. I—I thought my essential self, whatever that was, would at a certain moment pass a certain line and emerge on the other side; and the things would be rather as they had been on earth, thinner . . . spiritual. I should see faces, perhaps; forms, places, . . . all in a kind of delicate light. . . . What really happened was a complete surprise."

Mr. Bosanquet paused, and in a meditative kind of way winked several times at the fire. He showed no emotion. He seemed to me merely to be recalling the best phrases to use.

8 ROBERT H. BENSON

"Well," he said, "I have told this story before, and each time before telling it I have thought that I had got the point and could really describe what happened, and each time I have been disappointed. . . . Of course it must be so. There are simply no words or illustrations. I must do the best I can.

"Well, this process went on, and after a while I perceived plainly that my senses were fading. I believe I opened my eyes; so I was told afterwards—opened them wide; but, at any rate, I saw nothing this time except blurred lines and colors, rather like the reverse side of a carpet. They were rather bewildering; but they soon went, leaving nothing but a streaked grayness that darkened rapidly.

"I could no longer move my hands, or, in fact, recall to myself by feeling any material thing at all. I seemed to have lost relations with my body. Neither could I move my lips or tongue; taste had gone. I don't think I had ever understood before how taste depends on the will and the movement of the tongue—much more so than any of the other senses, which are, more or less, passive.

"And then quite suddenly I perceived that hearing had ceased also. There had been no drumming in my ears, as I had half expected; I think there had been at some time previously a clear singing of one high note, which had rather bothered me; and I suppose that it was then that hearing had gone, but I did not notice it till I thought about it.

"And then there was one more thing more strange than all. . . . I began to perceive that my will was not myself.

"Most of us are accustomed to think that it is. It is so closely united with that which is the very self that we usually identify them. Sometimes we are even more foolish, and identify our emotions with ourselves, and think that our moods are our character. The fact is, of course, that the intellect is the most superficial of our faculties; there are simply scores of things that we cannot understand in the least, but of which for all that we are as certain as of our own existence. Next to that comes the emotion: it is certainly nearer to us than intellect, though not much; and thirdly comes the will.

"Now the will is quite close to us; it is that through which we consciously act after having heard the reasons for or against action alleged by the other faculties. But the will is, after all, a faculty of self—not self itself.

"I began to see this from the way it was laboring, like an exhausted engine; it was throbbed and moved; it turned this way and that, directing the all but dead faculties outside to move in this or that direction—to think or to perceive. But I began to see clearly now that the real self was something altogether apart, existing simply in another mode. There, that is the point—*in another mode.* . . .

"Now, in this matter I feel hopeless. I simply cannot express what I knew, and know, to be the central fact of our existence. I can say no more than that. Self, that which lies far behind everything else, exists in as different a mode from all else, as—as the inner meaning of a phrase of music is apart from the existence of a dog walking up the street. There is simply no common term which can be applied to them both.

"Well, I perceived my will to be laboring, very slowly and clumsily, and I perceived that it would not be able to move much longer. (You must understand that this 'perceiving' as I call it was not the act of my intellect; it was simply a deep intuitive knowledge dwelling in that which I call Self.)

"Then I suddenly became aware that it was important for my will to fall in the right direction; I understood that this would make—well, the whole difference to me. . . . I knew that this would be my last conscious act. . . .

"You ask me how I knew what was the right direction. Well, I must go slowly here. . . ."

He paused for a moment, then he went on very slowly, picking his words.

"I began, I think I may say, to be clearly and vividly conscious of two *centres*; there was Self, and there was Another. This Other was at present completely hidden from me; I was only aware of it as one may be aware of the presence of a huge personality behind an impenetrable curtain. But I perceived that this Other was the only important thing. . . .

"Well, my will was reeling; there was no discomfort, no fear, or pain, or anxiety, and I—whatever that is—watched it as a man may watch a top in its last swift twistings on its side. I had still some control over it; I knew that it was my will; it still was linked to me in a way. . . . Then I put out my energy (remember, there was no conscious perception of anything; nothing but a perfectly blind instinct) and tried to wrench that rolling thing round to a position of rest—ah! how shall I put it?—a position of rest pointing toward this other centre.

"And as I made that effort I lost touch with it. I have no idea whether I succeeded, and at the same instant, if I may call it so, something happened."

Mr. Bosanquet leaned back and sighed.

"Every word is wrong," he said; "you understand that, do you not?"

I nodded two or three times. I kept my eyes on his face. He glanced round at the other two. Then he went on, shifting his attitude a little.

"Well, this something—I suppose I could give half a dozen illustrations, but none of them would be adequate. Let me give you two or three.

"When a man falls in love suddenly his whole centre changes. Up to that point he has probably referred everything to himself—considered things from his own point. When he falls in love the whole thing is shifted; he becomes a part of the circumference—perhaps even the whole circumference; some one else becomes the centre. For example, things he hears and sees are referred in future instantly to this other person; he ceases to be acquisitive; his entire life, if it is really love, is pulled sideways; he does not desire to get, but to give. That is why it is the noblest thing in the world.

"Secondly, imagine that you had lived all your life in a certain house, and had got to know every detail of it perfectly; you had walked about in the garden, too, and looked through the railings, and thought you knew pretty fairly what the country was like. Then one morning, after you had got up and dressed, you went to your bedroom door, opened it, and went out, and that very instant found yourself not in the passage, but on the top of a high mountain with a strange country visible for miles all round, and no house or human being near you.

"Thirdly (and this perhaps is the best illustration after all), imagine that you were looking at a picture, and had become absorbed in it, and then without any warning at all the picture suddenly became a chord of music which you heard, and which you recognized to be identical with the picture—not merely analogous to it, but the actual picture translated, transubstantiated, and transaccidentated into sound.

"Now, those are the three illustrations I generally use in telling this story; there are others, but I think these are the best.

"Well, it was like that; but you must please to remember that these are only like charcoal sketches of something which is color rather than shape. But briefly, those are the nearest similitudes I can think of.

"First, although I remained the same, I became aware that I simply was not the centre of what I experienced. It was not I who primarily existed at all. There was Something—I call it Something, because the word Person simply bears no resemblance to the Personality of this Other Existence; at least, no more than a resemblance, because this Other Personality was as different from and as far above our own as the personality of a philosopher is different from the corresponding thing in a people. I became aware—at least, this was what I told myself afterwards—I became aware of real Existence for the first time in my experience. I myself then became merely a speck in a circumference, yet—and this is why I spoke of love—I also became aware that while I had not lost my individuality, yet this Other Being was the only thing that mattered at all, and, further—well, I may as well say it outright, that in the very depth of this Existence was Human Nature; yes, Human Nature. I knew it instantly. I never before had had the faintest idea of what the Incarnation really meant.

"Secondly, the whole of everything was different—as startlingly different as the change of my second illustration. I had expected

to find a kind of continuation. There was, in one sense, no continuation at all; nothing in the least like what experience had led
me to expect. It was completely abrupt.

"Thirdly, in another sense, what I found was not only the con-
sequence of what had preceded, it was not simply the result, but it
was identical with what had preceded. It was the picture becoming
sound—the essence of my previous life was here in other terms. It
simply was. The whole thing was complete. You may call this Judgment; well, that will do; but it was a Judgment in which there was
no question of concurrence or protest. It was inevitably true.

"Let me take even one more illustration.

"Once I went with my brother into a glasshouse in autumn. He
smelled a certain flower, and then rather excitedly asked me to
smell it. I shut my eyes and smelled it. Practically instantly the
whole thing became sound and sight. I saw the terrace at home in
summer, and heard the bees. I looked up.

"'Well?' he said.

"'The terrace in summer,' I said.

"'Exactly.'

"Well, it was like that. There was no question about it.

"Now, I have taken some time to tell this; but I must make it
clear that there was absolutely no time in the experience—no sense
of progression. It was not merely that I was absorbed, but that time
had no existence. This is how I knew it.

"Simultaneously with all this I heard one noise; and immediately time began—I began to consider. Presently I heard another
noise, then another, like a great drum being beaten. Then the noises
went, and there was absolute silence of which I was aware; and
others came in—a rustling, a footstep, the sound of words. I was
entirely absorbed in these. I heard the sound of water, a door opening, the ticking of a clock. I was conscious of no consideration about
these things, and no sensation of any kind; it was as if my brain
had become one ear which heard. This went on—well, I may say it
was ten seconds or ten years. Time meant nothing to me. I only
knew even now that it existed because one thing followed another.
I did not reflect at all.

"At last, after this had gone on, it was as if a new note had struck; another sense began to move, the sense of sight. I first became aware of darkness, then came a glimmer, with a sensation of flickering. Then touch. I became aware of a constraint somewhere in the universe; it was a long time before I knew that I myself was feeling it. I did not perceive sensation; I was it.

"Well, these waxed and waxed; then my will stirred; and I became aware that I could choose, that I could acquiesce or resent. Then emotion, and I found myself disliking certain sensations. Then I began to wonder and question again, and ask myself why and what—"

Mr. Bosanquet broke off abruptly.

"Well, I needn't go on. To put it in a word, I was coming back to ordinary life. Half an hour after the doctor had said that I was dead, and about three minutes after the nurse had finished with me—just as she was looking at me, in fact, before going out of the room—I made a sound with my lips. The rest happened as you would expect; there was nothing interesting in that.

"But this is the point I want to make clear. Those noises I heard like a drum followed by the silence were without doubt the sounds my own body made in dying.

"It was at that point that I died; and the next sounds that I began to hear were the noises the nurse made in washing me and laying me out. There is no question about that. I asked about all the details minutely.

"But the thing that seemed to me so strange at first was the fact that I had died 'before' that, as we say. That complete change of the mode of existence undoubtedly marked death, and the particular instant of death must have been that at which I became aware of the change, and of the severance of my will from myself.

"But I understood it presently. The explanation, I think, must be this.

"There is always a certain space of time between an incident happening and our perception of it—infinitesimally small if we are observing it, but yet it is there. Well, when I made that final effort of will I died, but dying had begun before that. I had only regarded dying from the purely internal side; it took in my soul the form of severance from my will. At that same instant, since we must speak in terms of time, I was in the spiritual mode of existence, where there is simply no time but which includes all time and all one's previous experience; and in practically the same 'instant' I was back again, and experiencing the physical phenomena of dying. The drum-note was either my throat or heart, I suppose; the silence that followed was the body's perception of death worked out in terms of time.

"We may say, then, this, impossible as it sounds—that death had taken place at a given moment in time; that that inner real self behind the will which I have spoken of simultaneously experienced severance from the body, and was immediately in its own mode of existence, which, although reckoned as time, was an instant; was, in fact, simply eternity with its inevitable consequences. But after eternity had been experienced—since I suppose again I must say 'after'—it ceased to be experienced; and all this was enacted in time. Then—"

Mr. Bosanquet sat up, smiling suddenly.

"It is useless; I am boring you."

I roused myself to answer with an energy I had not expected.

"No; please—"

"Well, in one sentence: Then I died."

He leaned back with an air of finality.

"But—but one question," I protested, "you spoke of Judgment. Was the result happiness or unhappiness?"

He shook his head, smiling.

Father Macclesfield's Tale

Monsignor Maxwell announced next day at dinner that he had already arranged for the evening's entertainment. A priest whose acquaintance he had made on the Palatine was leaving for England the next morning, and it was our only chance, therefore, of hearing his story. That he had a story had come to the Canon's knowledge in the course of a conversation on the previous afternoon.

"He told me the outline of it," he said; "I think it very remarkable. But I had a great deal of difficulty in persuading him to repeat it to the company this evening. However, he promised at last. I trust, gentlemen, you do not think I have presumed in begging him to do so."

Father Macclesfield arrived at supper.

He was a little, unimposing, dry man, with a hooked nose and gray hair. He was rather silent at supper, but there was no trace of shyness in his manner as he took his seat upstairs, and without glancing round once began in an even and dispassionate voice:

"I once knew a Catholic girl that married an old Protestant three times her own age. I entreated her not to do so, but it was useless. And when the disillusionment came she used to write to me piteous letters, telling me that her husband had in reality no religion at all. He was a convinced infidel, and scouted even the idea of the soul's immortality.

"After two years of married life the old man died. He was about sixty years old, but very hale and hearty till the end.

"Well, when he took to his bed the wife sent for me, and I had half a dozen interviews with him, but it was useless. He told me plainly that he wanted to believe—in fact, he said that the thought of annihilation was intolerable to him. If he had had a child he would not have hated death so much; if his flesh and blood in any manner survived him he could have fancied that he had a sort of vicarious life left; but as it was, there was no kith or kin of his alive, and he could not bear that."

Father Macclesfield sniffed cynically and folded his hands.

"I may say that his deathbed was extremely unpleasant. He was a coarse old fellow, with plenty of strength in him, and he used to make remarks about the churchyard and—and, in fact, the worms, that used to send his poor child of a wife half fainting out of the room. He had lived an immoral life, too, I gathered.

"Just at the last it was—well, disgusting. He had no consideration. God knows why she married him! The agony was a very long one; he caught at the curtains round the bed, calling out, and all his words were about death and the dark. It seemed to me that he caught hold of the curtains as if to hold himself into this world. And at the very end he raised himself clean up in bed and stared horribly out of the window that was open just opposite.

"I must tell you that straight away beneath the window lay a long walk between sheets of dead leaves with laurels on either side and the branches meeting overhead, so that it was very dark there even in summer, and at the end of the walk away from the house was the churchyard gate."

Father Macclesfield paused and blew his nose. Then he went on, still without looking at us.

"Well, the old man died, and he was carried along this laurel path and buried.

"His wife was in such a state that I simply dared not go away. She was frightened to death; and, indeed, the whole affair of her husband's dying was horrible. But she would not leave the house. She had a fancy that it would be cruel to him. She used to go down twice a day to pray at the grave; but she never went along the laurel walk. She would go round by the garden and in at a lower gate and come back the same way, or by the upper garden.

"This went on for three or four days. The man had died on a Saturday and was buried on Monday; it was in July, and he had died about eight o'clock.

"I made up my mind to go on the Saturday after the funeral. My curate had managed alone very well for a few days, but I did not like to leave him for a second Sunday.

"Then on the Friday at lunch—her sister had come down, by the way, and was still in the house—on the Friday the widow said something about never daring to sleep in the room where the old man had died. I told her it was nonsense, and so on; but you must remember she was in a dreadful state of nerves, and she persisted. So I said I would sleep in the room myself. I had no patience with such ideas then.

"Of course she said all sorts of things, but I had my way and my things were moved in on Friday evening.

"I went to my new room about a quarter before eight to put on my cassock for dinner. The room was very much as it had been— rather dark because of the trees at the end of the walk outside. There was the four-poster, there with the damask curtains, the table and chairs, the cupboard where his clothes were kept, and so on.

"When I went to put my cassock on I went to the window to look out. To the right and left were the gardens, with the sunlight just off them, but still very bright and gay with the geraniums, and exactly opposite was the laurel walk, like a long, green shady tunnel, dividing the upper and lower lawns.

"I could see straight down it to the churchyard gate, which was about a hundred yards away, I suppose. There were limes overhead and laurels, as I said, on each side.

"Well, I saw some one coming up the walk, but it seemed to me at first that he was drunk. He staggered several times as I watched— I suppose he would be fifty yards away—and once I saw him catch hold of one of the trees and cling to it as if he were afraid of falling. Then he left it and came on again slowly, going from side to side, with his hands out. He seemed desperately keen to get to the house.

"I could see his dress, and it astonished me that a man dressed so should be drunk, for he Was quite plainly a gentleman. He wore a white top hat and a gray cutaway coat and gray trousers, and I could make out his white spats.

"Then it struck me he might be ill, and I looked harder than ever, wondering whether I ought to go down.

"When he was about twenty yards away he lifted his face, and it struck me as very odd; but it seemed to me he was extraordinarily like the old man we had buried on Monday; but it was darkish where he was, and the next moment he dropped his face, threw up his hands, and fell flat on his back.

"Well, of course I was startled at that, and I leaned out of the window and called out something. He was moving his hands, I could see, as if he were in convulsions, and I could hear the dry leaves rustling.

"Well, then I turned and ran out and downstairs."

Father Macclesfield stopped a moment.

"Gentlemen," he said abruptly, "when I got there there was not a sign of the old man. I could see that the leaves had been disturbed, but that was all."

There was an odd silence in the room as he paused, but before any of us had time to speak he went on.

"Of course, I did not say a word of what I had seen. We dined as usual. I smoked for an hour or so by myself after prayers and then I went up to bed. I cannot say I was perfectly comfortable, for I was not, but neither was I frightened.

"When I got to my room I lit all my candles and then went to a big cupboard I had noticed and pulled out some of the drawers. In the bottom of the third drawer I found a gray cutaway coat and gray trousers; I found several pairs of white spats in the top drawer and a white hat on the shelf above. That is the first incident."

"Did you sleep there, Father?" said a voice softly.

"I did," said the priest; "there was no reason why I should not. I did not fall asleep for two or three hours, but I was not disturbed in any way and came to breakfast as usual.

"Well, I thought about it all a bit, and finally I sent a wire to my curate telling him I was detained. I did not like to leave the house just then."

Father Macclesfield settled himself again in his chair and went on in the same dry, uninterested voice.

"On Sunday we drove over to the Catholic church, six miles off, and I said mass. Nothing more happened till the Monday evening.

"That evening I went to the window again about a quarter before eight, as I had done both on the Saturday and Sunday. Everything was perfectly quiet till I heard the churchyard gate unlatch and I saw a man come through.

"But I saw almost at once that it was not the same man I had seen before; it looked to me like a keeper, for he had a gun across his arm; then I saw him hold the gate open an instant, and a dog came through and began to trot up the path toward the house with his master following.

"When the dog was about fifty yards away he stopped dead and pointed.

"I saw the keeper throw his gun forward and come up softly, and as he came the dog began to slink backward. I watched very closely, clean forgetting why I was there, and the next instant something—it was too shadowy under the trees to see exactly what it was—but something about the size of a hare burst out of the laurels and made straight up the path, dodging from side to side, but coming like the wind.

"The beast could not have been more than twenty yards from me when the keeper fired, and the creature went over and over in the dry leaves and lay struggling and screaming. It was horrible! But what astonished me was that the dog did not come up. I heard the keeper snap out something, and then I saw the dog making off down the avenue in the direction of the churchyard as hard as he could go.

"The keeper was running now toward me, but the screaming of the hare, or of whatever it was, had stopped, and I was astonished to see the man come right up to where the beast was struggling and kicking and then stop as if he were puzzled.

"I leaned out of the window and called to him.

"'Right in front of you, man,' I said; 'for God's sake kill the brute.'

"He looked up at me and then down again.

"'Where is it, sir?' he said; 'I can't see it anywhere.'

"And there lay the beast clear before him all the while not a yard away, still kicking.

"Well, I went out of the room and downstairs and out to the avenue.

"The man was standing there still, looking terribly puzzled, but the hare was gone. There was not a sign of it. Only the leaves were disturbed, and the wet earth showed beneath.

"The keeper said that it had been a great hare; he could have sworn to it, and that he had orders to kill all hares and rabbits in the garden enclosure. Then he looked rather odd.

"'Did you see it plainly, sir,' he asked.

"I told him not very plainly; but I thought it a hare, too.

"'Yes, sir,' he said; 'it was a hare, sure enough; but do you know, sir, I thought it to be a kind of silver-gray, with white feet. I never saw one like that before!'

"The odd thing was that not a dog would come near. His own dog was gone, but I fetched the yard dog, a retriever, out of his kennel in the kitchen yard, and if ever I saw a frightened dog it was this one. When we dragged him up at last, all whining and pulling back, he began to snap at us so fiercely that we let go, and he went back like the wind to his kennel. It was the same with the terrier.

"Well, the bell had gone, and I had to go in and explain why I was late; but I didn't say anything about the color of the hare. That was the second incident."

Father Macclesfield stopped again, smiling reminiscently to himself. I was very much impressed by his quiet air and composure. I think it helped his story a good deal.

Again, before we had time to comment or question, he went on.

"The third incident was so slight that I should not have mentioned it, or thought anything of it, if it had not been for the others;

but it seemed to me there was a kind of diminishing gradation of energy which explained. Well, now you shall hear.

"On the other nights of that week I was at my window again, but nothing happened till the Friday. I had arranged to go for certain next day; the widow was much better and more reasonable, and even talked of going abroad herself in the following week.

"On that Friday evening I dressed a little earlier and went down to the avenue this time, instead of staying at my window, at about twenty minutes to eight.

"It was rather a heavy, depressing evening, without a breath of wind, and it was darker than it had been for some days.

"I walked slowly down the avenue to the gate and back again; and I suppose it was fancy, but I felt more uncomfortable than I had felt at all up to then. I was rather relieved to see the widow come out of the house and stand looking down the avenue. I came out myself then and went toward her. She started rather when she saw me and then smiled.

"'I thought it was some one else,' she said. 'Father, I have made up my mind to go. I shall go to town to-morrow, and start on Monday. My sister will come with me.'

"I congratulated her, and then we turned and began to walk back to the lime avenue. She stopped at the entrance, and seemed unwilling to come any further.

"'Come down to the end,' I said, 'and back again. There will be time before dinner.'

"She said nothing, but came with me, and we went straight down to the gate and then turned to come back.

"I don't think either of us spoke a word; I was very uncomfortable indeed by now, and yet I had to go on.

"We were half way back, I suppose, when I heard a sound like a gate rattling; and I whisked round in an instant, expecting to see some one at the gate. But there was no one.

"Then there came a rustling overhead in the leaves; it had been dead still before. Then, I don't know why, but I took my friend suddenly by the arm and drew her to one side out of the path, so that we stood on the right hand, not a foot from the laurels.

"She said nothing, and I said nothing; but I think we were both looking this way and that, as if we expected to see something.

"The breeze died, and then sprang up again, but it was only a breath. I could hear the living leaves rustling overhead, and the dead leaves underfoot, and it was blowing gently from the church-yard.

"Then I saw a thing that one often sees; but I could not take my eyes off it, nor could she. It was a little column of leaves, twisting and turning and dropping and picking up again in the wind, coming slowly up the path. It was a capricious sort of draught, for the little scurry of leaves went this way and that, to and fro across the path. It came up to us, and I could feel the breeze on my hands and face. One leaf struck me softly on the cheek, and I can only say that I shuddered as if it had been a toad. Then it passed on.

"You understand, gentlemen, it was pretty dark; but it seemed to me that the breeze died and the column of leaves—it was no more than a little twist of them—sank down at the end of the avenue.

"We stood there perfectly still for a moment or two, and when I turned she was staring straight at me, but neither of us said one word.

"We did not go up the avenue to the house. We pushed our way through the laurels and came back by the upper garden.

"Nothing else happened; and the next morning we all went off by the eleven o'clock train.

"That is all, gentlemen."

Father Stein's Tale

Old Father Stein was a figure that greatly fascinated me during my first weeks in Rome, after I had got over the slight impatience that his personality roused in me. He was slow of speech and thought and movement, and had that distressing grip of the obvious that is characteristic of the German mind. I soon rejoiced to look at his heavy face, generally unshaven, his deep twinkling eyes, and the ponderous body that had such an air of eternal immovability, and to watch his mind, as through a glass case, laboring like an engine over a fact that he had begun to assimilate. He took a kind of paternal interest in me, too, and would thrust his thick hand under my arm as he stood by me, or clap me heavily on the shoulder as we met. But he was excellently educated, had seen much of the world, although always through a haze of the Fatherland that accompanied him everywhere, and had acquired an exceptional knowledge of English during his labors in a London mission. He used his large vocabulary with a good deal of skill.

I was pleased then when Monsignor announced on the following evening that Father Stein was prepared to contribute a story. But the German, knowing that he was master of the situation, would utter nothing at first but hoarse ejaculations at the thought of his reminiscences, and it was not until we had been seated for nearly half an hour before the fire that he consented to begin.

"It is of a dream," he said; "no more than that; and yet dreams, too, are under the hand of the good God, so I hold. Some, I know, are just folly, and tell us nothing but the confusion of our own nature when the controlling will is withdrawn; but some, I hold, are the whispers of God, and tell us of what we are too dull to hear in our waking life. You do not believe me? Very well; then listen.

"I knew a man in Germany, thirty years ago, who had lived many years away from God. He had been a Catholic, and was well educated in religion till he grew to be a lad. Then he fell into sin, and dared not confess it; and he lied, and made bad confessions, and approached the altar so. He once went to a strange priest to tell his sin, and dared not when the time came; and so added sin to sin, and lost his faith. It is ever so. We know it well. The soul dare not go on in that state, believing in God, and so by an inner act of the will renounces Him. It is not true, it is not true, she cries; and at last the voice of faith is silent and her eyes blind."

The priest stopped and looked round him, and the old Rector nodded once or twice and murmured assent.

"For twenty years he had lived so, without God, and he was not unhappy; for the powers of his soul died one by one, and he could no longer feel. Once or twice they struggled, in their death agony, and he stamped on them again. Once, when his mother died, he nearly lived again; and his soul cried once more within him, and stirred herself; but he would not hear her; it is useless, he said to her; there is no hope for you; lie still; there is nothing for you; you are dreaming; there is no life such as you think; and he trampled her again, and she lay still."

We were all very quiet now. I certainly had not suspected such passion in this old priest; he had seemed to me slow and dull and not capable of any sort of delicate thought or phrase, far less of tragedy; but somehow now his great face was lighted up, his eyebrows twitched as he talked, and it seemed as if we were hearing of a murder that this man had seen for himself. Monsignor sat perfectly motionless, staring intently into the fire, and Father Brent was watching the German sideways; Father Stein took a deliberate pinch of snuff, snapped his box, and put it away, and went on.

"This man had lived on the sea coast as a child, but was now in business in a town on the Rhine, and had never visited his old home since he left it with his mother on his father's death. He was now about thirty-five years of age, when God was gracious to him. He was living in a cousin's house, with whom he was partner.

"One night he dreamed he was a child, and walking with one whom he knew was his sister who had died before he was born, but he could not see her face. They were on a white, dusty road, and it was the noon of a hot summer day. There was nothing to be seen round him but great slopes of a dusty country with dry grass, and the burning sky overhead, and the sun. He was tired, and his feet ached, and he was crying as he walked, but he dared not cry loud for fear that his sister would turn and look at him, and he knew she was a—a revenant, and did not wish to see her eyes. There was no wind and no birds and no clouds; only the grasshoppers sawed in the dry grass, and the blood drummed in his ears until he thought he would go mad with the noise. And so they walked, the boy behind his sister, up a long hill. It seemed to him that they had been walking so for hours, for a lifetime, and that there would be no end to it. His feet sank to the ankles in dust, the sun beat on to his brain from above, the white road glared from below, and the tears ran down his cheeks.

"Then there was a breath of salt wind in his face, and his sister began to go faster, noiselessly; and he tried, too, to go faster, but could not; his heart beat like a hammer in his throat, and his feet lagged more and more, and little by little his sister was far in front, and he dared not cry out to her not to leave him for fear she should turn and look at him; and at last he was walking alone, and he dared not lie down or rest.

"The road passed up a slope, and when he reached the top of it at last he saw her again, far away, a little figure that turned to him and waved its hand, and behind her was the blue sea, very faint and in a mist of heat, and then he knew that the end of the bitter journey was very near.

"As he passed up the last slope the sea-line rose higher against the sky, but the line was only as the fine mark of a pencil where sea and sky met, and a dazzling white bird or two passed across it and then dropped below the cliff. By the time he came near his sister the dusty road had died away into the grass, and he was walking over the fresh turf that felt cool to his hot feet. He threw himself down on the edge of it by his sister, where she was lying with her head on her hands looking out at the sea where it spread itself out, a thousand feet below; and still he had not seen her face.

"At the foot of the cliff was a little white beach, and the rocks ran down into deep water on every side of it, and threw a purple shadow across the sand; there were birds here, too, floating out from the cliff and turning and returning; and the sea beneath them was a clear blue, like a Cardinal's ring that I saw once, and the breeze blew up from the water and made him happy again."

Father Stein stopped again, with something of a sob in his old heavy voice, and then he turned to us.

"You know such dreams," he said; "I cannot tell it as—as he told me; but he said it was like the bliss of the redeemed to look down on the sea and feel the breeze in his hair, and taste its saltness.

"He did not wish his sister to speak, though he was afraid of her no more; and yet he knew that there was some secret to be told that would explain all—why they were here, and why she had come back to him, and why the sea was here, and the little beach below them, and the wind and the birds. But he was content to wait until it was time for her to tell him, as he knew she would. It was enough to lie here, after the dusty journey, beside her, and to wait for the word that should be spoken.

"Now, at first he was so out of breath and his heart beat so in his ears that he could hear nothing but that and his own panting; but it grew quieter soon, and he began to hear something else—the noises of the sea beneath him. It was a still day, but there was movement down below, and the surge heaved itself softly against the cliff and murmured in deep caves below, like the pedal note of the Frankfort organ, solemn and splendid; and the waves leaned over and crashed gently on the sand. It was all so far beneath that he saw the breaking wave before the sound came up to him, and he lay there and watched and listened; and that great sound made him happier even than the light on the water and the coolness and rest; for it was the sea itself that was speaking now.

"Then he saw suddenly that his sister had turned on her elbow and was looking at him; and he looked into her eyes, and knew her, though she had died before he was born. And she, too, was listening, with her lips parted, to the sound of the surge. And now he knew that the secret was to be told; and he watched her eyes, smiling. And she lifted her hand, as if to hold him silent, and waited, and again the sweet murmur and crash rose up from the sea, and she spoke softly.

"'It is the Precious Blood,' she said."

Father Stein was silent, and we all were silent for a while. As far as I was concerned, at least, the story had somehow held me with an extraordinary fascination, I scarcely knew why.

There was a movement among the others, and presently the Frenchman spoke.

"*Et puis?*" he said.

"The man awoke," said Father Stein, "and found tears on his face."

It was such a short story that there were still a few minutes before the time for night-prayers, and we sat there without speaking again until the clock sounded in the campanile overhead, and the Rector rose and led the way into the west gallery of the church. I saw Father Stein waiting at the door for me to come up, and I knew why he was waiting.

He took my arm in his thick hand and held it a moment as the others passed down the two steps.

"I was that man," he said.

Mr. Percival's Tale

When I came in from mass into the refectory on the morning following Father Stein's story, I found a layman breakfasting there with the Father Rector. We were introduced to each other, and I learned that Mr. Percival was a barrister, who had arrived from England that morning on a holiday, and was to stay at St. Filippo for a fortnight.

I yield to none in my respect for the clergy; at the same time a layman feels occasionally something of a pariah among them. I suppose this is bound to be so, otherwise I was pleased then to find another dog of my breed with whom I might consort, and even howl, if I so desired. I was pleased, too, with his appearance. He had that trim, academic air that is characteristic of the Bar, in spite of his twenty-two hours' journey, and was dressed in an excellently made gray suit. He was very slightly bald on his forehead, and had those sharp-cut, mask-like features that mark a man as either lawyer, priest or actor; he had, besides, delightful manners and even, white teeth. I do not think I could have suggested any improvements in person, behavior, or costume.

By the time that my coffee had arrived the Father Rector had run dry of conversation, and I could see that he was relieved when I joined in.

In a few minutes I was telling Mr. Percival about the symposium we had formed for the relating of preternatural adventures, and I presently asked him whether he had ever had any experience of the kind.

He shook his head.

"I have not," he said in his virile voice; "my business takes my time."

"I wish you had been with us earlier," put in the Rector. "I think you would have been interested."

"I am sure of it," he said. "I remember once—but you know, Father, frankly I am something of a sceptic."

"You remember?" I suggested.

He smiled very pleasantly with eyes and mouth.

"Yes, Mr. Benson; I was once next door to such a story. A friend of mine saw something; but I was not with him at the moment."

"Well, we thought we had finished last night," I said; "but do you think you would be too tired to entertain us this evening?"

"I shall be delighted to tell the story," he said easily. "But indeed I am a sceptic in this matter; I cannot dress it up."

"We want the naked fact," I said.

I went sight-seeing with him that day, and found him extremely intelligent and at the same time accurate. The two virtues do not run often together, and I felt confident that whatever he chose to tell us would be salient and true. I felt, too, that he would need few questions to draw him out; he would say what there was to be said unaided.

When we had taken our places that night he began by again apologizing for his attitude of mind.

"I do not know, reverend Fathers," he said, "what are your own theories in this matter; but it appears to me that if what seems to be preternatural can possibly be brought within the range of the natural, one is bound scientifically to treat it in that way. Now in this story of mine—for I will give you a few words of explanation first in order to prejudice your minds as much as possible—in this story the whole matter might be accounted for by the imagination. My friend, who saw what he saw, was under rather theatrical circumstances, and he is an Irishman. Besides that, he knew the history of the place in which he was; and he was quite alone. On the other hand, he has never had an experience of the kind before or since; he is perfectly truthful, and he saw what he saw in moderate daylight. I give you these facts first, and I think you would be perfectly justified in thinking they account for everything. As for my own theory, which is not quite that, I have no idea whether you will agree or disagree with it. I do not say that my judgment is the only sensible one, or anything offensive like that. I merely state what I feel I am bound to accept for the present."

There was a murmur of assent. Then he crossed his legs, leaned back and began:

"In my first summer after I was called to the Bar I went down South Wales for a holiday with another man who had been with me at Oxford. His name was Murphy; he is a J.P. now, in Ireland, I think. I cannot think why we went to South Wales; but there it is. We did.

"We took the train to Cardiff, sent on our luggage up the Taff Valley to an inn of which I cannot remember the name, but it was close to where Lord Bute has a vineyard. Then we walked up to Llandaff, saw St. Tylo's tomb, and went on again to this village.

"Next morning we thought we would look about us before going on, and we went out for a stroll. It was one of the most glorious mornings I ever remember, quite cloudless and very hot, and we went up through woods to get a breeze at the top of the hill.

"We found that the whole place was full of iron mines, disused now, as the iron is richer further up the country; but I can tell you that they enormously improved the interest of the place. We found shaft after shaft, some protected and some not, but mostly overgrown with bushes, so we had to walk carefully. We had passed half a dozen, I should think, before the thought of going down one of them occurred to Murphy.

"Well, we got down at last, though I rather wished for a rope once or twice, and I think it was one of the most extraordinary sights I have ever seen. You know, perhaps, what the cave of a demon-king is like in the first act of a pantomime. Well, it was like that. There was a kind of blue light that poured down the shafts, refracted from surface to surface, so that the sky was invisible. On all sides passages ran into total darkness; huge reddish rocks stood out fantastically everywhere in the pale light; there was a sound of water falling into a pool from a great height, and presently, striking matches as we went, we came upon a couple of lakes of marvelously clear blue water, through which we could see the heads of ladders emerging from other black holes of unknown depth below.

"We found our way out after a while into what appeared to be the central hall of the mine. Here we saw plain daylight again, for there was an immense round opening at the top, from the edges of which curved among the sides of the shaft, forming a huge circular chamber.

"Imagine the Albert Hall roofless; or, better still, imagine Saint Peter's with the top half of the dome removed. Of course, it was far smaller, but it gave an impression of great size, and it could not have been less than two hundred feet from the edge, over which we saw the trees against the sky, to the tumbled, dusty, rocky floor where we stood.

"I can only describe it as being like a great burnt-out hell in the *Inferno*. Red dust lay everywhere; escape seemed impossible; and vast crags and galleries, with the mouths of passages showing high up, marked by iron bars and chains, jutted out here and there.

"We amused ourselves here for some time by climbing up the sides, calling to one another, for the whole place was full of echoes, rolling down stones from some of the upper edges; but I nearly ended my days there.

"I was standing on a path, about seventy feet up, leaning against the wall. It was a path along which feet must have gone a thousand times when the mine was in working order, and I was watching Murphy, who was just emerging onto a platform opposite me, on the other side of the gulf.

"I put my hand behind me to steady myself, and the next instant very nearly fell forward over the edges at the violent shock to my nerves given by a wood-pigeon who burst out of a hole, brushing my hand as he passed. I gripped on, however, and watched the bird soar out across space, and then up and out at the opening; and then I became aware that my knees were beginning to shake.

So I stumbled along, and threw myself down on the little platform onto which the passage led.

"I suppose I had been more startled than I knew, for I tripped as I went forward, and knocked my knee rather sharply on a stone. I felt for an instant quite sick with the pain on the top of jangling nerves, and lay there saying what I am afraid I ought not to have said.

"Then Murphy came up when I called, and we made our way together through one of the sloping shafts, and came out onto the hillside among the trees."

Mr. Percival paused; his lips twitched a moment with amusement.

"I am afraid I must recall my promise," he said. "I told you all this because I was anxious to give a reason for the feeling I had about the mine, and which I am bound to mention. I felt I never wanted to see the place again—yet in spite of what followed I do not necessarily attribute my feelings to anything but the shock and the pain that I had had. You understand that?"

His bright eyes ran round our faces.

"Yes, yes," said Monsignor sharply; "go on, please, Mr. Percival."

"Well, then!"

The lawyer uncrossed his legs and placed them the other way.

"During lunch we told the landlady where we had been, and she begged us not to go there again. I told her that she might rest easy; my knee was beginning to swell. It was a wretched beginning to a walking tour.

"It was not that, she said; but there had been a bad accident there. Four men had been killed there twenty years before by a fall of rock. That had been the last straw on the top of ill-success, and the mine had been abandoned.

"We inquired as to details, and it seemed that the accident had taken place in the central chamber, locally called 'The Cathedral,' and after a few more questions I understood.

"'That was where you were, my friend,' I said to Murphy; 'it was where you were when the bird flew out.'

"He agreed with me, and presently when the woman was gone announced that he was going to the mine again to see the place. Well, I had no business to keep him dangling about. I couldn't walk anywhere myself, so I advised him not to go on to that platform again, and presently he took a couple of candles from the sticks and went off. He promised to be back by four o'clock, and I settled down rather drearily to a pipe and some old magazines.

"Naturally, I fell sound asleep. It was a hot, drowsy afternoon and the magazines were dull. I awoke once or twice, and then slept again deeply.

"I was awakened by the woman coming in to ask whether I would have tea; it was already five o'clock. I told her Yes. I was not in the least anxious about Murphy; he was a good climber, and therefore neither a coward nor a fool.

"As tea came in I looked out of the window again and saw him walking up the path, covered with iron dust, and a moment later I heard his step in the passage, and he came in.

"Mrs. What's-her-name had gone out.

"'Have you had a good time?' I asked.

"He looked at me very oddly and paused before he answered.

"'Oh, yes,' he said; and put his cap and stick in a corner.

"I knew Murphy.

"'Well, why not?' I asked him, beginning to pour out tea.

"He looked round at the door, then he sat down without noticing the cup I pushed across to him.

"'My dear fellow,' he said, 'I think I am going mad.'

"Well, I forget what I said, but I understood that he was very much upset about something, and I suppose I said the proper kind of thing about his not being a damned fool.

"Then he told me his story."

Mr. Percival looked round at us again, still with that slight twitching of the lips that seemed to signify amusement.

"Please remember—" he began, and then broke off. "No; I won't—"

"Well.

"He had gone down the same shaft that we went down in the morning, and had spent a couple of hours exploring the passages. He had found an engine-room with tanks and rotten beams in it and rusty chains. He had found some more lakes, too, full of that extraordinary electric-blue water; he had disturbed a quantity of bats somewhere else. Then he had come out again into the central hall, and on looking at his watch had found it after four o'clock, so he thought he would climb up by the way we had come in the morning and go straight home.

"It was as he climbed that his odd sensations began. As he went up, clinging with his hands, he became perfectly certain that he was being watched. He couldn't turn round very well, but he looked up as he went to the opening overhead, but there was nothing there but the dead-blue sky, and the trees very green against it, and the red rocks awning away on every side. It was extraordinarily quiet, he said; the pigeons had not come home from feeding, and he was out of hearing of the dripping water that I told you of.

"Then he reached the platform and the opening of the path where I had my fright in the morning, and turned round to look.

"At first he saw nothing peculiar. The rocks up which he had come fell away at his feet down to the floor of the 'Cathedral' and to the nettles with which he had stung his hands a minute or two before. He looked around at the galleries overhead and opposite, but there was nothing there.

"Then he looked across at the platform where he had been in the morning and where the accident had taken place.

"Let me tell you what this was like. It was about twenty yards in breadth and ten deep, but lay irregular and filled with tumbled rocks. It was a little below the level of his eyes, right across the gulf, and in a straight line would be about fifty or sixty yards away, It lay under the roof, rather retired, so that no light from the sky fell directly on to it; it would have been in complete twilight if it hadn't been for a shaft smaller above it, which shot down a funnel of bluish light, exactly like a stage effect. You see, reverend Fathers, it was very theatrical altogether. That might account, no doubt—"

Mr. Percival broke off again, smiling.

"I am always forgetting," he said. "Well, we must go back to Murphy. At first he saw nothing but the rocks and the thick, red dust and the broken wall behind it. He was very honest, and told me that as he looked at it he remembered distinctly what the landlady had told us at lunch. It was on that little stage that the tragedy had happened.

"Then he became aware that something was moving among the rocks, and he became perfectly certain that people were looking at him; but it was too dusky to see very clearly at first. Whatever it was was in the shadows at the back. He fixed his eyes on what was moving. Then this happened."

The lawyer stopped again.

"I will tell you the rest," he said, "in his own words so far as I remember them.

"'I was looking at this moving thing,' he said, 'which seemed exactly of the red color of the rocks, when it suddenly came out under the funnel of light, and I saw it was a man. He was in a rough suit all iron stained, with a rusty cap, and he had some kind of a pick in his hand. He stopped first in the centre of the light, with his back turned to me, and stood there looking. I cannot say that I was consciously frightened; I honestly do not know what I thought he was. I think that my whole mind was taken up in watching him.

"'Then he turned round slowly and I saw his face. Then I became aware that if he looked at me I should go into hysterics or something of the sort, and I crouched down as low as I could. But he didn't look at me; he was attending to something else, and I could see his face quite clearly. He had a beard and moustache, rather ragged and rusty; he was rather pale, but not particularly. I judged him to be about thirty-five.' Of course," went on the lawyer, "Murphy didn't tell it me quite as I am telling it to you. He stopped a good deal; he drank a sip of tea once or twice and changed his feet about.

"Well, he had seen this man's face very clearly, and described it very clearly.

"It was the expression that struck him most.

"'It was a rather amused expression,' he said; 'rather pathetic and rather tender, and he was looking interestedly about at everything

—at the rocks above and beneath; he carried his pick easily in the
crook of his arm. He looked exactly like a man whom I once saw
visiting his home where he had lived as a child.' (Murphy was very
particular about that, though I don't believe he was right.) 'He was
smiling a little in his beard and his eyes were half shut. It was so
pathetic that I nearly went into hysterics then and there,' said
Murphy. 'I wanted to stand up and explain that it was all right, but
I knew he knew more than I did. I watched him, I should think, for
nearly five minutes; he went to and fro softly in the thick dust,
looking here and there, sometimes in the shadow and sometimes
out of it. I could not have moved for ten thousand pounds and I
could not take my eyes off him.

"'Then just before the end I did look away from him. I wanted
to know if it was all real, and I looked at the rocks behind and the
openings. Then I saw that there were other people there; at least,
there were things moving of the color of the rocks.

"'I suppose I made some sound then; I was horribly frightened.
At any rate, the man in the middle turned right round and faced
me, and at that I sank down with the sweat dripping from me, flat
on my face, with my hands over my eyes.

"'I thought of a hundred thousand things—of the inn and you
and the walk we had had—and I prayed—well, I suppose I prayed.
I wanted God to take me right out of this place. I wanted the rocks
to open and let me through.'"

Mr. Percival stopped. His voice shook with a tiny tremor. He
cleared his throat.

"Well, reverend Fathers, Murphy got up at last and looked about
him, and of course there was nothing there but just the rocks and
the dust and the sky overhead. Then he came away home the short-
est way."

It was a very abrupt ending, and a little sigh ran round the
circle.

Monsignor struck a match noisily and kindled his pipe again.

"Thank you very much, sir," he said briskly.

Mr. Percival cleared his throat again, but before he could speak
Father Brent broke in.

"Now, that is just an instance of what I was saying, Monsignor, the night we began. May I ask if you really believe that those were the souls of the miners? Where's the justice of it? What's the point?"

Monsignor glanced at the lawyer.

"Have you any theory, sir?" he asked.

Mr. Percival answered without lifting his eyes.

"I think so," he said shortly; "but I don't feel in the least dogmatic."

Father Brent looked at him almost indignantly.

"I should like to hear it," he said. "If you can square that—"

"I do not square it," said the lawyer. "Personally I do not believe they were spirits at all."

"Oh?"

"No, I do not, though I do not wish to be dogmatic. To my mind it seems far more likely that this is an instance of Mr. Hudson's theory—the American, you know. His idea is that all apparitions are no more than the result of violent emotions experienced during life. That about the pathetic expression is all nonsense, I believe."

"I don't understand," said Father Brent.

"Well, these men, killed by the fall of the roof, probably went through a violent emotion. This would be heightened in some degree by their loneliness and isolation from the world. This kind of emotion, Mr. Hudson suggests, has a power of saturating material surroundings, which under certain circumstances would once more, like a photograph, give off an image of the agent. In this instance, too, the absence of other human visitors would give this materialized emotion a chance, so to speak, of surviving; there would be very few cross-currents to confuse it. And finally, Murphy was alone; his receptive faculties would be stimulated by that fact, and all that he saw, in my belief, was the psychical wave left by these men in dying."

"Oh! Did you tell him so?"

"I did not. Murphy is a violent man."

I looked up at Monsignor, and saw him nodding emphatically to himself.

My Own Tale

I must confess that I was a little taken aback on my last evening before leaving for England when Monsignor Maxwell turned on me suddenly at supper and exclaimed aloud that I had not yet contributed a story.

I protested that I had none; that I was prosaic person; that there was some packing to be done; that my business was to write down the stories of other people; that I had my living to make and could not be liberal with my slender store; that it was a layman's function to sit at holy and learned priests' feet, not to presume to inform them on any subject under the sun.

But it was impossible to resist; it was pointed out to me that I had listened on false pretences if I had not intended to do my share, that telling a story did not hinder my printing it. And, as a final argument, it was declared that unless I occupied the chair that night all present withdrew the leave that had already been given to me to print their stories on my return to England.

There was nothing, therefore, to be done; and as I had already considered the possibility of the request, I did not occupy an unduly long time in pretending to remember what I had to say.

When I was seated upstairs and the fire had been poked according to the ritual and the matches had gone round, and buckled shoes protruded side by side with elastic-ankled boots, I began.

"This is a very unsatisfactory story," I said, "because it has no explanation of any kind. It is quite unlike Mr. Percival's. You will see that even theorizing is useless when I have come to the end. It is simply a series of facts that I have to relate; facts that have no significance except one that is supernatural, but it is utterly out of the question even to guess at that significance.

"It is unsatisfactory, too, for a second reason, and that is, that it is on such very hackneyed lines. It is simply one more instance of that very dreamy class of phenomena, named 'haunted houses,' except that there is no ghost in it. Its only claim to interest is, as I have said, the complete futility of any attempt to explain it."

This was rather a pompous exordium, I felt, but thought it best not to raise expectations too high, and I was therefore deliberately dull.

"Sixteen years ago from last summer I was in France. I had left school, where I had labored two hours a week at French for four years, and gone away in order to learn it in six weeks. This I accomplished very tolerably, in company with five other boys and an English tutor. Our general adventures are not relevant, but toward the end of our stay we went over one Sunday from Portrieux in order to see a French chateau about three miles away.

"It was a really glorious June day, hot and fresh and exhilarating, and we lunched delightfully in the woods with a funny, fat little French count and his wife, who came with us from the hotel. It is impossible to imagine less uncanny circumstances or companions.

"After lunch we all went cheerfully to the house, whose chimneys we had seen among the trees.

"I know nothing about the dates of houses, but the sort of impression I got of this house was that it was about three hundred years old; but it may equally have been four, or two. I did not know then and do not know now anything about it except its name, which I will not tell you; and its owner's name, which I will not tell you either, and—and something else that I will tell you. We will call the owner, if you please, Comte Jean Marie the First. The house is built in two courts, the right-hand court, through which we entered, was then used as a farm-yard; and I should think it probable that it is still so used. This court was exceedingly untidy. There was a large manure heap in the centre, and the servants' quarters to our right

looked miserably cared for. There was a cart or two with shafts
turned up, near the sheds that were built against the wall opposite
the gate; and there was a sleepy old dog with bleared eyes that
looked at us intensely from his kennel door.

"Our French friend went across to the servants' cottages with
his moustache sticking out on either side of his face; and presently
came back with two girls and the keys. There was no objection, he
exclaimed dramatically, to our seeing the house!

"The girls went before us, and unlocked the iron gate that led
to the second court; and we went through after them.

"Now we had heard at the hotel that the family lived in Paris;
but we were not prepared for the dreadful desolation of that inner
court. The living part of the house was on our left; and what had
once been a lawn to our right; but the house was discolored and
weather-stained; the green paint of the closed shutters and door
was cracked and blistered; and the lawn resembled a wilderness;
the grass was long and rank; there were rose-trees trailing along
the edge and across the path; and a sun-dial on the lawn reminded
me strangely of a drunken man petrified in the middle of a stagger.
All this, of course, was what was to be expected in an adventure of
this kind. It would do for a Christmas number.

"But it was not our business to criticize; and after a moment or
two, we followed the girls who had unlocked the front door and
were waiting for us to enter.

"One of them had gone before to open the shutters.

"It was not a large house, in spite of its name, and we had soon
looked through the lower rooms of it. They, too, were what you
would expect; the floors were beeswaxed; there were tables and
chairs of a tolerable antiquity; a little damask on the walls and so
on. But what astonished us was the fact that none of the furniture
was covered up, or even moved aside; and the dust lay, I should
say, half an inch thick on every horizontal surface. I heard the
Frenchman crying on his God in an undertone—as is the custom of
Gauls—" (I bowed a little to Father Meuron)— "and finally he burst
out with a question as to why the rooms were in this state.

"The girl looked at him stolidly. She was a stout, red-faced girl.

"'It is by the Count's orders,' she said.

"'And does the Count not come here?' he asked.

"'No, sir.'

"Then we all went upstairs. One of the girls had preceded us again and was sitting with her hand on a door to usher us in.

"'See here is the room the most splendid!' she said; and threw the door open.

"It was certainly the room the most splendid. It was a great bed-chamber hung with tapestry; there were some excellent chairs with carved legs; a splendid gold-framed mirror tilted forward over the carved mantle-piece; and, above all, and standing out from the wall opposite the window was a great four-posted bed, with an elaborately carved head to it, and heavy curtains hanging from the canopy.

"But what surprised us more than anything that we had yet seen, was the sight of the bed. Except for the dust that lay on it, it might have been slept in the night before. There were actually damask sheets upon it, thrown back, and two pillows. All gray with dust. These were not arranged but tumbled about, as a bed is in the morning before it is made.

"As I was looking at this, I heard a boy cry out from the washing-stand.

"'Why, it has had water in it,' he said.

"This did not sound exceptional for a basin, but we all crowded round to look; and it was perfectly true; there was a gray film round the interior of it; and when he had disturbed it as a boy would with his finger we could see the flowered china beneath. The line came two-thirds of the way up the sides of the basin. It must have been partly filled with water a long while ago, which gradually evaporated, leaving its mark in the dust that must have collected there week after week.

"The Frenchman lost his patience at that.

"'My sacred something!' he said, 'why is the room like this?'

"The same girl who had answered him before, answered him again in the same words. She was standing by the mantle-piece watching us.

"'It is the Count's orders,' she said stolidly.

"'It is by the Count's orders that the bed is not made?' snapped the man.

"'Yes, sir,' said the girl simply.

"Well, that did not content the Frenchman. He exhibited a couple of francs and began to question.

"This is the story that he got out of her. She told it quite simply.

"The last time that Count Jean Marie had come to the place, it had been for his honeymoon. He had come down from Paris with his bride. They had dined together downstairs, very happily and gaily; and had slept in the room in which we were at this moment. A message had been sent out for the carriage early next morning; and the couple had driven away with their trunks leaving their servants behind. They had not returned, but a message had come down from Paris that the house was to be closed. It appeared that the servants who had been left behind had had orders that nothing was to be tidied; even the bed was not to be made; the rooms were to be locked up, and left as they were.

"The Frenchman had hardly been able to restrain himself as he heard this unconvincing story; though his wife shook him by the shoulders at each violent gesture that he made, and at the end he had put a torrent of questions.

"'Were they frightened then?'

"'I do not know, sir.'

"'I mean the bride and bridegroom, fool!'

"'I do not know, sir.'

"'Sacred name!—and—and—why do you not know?'

"'I have never seen any of them, sir.'

"'Not seen them! Why you said just now.'

"'Yes, sir; but I was not born then. It was thirty years ago.'

"I do not think I have ever seen people so bewildered as we all were. This was entirely unexpected. The Frenchman's jaw dropped; he licked his lips once or twice; and turned away. We all stood perfectly still a moment, and then we went out."

I indulged myself with a pause just here. I was enjoying myself more than I thought I should. I had not told the story for some while; and had forgotten what a good one it was. Besides, it had the advantage of being perfectly true. Then I went on again with a pleased consciousness of faces turned to me and black-ended cigarettes.

"I must tell you this," I said. "I was relieved to get out of the room. It is sixteen years ago now; and I may have embroidered on my sensations; but my impression is that I had been just a little uncomfortable even before the girl's story. I don't think that I felt that there was any presence there, or anything of that kind. It was rather the opposite; it was the feeling of an extraordinary emptiness."

"Like a Catholic Cathedral in Protestant hands," put in a voice.

I nodded at the zealous, convert-making Father Brent.

"It was very like that," I said, "and had, too, the same kind of pathos and terror that one feels in the presence of a child's dead body. It is unnaturally empty, and yet significant; and one does not quite know what it signifies."

I paused again.

"Well, reverend Fathers, that is the first Act. We went back to Portrieux; we made enquiries and got no answer. All shrugged their shoulders, and said that they did not know. There were no tales of the bride's hair turning white in the night, or of any curse or ghost or noises or lights. It was just as I have told you. Then we went back to England; and the curtain came down.

"Now generally such curtains have no resurrection. I suppose we have all had fifty experiences of First Acts; and we do not know to this day whether the whole play is a comedy or a tragedy; or even whether the play has been written at all."

"Do not be modern and allusive, Mr. Benson," said Monsignor.

"I beg your pardon, Monsignor, I will not. I forgot myself. Well, here is the Second Act. There are only two, and this is a much shorter one.

"Nine years later I was in Paris, staying in the Rue Picot with some Americans. A French friend of theirs was to be married to a man; and I went to the wedding at the Madeleine. It was—well, it was like all other weddings at the Madeleine. No description can be adequate to the appearance of the officiating clergyman and the altar and the bridesmaids and the French gentlemen with polished boots and butterfly ties, and the conversation, and the gaiety, and the general impression of a confectioner's shop and a milliner's and a salon and a holy church. I observed the bride and bridegroom and forgot their names for the twentieth time, and exchanged some remarks in the sacristy; with a leader of society who looked like a dissipated priest; with my eyes starting out of my head in my anxiety not to commit a *solécisme* or a *barbarisme*. And then we went home again.

"On the way home we discussed the honeymoon. The pair were going down to a country house in Brittany. I enquired the name of it; and, of course, it was the chateau I had visited nine years before. It had been lent them by Count Jean Marie the Second. The gentleman resided in England, I heard, in order to escape the conscription; he was a connection of the bride's; and was about thirty years of age.

"Well, of course, I was interested; and made enquiries and related my adventure. The Americans were mildly interested, too, but not excited. Thirty-nine years is ancient history to that energetic nation." (I bowed to Father Jenks, before I remembered that he was a Canadian; and then pretended that I had not and went on quickly, and missed a dramatic opportunity.) "But two days afterward they were excited. One of the girls came into déjeuner, and said that she had met the bride and bridegroom dining together in the Bois. They had seemed perfectly well; and had saluted her politely. It seemed that they had come back to Paris after one night at the chateau, exactly as another bride and bridegroom had done thirty-nine years before.

"Before I finish let me sum up the situation.

"In neither case was there apparently any shocking incident, and yet something had been experienced that broke up plans and sent away immediately from a charming house and country two pairs of persons who had deliberately formed the intention of living there for a while. In both cases the persons in question had come back to Paris.

"I need hardly say that I managed to call with my friends upon the bride and bridegroom, and, at the risk of being impertinent, asked the bride point-blank why they had changed their plans and come back to town.

She looked at me without a trace of horror in her eyes, and smiled a little.

"'It was *triste*,' she said; 'a little *triste*. We thought we would come away; we desired crowds.'

I paused again.

"'We desired crowds,' I repeated. "You remember, reverend Fathers, that I had experienced a sense of loneliness, even with my friends, during five minutes spent in that upstairs room. I can only suppose that if I had remained longer I should have experienced such a further degree of that sensation that I should have felt exactly as those two pairs of brides and bridegrooms felt and have come away immediately. I might even, if I had been in authority, have given orders that nothing was to be touched except my own luggage."

"I do not understand that," said Father Brent, looking puzzled.

"Nor do I altogether," I answered; "but I think I perceive it to be a fact for all that. One might feel that one was an intruder, that one had meddled with something that desired to be left alone, and that one had better not meddle further in any kind of way."

"I suppose you went down there again," observed Monsignor Maxwell.

"I did; a fortnight afterwards. There was only one girl left; the other was married and gone away. She did not remember me; it was nine years ago, and she was a little redder in the face and a little more stolid.

"The lawn had been clipped and mown, but was beginning to grow rank again. Then I went upstairs with her. The room was comparatively clean; there was water in the basin; and clean sheets on the bed; but there was just a little film of dust lying on everything. I pretended I knew nothing and asked questions; and I was told exactly the same story as I had heard nine years before; only this time the date was only a fortnight ago.

"When she had finished she added:

"'It happened so once before, sir; before I was born.'

"'Do you understand it?' I said.

"'No, sir; the house is a little *triste* perhaps. Do you think so, sir?'

"I said that perhaps it was. Then I gave her two francs and came away.

"That is all, reverend Fathers."

There was silence for a minute. Then Padre Bianchi made what I consider a tactless remark.

"Bah! that does not terrify me," he said.

"'Terrify' is certainly not the word," remarked Monsignor Maxwell.

"I am not quite sure about that," ended Father Brent.

The bell rang for night-prayers.

"Sum up, Father Rector," said Monsignor without moving. "You have heard all the stories and Mr. Benson is going to-morrow."

The old priest smiled as he stood up; and was silent for a moment, looking at us all.

"I can only sum up like this, with the sentiments with which Monsignor began," he said: "The longer I live and the more I hear and see, the greater I feel my ignorance to be. I heard a man say the other day that Catholics were the only genuine agnostics alive; and that he respected them for it. They knew some things that others did not; but they did not pretend to affirm or to deny that of which they had no possibility of judging. Is that what you meant me to say, Monsignor."

Monsignor nodded meditatively.

"I think that is a sound conclusion," he said. "It is understood then, Mr. Benson, that if you print these stories, you will add that not one of us commits himself to belief in any of them—except, I suppose, each in his own."

"I will mention it," I said."

"Perhaps you might say that we do not even commit ourselves to our own. You can say what you like about yours, of course."

"I will mention that, too," I said, "and I will class myself with the rest. The agnostic position is certainly the soundest in all matters outside the deposit of faith. We all stand, then, exactly where we did at the beginning?"

"Certainly I do," said Padre Bianchi.

"We all do," said a number of voices.

Then we went to night-prayers together for the last time.

Coachwhip Publications

CoachwhipBooks.com

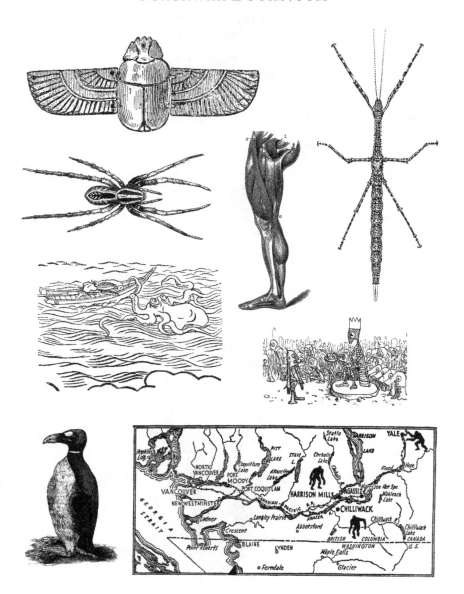

Shadows from a Veiled Creation
Classic Tales of Supernatural Fiction
in the Christian Tradition

44 Stories
ISBN 1·930585·26·8

CPSIA information can be obtained
at www.ICGtesting.com
Printed in the USA
BVHW032122070122
625741BV00001B/10

9 781616 460044